FANON

Books by John Edgar Wideman

FANON

JOHN EDGAR WIDEMAN

HOUGHTON MIFFLIN COMPANY

BOSTON • NEW YORK

2008

For information about permission to reproduce selections from
this book, write to Permissions, Houghton Mifflin Company,
215 Park Avenue South, New York, New York 10003.

www.houghtonmifflinbooks.com

Library of Congress Cataloging-in-Publication Data

Wideman, John Edgar.

Fanon / John Edgar Wideman.

p. cm.

ISBN-13: 978-0-618-94263-3

ISBN-10: 0-618-94263-7

1. Fanon, Frantz, 1925–1961—Fiction. I. Title.

PS3573.I26F36 2007

813'.54—dc22   2007009420

Printed in the United States of America

Book design by Robert Overholtzer

MP 10 9 8 7 6 5 4 3 2 1

DEDICATED TO FRANTZ FANON

1925–1961

The imaginary life cannot be isolated from real life, the concrete and the objective world constantly feed, permit, legitimate and found the imaginary. The imaginary consciousness is obviously unreal, but it feeds on the concrete world. The imagination and the imaginary are possible only to the extent that the real world belongs to us.

—FRANTZ FANON, 1956

PART I

A LETTER TO FRANTZ FANON

I'M SITTING with the last of a glass of red wine in the small garden of a small house in Brittany. I spent the morning of this day as I've spent most mornings this summer, trying to save a life, adding a few words, a few sentences to the long letter I'm addressing to you, Frantz Fanon, dead almost half a century before I begin writing to you, writing just about every day, outdoors when weather permits, sitting each morning in the garden of a house in France, the country you claimed, Fanon, as your nation, fought and bled for, wounded near Lyon in 1944, and then fought against during the war for Algerian independence until you died of leukemia, they say, in 1961, in a hospital in America, the country I claim as mine. France your country, French your language, though you were born in Martinique, a Caribbean island thousands of miles away from where I sit this evening thinking about you, Fanon, about your short, more than full life, about the fact that sixty-five years of my very full life have passed no less swiftly than the thought of them that just now passed through my mind. Though your story's extraordinary, it's also like mine, like anybody's, just another story, but since I've chosen to tell it or it's chosen me, for reasons I'm still attempting to figure out as I proceed, reasons that may be why I proceed, I know a life's at stake. Whose life and why are other things I'm trying to figure out.

I intend to say more about this particular evening, Fanon, but first I need to speak to you about the project that's been on my mind for many years, forty years at least, ever since I read your final book, *The Wretched of the Earth,* for the first time. Although the worrisomeness I'm calling a Fanon project has assumed various forms, it began clearly enough as a determination to be like you, that is, to become a writer committed to telling the truth about color and oppression, a writer who exposes the lies of race and reveals how the concept of race is used as a weapon to destroy people. I wanted to be somebody, an unflinchingly honest, scary somebody like Frantz Fanon whose words and deeds just might ignite a revolution, just might help cleanse the world of the plague of racism. Over the years I gradually resigned myself to the fact that I couldn't measure up to your example, and my Fanon project shifted to writing about disappointment with myself and my country, about shame and guilt and lost opportunities, about the price of not measuring up to announced ideals. Of course my perceptions of you changed as I changed and the world changed around me. The Fanon project continued to simmer, however, never forgotten, never achieved, often lamented, less a model for guiding my actions than a source of anxiety and unfulfilled ambition, deep dread that someday my nation and I must endure a shattering reckoning. I published numerous books during this period, always hoping they didn't dishonor Frantz Fanon nor compromise unforgivably my original project. Then about six years ago, the Fanon project took another turn — if I couldn't live Fanon's life, maybe I could write it. On Martinique I encountered your stenciled, spray-painted image, an image like my project, almost effaced, so I didn't recognize you until two days after you popped up in the middle of nowhere, a field where cows grazed near the beach, your face on a concrete minibunker belonging to an energy company supplying electricity to the section of the island, Sainte-Anne's Parish, where I was staying in a resort hotel, on holiday with a Frenchwoman I'd recently met, rapidly fallen in love with, and would eventually marry. The rest of the story of catching up with my Fanon project may or may not be in the following pages. I'm hoping it will be. Hoping there's still time to connect with you.

My sense of urgency about connecting would require many books to express, and I realize time's running out. I won't be writing many more books, if any. The plague of race continues to blight people's lives, becoming more virulent as it mutates and spreads over the globe. When I ask myself if your example made any difference, Fanon, ask if your words and deeds alleviate one iota the present catastrophe of hate, murder, theft, and greed, where else should I start looking besides the mirror. Where should I search if not in faces of people I love. Will I find an answer in your eyes, behind me in the mirror, gazing into the face I see seeing yours.

Once upon a time I believed fiction writing was a privileged, not a suspect, activity. I thought writing fiction could establish a stable identity for me in the everyday world where people need to eat, wear clothes, work, etc., and at the same time free me to entertain myself and others, maybe, by creating alternative lives in my fiction. Real worlds and imaginary worlds weren't necessarily antagonistic, I thought. They could complement each other, engage in open-minded, open-ended conversation and exchange. Fact and fiction need each other, don't they. You can't have one without the other. I wasn't wrong. Just naive. Writing fiction marginalized me as much as I was marginalized by the so-called fact of my race. Your witness, Fanon, of the separate domains of settler and native, black and white, your understanding of how that separation exploits the native, appropriates the native's land, and stultifies the being of both settler and native, taught me how divided from myself and others I've become.

Stipulating differences that matter between fact and fiction — between black and white, male and female, good and evil — imposes order in a society. Keeps people on the same page. Reading from the same script. In the society I know best, mine, fact and fiction are absolutely divided, one set above the other to rule and pillage, or, worse, fact and fiction blend into a tangled, hypermediated mess, grounding being in a no-exit maze of consuming: people as a consuming medium, people consumed by the medium.

Fiction writing and art in general are scorned, stripped of relevance to people's daily lives, dependent on charity, mere playthings of power, privilege, buying and selling.

My society polices its boundaries with more and more self-destructive manichean violence now that its boundaries are exposed not as naturally or supernaturally ordained but organized through various sorts of coercion by some members of the society to benefit themselves and disadvantage others.

Under what rock, whose skirts have I been hiding, you might be wondering, not to have learned those truths before I began zipping up my own trousers. A good question, Fanon. A more difficult question: if I truly understand all the above, why am I still writing.

You feared, Fanon, that winning a war of independence in Algeria, no matter how protracted and bloody the struggle, would be less difficult than maintaining a clear vision of the goals that had made declaring war against France a necessity for colonized Algerians and eventually for you. You realized that oppressed people could be convinced to sacrifice their lives for the promise of freedom, dignity, and self-determination and also that it's easier to die for such ideals than to live them, live with them embedded, uncompromised, in place day by day, choice by choice in the institutions of society, in the consciousness of individuals and the spirit of a culture.

Ratcheting down many degrees from a colonial war for national independence but also always ratcheting up in the sense of keeping in mind the aspirations that justify risking all, my small struggle is to write your life, word by word, sentence by sentence, and not lose sight of why I've set myself an impossible task. I want to be free. I want to write a life for myself, fact and fiction, to open possibilities of connecting with your life, other lives.

When I was a kid I owned a magic slate. The magic of it, I understood back then, being you could lift the blue-gray plastic sheet you drew upon with your plastic stylus and every mark you'd etched on the slate would disappear. A magically clean page each time, any time you wished. A man named Thomas, who lives only in his stalled novel which doesn't have a name, also possessed a magic slate when he was a boy. Yesterday Thomas was reminded of his slate and his old habit of drawing nasty pictures and writing obscene words on it, a memory I inserted in his thoughts when a UPS guy delivered a severed human head (maybe) to Thomas's New York apartment door, a memory triggered specifically by an electronic pad Thomas had to sign to indicate he received a package. Attached by a curly cord to an electronic pen, just as my slate was attached to a plastic stylus, the UPS man's pad was a bit smaller but exactly the same color and shape as Thomas's slate and mine. And like the slate, the deliveryman's toy performs a rather impressive trick. Before Thomas completes the second letter of his signature, the first letter registers in a databank in Bombay. On the other hand — not the hand signing an electronic receipt for a package that might contain a head, nor the hand busy writing Thomas's story, nor the hand composing this letter, and not exactly the hand that would hurt me a lot if somebody whacked it with a hammer — on the other hand, the one both astounded and dismayed by the marvels of modern communication, I wonder what could be more magical than a clean slate. More intimidating. More devastating.

I don't introduce Thomas simply to erase him. He's crucial to my project. Thomas leads as often as he follows. Writes as much as he's written. Since you're a writer, Fanon, you'll understand what I mean when I say that inventing Thomas helps invent the person who's able to write what you're reading. And though I wish to grant Thomas all due credit, I must also admit that Thomas is a fiction, that I'm responsible for any Fanon portrait this project paints, not Thomas or anybody else, that Thomas intends to write a book about Fanon and never will, nor will he ever write his own life into a fiction, try, try as he might. I depend on you and any serious reader to remember this without forgetting, on the other hand, that I would absolutely welcome Thomas, would be grateful for his participation if he performed no function beyond reminding me and anyone reading these words not to ignore the fictive nature of any and all enterprises we undertake. Opening a novel, opening our eyes, opening our minds, hearts, legs, wallets, we are opening ourselves to a reality not unlike a magic slate where one unvarying condition of our appearance is that we are condemned, sooner or later, to disappear and never be seen or heard again.

The Igbo of Nigeria, a people you no doubt encountered during your frequent diplomatic missions on behalf of Algeria, say a person doesn't die until the living stop remembering, stop telling stories about the person. Also, in Igbo tradition the age-mates or age-set of a freshly deceased peer scour their village, rushing hither and thither, searching for their missing comrade everywhere he once would be sure to have been found, the search increasingly intense and frantic as the age-mates run disappointed, back and forth from one familiar, intimate place to another, and their entreaties, their lamentations fail to coax the missing one from hiding.

I'm not suggesting I consciously mine Igbo lore to organize my project. I cite the Igbo to acknowledge my unanticipated good fortune, my gratitude for the presence of what might be called ancestors (like you) waiting to be discovered. Ancestors who speak, not on demand, but if and when they choose. The simultaneous loss and discovery of their presence defines a space I might inhabit if I learn how, a vast solitude, a space less alone, less silent perhaps because others once occupied it and I've been expected.

Think of me, of Thomas, as your age-mates, Fanon, playing a deadly serious game of chasing your spirit. Think of us hurrying along real streets, knocking on real doors, peeking in real windows, asking real people if they've seen our friend, our brother, visible now only in our search, our hunger for him. Imagine a gang of us, a posse of the bereaved, each person making separate forays or the whole bunch driven by a single thought or stalled, huddling together for mutual comfort, some hopeful, some resigned, some frayed, some disbelieving, others intoxicated by the effort, every one of us so full of pain, fear, longing, memories that our bodies droop and collapse in a heap like shed costumes or skins at the end of a night of seeking since dawn our lost companion. The one we won't save. Won't let go. Can't. Imagine how deeply we might sleep, how sealed in darkness, oppressed by the weight of our sorrow, how weightless our dreams, as weightless, bodiless, remote and close as we seem to our fellow villagers or a curious stranger passing by who witnesses us, grown men behaving like spooked chickens or a band of orphaned children, noisy phantoms slipping, gliding through the compound's paths and shadows, then fading into the bush, ghosts in pursuit of a ghost, wailing, crying out in tongues, marking our trail with wet, glistening tears, real and far away as stars.

THE BELL RINGS

WHEN THE DOORBELL rings it catches Thomas imagining how a head, bloody and real, might arrive at his door. Just a coincidence, he tells himself on his way from his desk to the apartment door, the bell ringing in the midst of his daydreaming about the delivery of a head. A coincidence, he repeats, smiling at the gullible part of himself who believes he sees a delivery person in the hall holding a head-sized box squeezed under one arm. Strictly a coincidence Thomas assures himself, like when you think about someone you haven't run into for a long while and in the next instant the imagined someone appears. A coincidence, never mind the fact that it feels like the opposite of coincidence. Like timing's off. Like two different worlds have gotten tangled up, squeezed together. A traffic jam. Or traffic accident. Everything coincidental, Thomas thinks, impatient with the impatient pounding on his door. Everything happens at once, once and only once. No stops. No starts. No chance to escape like the unexpected grains of rice yesterday spilling, skittering helter-skelter across the kitchen floor when he lifted from the cupboard shelf a bag of Uncle Ben's with a hole he didn't see in the bottom.

Thomas opens his door, and before he can speak — while he's concluding faster than the speed of light that time's timing can't be off and that he doesn't understand even a little bit what the word *coincidence* means and furthermore that trying to conceive how his life passes through time is like imagining a solid brick wall and stepping through before realizing that he can't step through a brick wall though he might very well have arrived on the far, unimaginable side — before Thomas can utter a word, a brown guy in a brown UPS suit apologizes for not phoning the apartment from the lobby to alert Thomas and confirm that Thomas exists and is indeed the person who inhabits #M901 or confirm #M901 as indeed the apartment where a package addressed to Thomas should be conveyed and someone will sign for it in the event Thomas is not present or does not exist, working out to the same thing from the delivery person's perspective, and today being a busy day, he's would you believe it behind schedule already at 10 A.M. so once past the security desk he jumped into an elevator just as its door began to slide shut and rode express to the ninth floor without calling on his cell phone (brown matching his brown uniform) to ascertain if anybody home.

Sign here, please, sir.

Sign right here. No mention of a head inside the hatbox-sized box, way too heavy for a hat when he passes it to Thomas.

You sure it's not ticking, ha-ha, Thomas says occasionally to delivery people to be funny, ha-ha. Delivery people usually don't get it or ignore it or don't like it or hold Thomas in contempt these days of terror, *Not funny, asshole,* scolding him with their magistrate's eyes. Would this delivery person have a sense of humor or at least extend to Thomas the benefit of the doubt, a slight I'm-the-friendly-delivery-person-with-a-smile-for-whatever-stupid-shit-the-customer-says smile. No joking around with today's brown person at the door. Thomas has delayed him long enough. Is he supposed to notice the brown head above the brown uniform. Only thing matters supposed to be the outfit, not who's in it. Outfit trumps infit, right. Or the reverse, maybe. Confusing is what Thomas thinks. Like skin color doesn't matter these days they say, grinning and squinting colorblind like you're welcome on their doorstep no matter what your color, gender, creed, delivering a pizza or an opportunity *surprise surprise* to open a package today from the Big World that just might save their lives. *Sign here, please.*

Without comment Thomas signs and looks a pleasant look to cover up his unease, his uncertainty about tipping protocol, whether a tip is expected or optional in these situations, how large or small, should he offer a tip whether it's required or not, and if he doesn't, will he be sent to hell as a cheap bastard in the brown uniformed messenger's brown thoughts. Is brown-on-brown tipping a special case requiring a huge tip or maybe only a brother-to-brother wink, a deeply satisfying exchange worth more than money can buy with the delivery person standing there holding an electronic tablet Thomas must mark with an electronic pen which agitates neurons and electrons, the first letter of Thomas's name spinning away to register in Hong Kong before he finishes scratching the second letter on the miniscreen whose bluish gray glow reminds him of those magic slates when he was a kid. Remember. With a plastic stylus you wrote on a plasticky transparent cover sheet and the marks appeared on the gray-blue page beneath. Lifting the top sheet erased the nasty drawings and swear words Thomas liked to practice back then anywhere anonymous, like fences or walls of abandoned buildings or like on the carbon-backed magic page where he wouldn't be caught, except one day, raising both sheets with thumb and finger, he noticed the stiff purple slab retained a copy of his evil scribble-scrabble, not only the latest production but layer upon layer accumulated over days and weeks, of sinful ideas and dirty pictures and curses good boy Thomas knew he wasn't supposed to know, let alone express, preserved there to expose him to punishment or worse, ridicule. Thomas's tender secrets unveiled, betraying him like the credit card bill his ex-wife, apoplectic, once waved in his face as unimpeachable evidence of Thomas rendezvousing in a fancy restaurant with some female not her.

You never learn, do you, Thomas. Busted again the instant you signed the tiny window of the UPS guy's gadget. Now it's your head, forever. If there is a head in the box. Never trust technology's toys. No more than you trust the novels you toy with, the novels toying with you. One thing always connected to other things, endless chains of words and messages looping backward, forward, sideways, rope around your neck. Remember the exhibit of sepia photos, the droopy-headed brown victims of lynching, crackers leering at the victim's limp private parts. Keep your business to yourself, Thomas, or your business everybody's business, nobody's business. If you're not careful, your business displayed word by word, scratch by scratch, and you're dead. No magic sheet to lift. The evidence of your guilt indelible everywhere you believed, foolish boy, you could safely spray your tag.

Your signature now belongs to the ages. One small step for you, Thomas, a giant leap for mankind. Like Michael's moonwalk. Like this thing. This head (if there is one) in a box belongs to you for eternity once the delivery person, after a proper credentializing, passes it to you and *Sayonara* backpedals into the hallway, pushing the door shut behind his Japanese-sampling brown self.

The narrative forges ahead. And doesn't. Giving Thomas a headache either way. A bad head. Stop, Thomas. Nothing funny here. One more atrocious head pun and it's off with yours.

Wordplay a common symptom of aftershock. Nothing to be ashamed of, Thomas responds. Could happen to anybody. A natural reaction, the studies say. The mind dividing to protect itself while performing unbearably grim duties. A means of buying time, creating a little distance, you know. Yaketty-yak. Entire nations and epochs have employed the stratagem. How else are people supposed to cope with horror beyond comprehension. Wordplay better than completely numbing out. You know, like that numb look Igbo slaves got in their eyes before they hanged themselves.

Words, however, don't help much, do they. Neither does time. Minute by minute passing, none of them altering the unalterable truth that Thomas may have received, accepted, and signed for a package containing a human head and it's his head now on the desk, daring him to look. He's run out of words, excuses, patience with himself, and the box still sits. Patient. Beyond words. Not speaking. Unspeakable. He must deal with it. Where's his magic slate. Each day dawning a new page to scribble on. A new Thomas. No questions asked. Now only one question: what's in the box. Why not return the package unopened to UPS. Let them deal with it. Well, if you don't open the box, Thomas, no story. Nothing. Zero. No Thomas. Who would want to hear your story without a bloody head in it. Without terrorists, torture, sizzling sex. Without an intricate plot linking Thomas to a secret brotherhood with a plan to destroy civilization as we know it, a diabolical plan linking the brotherhood to Frantz Fanon, linking the devil Fanon to you, Thomas. Who would pay to read what Thomas thinks about Thomas. Thomas knows the answer to that one. Hears the crinkle of the plastic sheet the reader's raising to expose him, erase him.

THOMAS OPENS THE BOX

NO MORE DODGING. No more reprieves. Get busy, Thomas. Innocent people are being slaughtered and mutilated daily. If not in your neighborhood, if not next door, the horror's much closer than you think. This head in a box somebody's crude way of announcing the fact to you. In your face, Thomas. Somebody powerful and ruthless has gone to an awful lot of trouble and not inconsiderable expense to deliver awful news to your door. Remember the guy in *The Godfather* screaming when he wakes up next to a severed head on his pillow. But that was just a movie, wasn't it, and this isn't. Not yet anyway. Somebody sent you a head in a box, and it doesn't belong to an Arabian racehorse. It's your head. You're sure now, aren't you. Sure. Sure of what. Do you really want to know, Thomas. The whole truth. Whole story. The perpetrators. The victim. Friend or foe. Colored or not. Could it be you, Thomas. Hurry up. Open the goddamn box . . .

He spreads last week's *Village Voice* over the metal-topped kitchen table, no incriminating booties or boobs from the personals when he sets down the box containing the head (does it really). On the way from desk to table the box weighs more than when the UPS guy passed it through the door, more than it weighed when Thomas carried it to his desk. Does blood with no place to drain become darker, heavier, the longer it sits. Though it's morning, the city already somber through the smidgen of kitchen window. Is everybody's dread leaking, leaking with no place to go, piling up, darker, heavier, higher than his building.

How long before the head begins to stink. Did the delivery person smell it. Is Thomas being spared by his chronically clogged sinuses. How long has he been sitting, staring. Talking to himself. A serrated steak knife purchased at K-mart rests on a headline next to the box. What color is the knife. What color is the head. Do you really want to know. Not too late to call the cops. Let the cops unpack the box. You're innocent, Thomas. Nothing to fear but fear itself. Look. Don't look. Flip a coin. Maybe it will come up tails.

With determination and tongue in cheek like the other Michael when a big hoop game winds down, he slices through all four corners of the box. Slowly, carefully sawing so what's inside doesn't roll off the table. He's not ready to touch it. Uses one loose cardboard wing of the box to nudge *it,* steady *it,* while the blade gnaws through the final corner. Why does he believe it's real. Could be a cabbage, a hunk of carved wood, a plaster mannequin's head beneath the plastic shrinkwrap. Whatever it is, he wouldn't actually be touching *it,* would he, if he only touches the wrapping. Thomas doesn't take the risk. The head or whatever it is, outside the box now. Or rather, no box now. Box deader than the head. Except you could tape the sides together again. Box good as new.

With plastic tight as a condom mashing its features the head (what else could it be) looks like it's trying to suck air through its covering. A bank robber wearing a stocking over his face. An Igbo mask to scare away an egwugwu. A face slammed into a windshield at 80 mph. Emmett Till's gnawed, nibbled face when they dragged his body from the Tallahatchie River.

A man's head for sure. A pig-faced man. How can you be sure of gender, color of anything unless you remove the plastic. Will you be sure if you remove the wrap. And you don't want to remove the wrap, do you, scaredy-cat Thomas. Afraid you'll find yourself staring at yourself many days dead in the East River. You'll never remove the mask, will you.

No. You would rather write about an imaginary head, right. Dream up words for its awfulness and send them hurrying after it, chasing it, chasing yourself so Thomas doesn't get away and never return. Writing it until you get it right. Until its words, a story, not Thomas coming apart, not something words can't grasp. Maybe you only need to tell the story once. If you can write it perfectly once, the horror will be words, the words appearing, the horror disappearing. The ordinary world real again. You real again. Then you'll be able to walk out the door and never come back. Leave the damned thing sitting on the kitchen table. Leave it alone. Forget it. Alone. Alone.

No room in the freezer compartment. If Thomas shifts the red-and-white plastic salad spinner clotted with shreds of rotting arugula, gets rid of the rack the spinner rests on, the head might fit in the fridge. Balled-up paper protects his fingers as he lifts the thing from the table. Tomorrow he'll buy disposable gloves. He'll buy a fridge with a larger freezer. Buy another apartment. Buy another city. Another name. Leave this nasty motherfucker on ice to whine its sorry tale to anybody dumb enough to listen.

A NOTE

THOMAS DOESN'T TRUST the white envelope enclosed in the box. Why should he trust anything arriving in a package with a severed head. Don't touch that envelope, Thomas. Full of anthrax, I bet. The head a trick to lower your defenses. Some super-slick terrorist somewhere has anticipated your response to a grisly head. After the shock of a head in a box, why would anybody worry about a little innocent-looking white envelope. Who wouldn't snatch it up and rip it open. Who wouldn't be anxious to read the message. Are human heads so cheap, so easy to obtain, the person or persons unknown sending this one can afford to use it as bait.

Thomas considers pinning down the envelope with a fork, slitting it open with the knife. His hands are too shaky. C'mon. No harder than boning a fish. He'd almost missed the envelope in the mess of packing he'd guided by knife blade off the table's edge into a black plastic garbage bag. Why hadn't the envelope been secured inside or outside the box. With one end of the envelope squeezed in a pot-holder, gingerly, he scissors off the other end and shakes out the contents. No sprinkle of white powder. Just a note, handwritten on a 3-by-5 index card.

> *We must immediately take the war to the enemy,*
> *leave him no rest, harass him. Cut off his breath.*

Just a second, Thomas. Are you sure a Fanon quote a good idea here. Why add to Fanon's bad rap as apostle of violence, hater of whites, spawner of terrorists. Posterity already blames the messenger for his message. Like the pharaohs used to kill bearers of bad news to scare bad news away. One death not enough to chase Fanon. His reputation lynched. Reading Fanon's critics, you'd think he committed the crimes against humanity his words accuse others of perpetrating. I understand why you need Fanon in your story, why you're anxious to hook up with him by any means possible, but think about the consequences of introducing Fanon in this manner. And Thomas thinks. Or would he. Think. With a human head (or what he believes is a head) on his kitchen table, wouldn't Thomas be feeling rather than thinking. Feel chilled. Queasy. Scared. Scared of what. Whom. Of everything and nothing. Of himself. The worst kind of fear.

Formless. All encompassing. Thought trumped, he listens to himself thinking anyway, clickety-click, blah-blah-blah.

If the Fanon quote fits, if it pumps up the action . . . so what if Fanon guilty by association. Fanon's reputation not Thomas's problem. Not in this scene, anyway. Later, maybe. In a different scene, another story. In the Fanon book he's intending to write. If he ever starts it. If he ever finishes the fiction he's writing now. If he ever finishes reading everything he's able to lay his hands on about Fanon and Martinique and the Algerian revolution. With Fanon so much on his mind, no wonder Fanon's bleeding into everything Thomas writes. Fanon his hero. Pinpoint of light in a darkening world. Doctor, philosopher, freedom fighter, writer, a man of color, man of peace who said no to color, no to peace if the price of color or peace is hiding behind a mask. But how would the sender of the note be aware of his plan for a Fanon book. Beyond mentioning the possibility to his brother and mom, he's told no one (except Fanon) about his project. Not even himself, exactly. Who's spying on Thomas. Listening in on his thoughts. Who knows the head's name. Who's reading stuff Thomas hasn't written yet. The plot thickens.

Why not some other message in the box with the head. A love quote, since whatever story he writes he wants love in it. The nice bit from Rilke, for example, which an Episcopalian priest recited during a wedding ceremony Thomas attended recently, something about love being when two people appoint themselves guardians forever of each other's solitude. Or Fanon's warning from *Les Damnés de la Terre*, his prescient words, ignored when they were written and still unheeded over four decades later, the quote about a long-suffering Third World stepping forward, an awakening Colossus in Europe's face, determined to resolve problems for which Europe has offered no solutions, words quoted in a Fanon biography Thomas just happened to be reading the morning he saw smoke billowing from the Twin Towers. Or another, less confrontational Fanon quote. *Oh, my body. Make of me a man who questions,* Thomas thinks. Would he think that thought with a head on a platter staring at him. For sure, he'd be asking questions. Question after scared question. Where's the rest of the body. Whose body is it. Who disposed of the body after detaching the head and sending it to Thomas. Who indeed. Who doesn't like Thomas very much. Why not. Isn't Thomas struggling valiantly to make the best of a bad situation. Isn't his life, his fate, like everybody else's in these days of hate and terror, out of his hands — anybody's hands. Too late for Fanon or any other savior to salvage. Doesn't the crawl say so daily in the small packets of information flowing across our screens. Yes. No. Yes. Thomas spinning in place like the hip-hop Sambo kids in the subway for tips. Slow down, Thomas. Nothing to fear but fear itself. But I already used that quote, didn't I, Thomas thinks. You're not responsible for the mess, Thomas. Neither is Fanon. This is work-in-progress, not a story anybody's written. Too early to tell what's going to happen next. Will I be the book's hero, the head inquires. Hold on, my friend. Can't give away the ending. Let's say the Fanon quote, *take the war to the enemy,* etc., included in the box to heighten suspense. Thicken the soup. Teach somebody a lesson. Who. Who knows. Who sez.

POINT OF VIEW

LET'S GET IT STRAIGHT then. Once and for all. If Thomas is imagining Thomas receiving a head in a box, who imagines receiving the thoughts of Thomas. Who's dead. Who survives and imagines me. Thomas for one for sure because it's his story and for his story or anybody else's story to be written, somebody must imagine a second self, a made-up self like Thomas makes up, outside Thomas, imagining that other somebody as we each imagine ourselves, a she or he, black or white, old or young, alive or dead, a second self imagining. Where. Inside the first self which must be imagined first so it believes it could be the author of the second or third or however many other selves the story we imagine requires. Are we making progress here. Precious little, I'm afraid. Where are we. Where do we wish to go. Someplace simple, I hope. A story with an arc and ending. Fanon's story, the one Thomas can't write.

An old friend, my idol and housemate one year during college, Charley T., whose misfortune was to love Pat, a girl who gave any guy who smiled and asked nicely a hand job because it was such a small, easily managed task for her and seemed such a big happy deal for the guy, Charley decided that his fellow painters who worked the medium of watercolors had things assbackwards. Reversing the traditional practice of moving from light to dark by gradually deepening shade and adding color with washes of paint that conspire with a canvas's original pristine bright white, Charley started by painting his canvases a muddy blue-black. Then with the ass end of his brushes, with sticks, rags, spatula, razor, fingernails, kitchen utensils, an X-Acto blade, sponges, and occasionally paint on the bristles of his brushes, Charley worked darkness back to light. Inevitably the wear and tear of scrubbing, rubbing, scraping, licking, erasing, flogging, and washing destroyed not only the dark skin he'd applied. At some point along the way at the slightest touch from one of Charley's implements the tortured canvas would collapse in tatters and droop from its frame. There it would hang for weeks, months sometimes, until Charley talked himself into beginning again, stripping the old skin, stretching and thumbtacking a new one in place, propping the frame back on the easel. The last time I saw Charley he remained as adamant as ever about the superiority of his method and just as critical of the old way. And remained just as hopelessly in love with Pat, missing for years, presumed dead in a bus crash in Mexico. Charley still optimistic, digging a hole and burying himself like

Houdini in boxes, blindfolds, and handcuffs, a hole deep within the darkness of the canvas, convinced he can burrow out and bring back alive the fabulous light people swear sleeps down there at the end of the tunnel. Hey Charley, mi amigo, say hello if you bump into my head down there.

Romare Bearden, the world-famous painter who attended Peabody, the same high school in Pittsburgh my incarcerated brother and I attended, said that at the beginning of the Italian Renaissance some artists resisted the demands of their patrons for paintings conforming to the rules of perspective that had become fashionable. Artists feared the deep thrusts cut into their paintings by the new science and math of rendering space. Tintoretto, for example, screwed up on purpose. He believed that illusory holes in a painting could become real holes in which the gaze, maybe the gazer's body and soul, might plunge and be lost forever. Who knew. The point is resist. Painters might tumble in too. Bearden relates how a buddy and mentor of his, Robert Holty, hipped him to an example of resistance one afternoon as they stood studying Tintoretto's "Finding the Body of St. Mark." Holty pointed and whispered something like, See, this goes back and then something happens up here so that you have an hourglass effect. Instead of going right into the depth here — Tintoretto could have if he'd wanted to, he certainly possessed the chops — he made it like this . . . so you don't get too much of the illusion of space receding.

Romare Bearden's collages remind me of how my mother, another one of my idols — a life-saver like Fanon — talks. Her stories flatten and fatten perspective. She crams everything, everyone, everywhere into the present, into words that flow, intimate and immediate as the images of a Bearden painting. When she's going good my mom manages to crowd in lots and lots of stuff without creating a feeling of claustrophobia. She fills space to the brim without exhausting it. Without surrendering the authority of her long life, she always talks about the precise moment she's inhabiting. Makes the moment present and large enough, thank goodness, to include everybody listening. Bearden's collages and my mother's narratives truly democratic — each detail counts equally, every part matters as much as any grand design. Size and placement don't highlight forever some items at the expense of others. Meaning equals point of view. Stop. I sound like a museum audiocassette guide when all I really need to say is *dance* — my mom talking or Bearden at the turntable mixing cutouts with paint with fabric with photos with empty space are works-in-progress inviting me to dance.

And speaking of guides, perhaps Thomas should change his protagonist's name to Tristram, you know, as in Tristram Shandy, the eponymous hero of Sterne's backasswards novel. Except *Tristram*'s a clue fingerpointing in the wrong direction. Blaming the dead. As if Fanon and Tristram don't have enough troubles, their own wounds, wars, and ghosts to account for.

Helicopters whomp, whomp, whomp-whomping in the distance across a gray sky. They look like insects skimming the tops of tall buildings, sniffing and declining whatever goodies the towering stamens and pistils offer. An unusually busy traffic of choppers. Are they practicing. Has the shit hit the fan. Vehicles burning, a restaurant car-bombed. Are the helicopters ferrying survivors to emergency wards or bearing newscams to broadcast a spectacular accident, report a traffic jam, a power plant exploding, a flood, a parade, you never know anymore, the sound of choppers may be innocent but once bitten you never look at stray dogs the way you once did.

In the playground below my ninth-floor window an Asian guy heaves a long shot at the basket and when the ball knocks through the hoop the man thrusts both arms into the air. *Three.* A little extra spring in his step as he lopes to retrieve the ball. The guy doesn't hear choppers whomping overhead. Couldn't care less about the choppers' mission, the mission of terrorists, the bodies squirming in agony or hunger or smoldering beside a highway or suffocating in elevators filling up with smoke. Thank you, Jesus, for blindness that every once in a great while allows one of us to hit the target.

THOMAS TEACHES WRITING IN MY OLD SCHOOL

THERE ARE RULES for making a novel, says Thomas, standing assbackwards to his creative writing students, muttering rules over his shoulder while he jots them on the blackboard. On this, our first day together, and thus a sort of birthday, let's begin with point of view, the telling voice, the voice telling the story, the narrative heart that must always be alive, beating at the telling center or there would be no story, no novel, and to illustrate his point, various diagrams and underlined words with arrows like guided missiles connecting the dots begin to appear on the dusty blackboard — green not black its actual color — at the front of a small classroom holding a dozen or so hopeful white college students — their actual color not white nor any other paintbox color — who have gathered together in the name of fiction, a crew of wannabes yearning to learn the secret of doing what Thomas has done — break into print — break into the conversation about their lives books have been conducting since long before the students were born, books unread by them, books whose authors are mostly dead or much older and therefore not exactly qualified to speak about present lives. Does Thomas concur, hearing the nub of chalk in his hand tap-tap-tapping, as if the green chalkboard's a wall between cells and he's tapping a message to a fellow prisoner or the board a door he humbly taps, seeking permission to enter the office of a senior colleague, much older, smarter, more distinguished than Thomas will ever be, the chalk a blind man's cane tap-tap-tapping the way French impressionists composed a world with dots of color, and sure enough, a picture, familiar and embarrassing, greets Thomas when he steps back to regard his boardwork, a photo remembered from a thirty-year-old article in the alumni magazine of the college where he copped his first gig, a feature about neophyte instructors, featuring rare Thomas, the only member of his race on the faculty, Thomas wearing a sharp, Ivy League–cut herringbone suit, facing a class, the late-sixties shaggy backs of student heads in the foreground, and behind Thomas in the photo's background the rules for writing a novel sketched on a chalkboard — actual color unknown, since the photo's black and white — rules appearing just as slapdash, as spontaneously improvised and freshly minted in the ancient picture as they seem today, same ole, same ole shit recycled almost exactly, startling then shaming Thomas.

What if a former student fast-forwarded to this classroom or one of his present students bumped into the old photo. Would she or he demand a tuition rebate. Demand Thomas's head. On the other hand, don't all professors teach from yellowed lecture notes, scruffy index cards, falling-apart looseleaf notebooks, manila folders stuffed with brown-around-the-edges clippings. Why not. What else do you have to teach, if not the truth of your experience, your witness. Your old school theories precious like the music you grew up listening to, dancing to, fucking to. Midnighters. Five Royales. Turbans, Dells, Diablos, Spaniels, Flamingos. Oldies but goodies. Better now. Right on. All the questions and answers in one harmonized, swooning, do-wah falsetto riff. Same truth. Same greasy teenage fingers dipping nonstop into a bowl of potato chips because gobbling chips and day-dreaming safer than getting out on the floor and dancing. Same hopeless wishes and lost, lost loves. All good. All true then and now. Word.

Rules are truth, aren't they. Rules remember truth and pass it on. They are called *rules* because they truly work. Because truth and beauty mate when we apply the rules. Sometimes. Do. Wah. Why would the rules change each semester. Each decade. Each century.

Now don't get me wrong, folks. What I've scribbled on the board is neither a suicide note nor a foolproof set of instructions for assembling a novel. Rather, I'm suggesting, no, asserting, there's some, I repeat, *some* method in the writing madness. Writing madness. Isn't that precisely what we do. On another day we might begin class just as profitably there, with the madness, and accomplish as much, maybe more than beginning with method. Two sides of the same coin. Same shield, the Igbo would say. Can't brandish one side without lifting the other. Remember Otis singing his fa-la-la sad happy song.

Not guilty, Thomas pleads. Though the rules decorating a blackboard in the photo your classmate Ms. Jones or Mr. Smith unearthed and kindly distributed to each of you may resemble the rules I've outlined on the board today, I assure you, girls and boys, they ain't the same. Not the same no matter how much they look the same. I'm a different man today. Times have changed. You're different today than you were yesterday. None of you kiddies born yet that day thirty-five years ago in Philadelphia when I scribbled rules on a U of P green blackboard.

It had never happened. No need to defend yourself, Thomas. No disgruntled, vengeful, ungrateful student had stumbled upon sensitive material and busted you, Thomas. No terrorist had attempted to jack your class. A very unlikely circumstance. As unlikely as receiving a severed human head in the mail. (A very, very, very unlikely event that did happen to Thomas, but only once.)

Anyway, Thomas looks good in his herringbone suit. The Bible told him so. The Bible of his ex-wife's mouth, a Bible because in the courtroom she swore no lie had ever crossed her lips, then enumerated the many untruths Thomas had inflicted upon her, his sins just cause for the extortionate alimony payments she argued the judge should award. She'd told Thomas he looked good in his herringbone suit one morning when as usual he'd left himself not a minute to spare, his legs and heart already rehearsing the brisk twenty-block walk from the apartment beside Regent Park to his university office. He didn't say she looked good that morning, but she surely did look good, just out of the shower, wearing a green shorty robe, her curly feet and calves bare, snuggled up on the couch. On his way to the door he'd paused, unable to resist a last pat of her damp black hair. She'd laid down her book and grabbed something, probably the tail of the herringbone suit's jacket, and like Tarbaby wouldn't let go. Before he could say what they both knew he must say, *Gotta run,* she had his zipper down and was rummaging inside the baggy herringbone tweed trousers with an enthusiasm reminding him of Charley's Pat, working his penis through the slit in his boxers. The surprise kiss froze him in his tracks, especially since she planted her lips on a part of him her mouth, unsolicited, rarely visited. Standing next to the couch, herringbone elegant and formal, he felt awkward, a little like a soldier unexpectedly called to attention. Earlier, glancing up from reading her book when Thomas had been fluttering around the room searching for a paper or book he'd need at school, she'd said, *My, my. You look handsome this morning in your herringbone suit, professor.* The kiss brief. A kind of mouth caress, a bit of friction, a squeeze. His joint just starting to swell as she tucked it back in his shorts, then a bulge under his herringboned fly she grinned at and rubbed through the rich fabric after she'd zipped him up.

Whose life. A scene floating up from a novel's turning pages. One among a string of easy, page-turner scenes, he almost hears the music scoring them, assuring the audience that an author's in charge and things will work out just fine or disastrously, perfectly unfine, just keep reading. Why couldn't he write this novel. Or even better, why not live it. Love it or leave it, Thomas.

THOMAS LEAVES

FRANCE FLIES PAST through the window of the train. Does it, now. Is that what France does. Did, will do. Fly past. Fly fast-forward through a train window while Thomas, Fanon manuscript in his suitcase, daydreams other times, other places. For instance Philadelphia, his first university gig, city of love, of fire. How large the window. How many pages in his Fanon book. How small France. What speed flying. Who says so. *What happened to the head.* All of France in the window. An unfurling panoramic scroll of the entire nation present and past. Or one postcard scene at a time. Be specific. Well, more like one colorful postcard at a time, the cards succeeding each other very rapidly, so quickly, twenty-four frames per second, we experience an illusion of motion and also of standing still as we watch and can't tell which. Where are we. Why quibble. The view pretty either way. France flies through the train window or we fly by France, the country collapsing in ruins behind us, each card, toppled by the weight of the scene it bears, knocks over the next card in line, and the next and the next, nothing will ever be the same after the train flies down the rails. A bullet through the heart of the country. Through Thomas's head. Mile after mile of France disappearing into eyes trained through a window, eyes riveted on nature flowing or flying or galloping past. Out there beyond the train, on the other side of the glass, sits a world apart, but it also flies through the window and, like the head, lands in Thomas's lap, France beyond and within this steel time capsule of TGV racing express from Paris, Gare Montparnasse to Vannes, Gare Vannes, from the metropolitan center toward rural south and west, past cows, fields, chateaus, barns, factories, silos, huts, bridges, sheep, thousand-year-old thatch-roofed villages, horses of various ages, sizes, colors, no people to speak of for vast welcome stretches on the unfurling scroll until a large town closes like a fist around the train and then it's all about people, the visible ones, more or less his size, passenger size, scattered here and there along a station platform or the uncountable tiny invisibles populating the opaque-windowed belly of this town beast hunkered down over the tracks, an immense cold shadow blanketing our carriage, darkening our sky, brightening the train's merciless interior lights till the TGV creeps past the urban zone after stopping a minute to take on fuel and passengers, who knows what else, maybe a tariff's due or the engineer fell asleep — or maybe he's paying homage *toot-toot* to his crippled mother who lives here on the sixth floor of one of the government-subsidized apartment buildings, *toot-toot*, the views shuttling through the window too much of the same thing so he doesn't look, doesn't notice when or if the TGV is moving or not, not flying for sure, remember, remember France flying by through the window. Ooh-la-la. Like a snowstorm. Or firestorm. Oh. Oh where. Where is she now.

On one of his early morning walk/runs beside the East River the bright idea was born of carrying the yet-to-be-written book about Frantz Fanon to a famous, infamous film director who lives somewhere in southern France or perhaps in a chalet near his birthplace in Switzerland. Either (a) an actual journey to France with the manuscript in his bag — which would of course entail writing the Fanon book or (b) imagining such a trip and imagining a book, both fictions facts in the larger fiction of a life he constructs daily. Neither option (a) nor (b) an easy task. Neither extricates him from the burden of the alternative hovering in the wings. (A) and (b) in each other's way. Either way all voyages end nowhere. After a lot of bother, sooner or later you're home again, with more (and less) time on your hands to kill so why not kill time softly, gently, like the song advises. Travel like the hero of *Au Rebours* who never left home. Let your fingers do the walking. Click. Click. Click. A world delivered twenty-four-seven to your door.

Out the window, maxed to warp speed again, the countryside shudders past. Green fields, fields plowed black, straw-colored fallow fields, heather purplish fields under a single, seamless blue sky, a patchwork quilt of earth tones rippling, jostled, set in motion by our thunderous passing, the train a thread jerked through a needle's eye by a palsied hand, oh lord, this seems like the right thing to write at this moment though tomorrow tomorrow who knows about tomorrow you do lord of course but I mean us, me, we terrestrials pressed under the glass of imperturbable blue, what the fuck do we know. The fleetingness feels such and such a way right now, this instant that I write it on the page, though you know lord and even little ole ignorant me knows I'll be sorry tomorrow, maybe sorry everafter for whatever I write jiggedy-jig today sitting in my seat on the TGV through rural France, fair weather today, tomorrow who knows.

Serene above networks of circling choppers, planes are flying in New York City's airspace again. A decision disrespectful of the 9/11 dead and dangerous for the living. Old flight paths resumed because they maximize fuel efficiency and profit. Business as usual. New tower, tallest in the world, they promise, will rise to replace the old ones. Each silver plane a mad cow. Poisoning the sky as it's been poisoned by being fed its bones, its wastes.

Three new stories in the news catch my eye — faith-based prisons, cell phones with tracking chips, a man arrested for raising a tiger and an alligator in a Harlem apartment. The same story really. The Big Squeeze at both ends, so nothing left alive inside people's heads. Those three stories in the news and the fate of certain stories no longer in the news trouble Thomas too. Whatever happened to South Africa. He'd always hoped to see South Africa before he died. South Africa a good destination, perhaps, for his orphaned head.

I walk a lot to stay fit and focus my thoughts. Thomas follows or some days leads, and on good days Frantz Fanon joins us. He gets a chance to sightsee in New York City, an opportunity not offered by his other life. The only America Fanon saw firsthand a huge hospital. I study his eyes, wonder what he thinks as I narrate our tour.

If you cross over the FDR highway on the pedestrian ramp just south of Williamsburg Bridge, descend the temporary wooden steps (probably concrete and permanent by now), hang a quick left through the ornate gateway of a tall black wrought-iron fence, then continue to bear left toward the water by following paths or cutting catty-corner through construction, you'll find after a minute or so an unbarricaded entrance to the walkway along the East River. Turn right on the walkway and soon you'll see the Manhattan Bridge about a mile ahead, and beyond it, seemingly beneath it from this perspective, the Brooklyn Bridge. A half-minute more on the rusty-railed walkway edging the river and you reach a vantage point allowing your eyes to follow the course of the river south, downstream. You'll see the East River doesn't run in a straight line, it bends and bulges on the way to the sea, a thick, meandering serpent, friend to a pilot who employs the river and bridges spanning it to guide his plane to its target. The river widening finally to a broad plain, shimmering sometimes, sometimes misty, the horizon visible only if you imagine it out there, a line where water touches sky and Manhattan Island ends and the East River merges with the Atlantic Ocean, where even in the clearest weather your eyes can't tell land from sea from air — out there just before all details are extinguished, on most days you can see the Statue of Liberty.

As you proceed on the walkway, the Statue of Liberty remains visible for only about two hundred yards before a large abandoned warehouse on Pier 40 blocks your view. Cut off from seeing very far downriver, your gaze shifts naturally to the opposite shore, its docks, giant loading cranes, the jumble of tall smokestacks, billboards, factories, storage tanks, or you may check out boat traffic — the *Zephyr*,

Sea-Streak, yellow water taxis, tugs, NYPD launches, garbage barges inching to the sea — or glance down over the railing at water you hear splashing the river's concrete channel. The walkway doglegs, detouring Pier 40's backyard of clutter and ruin enclosed by Cyclone fencing. You're underneath the noisy canopy of FDR Drive, the least attractive stretch of the walkway, on South Street, where a series of hangarlike municipal buildings and parking lots for official vehicles — garbage trucks, EMT vans, fire engines, cop cars, ambulances — prevent access to the river for about a half-mile until a break in the fence lets you go left, following freshly painted white lines of a bike path. Here at the foot of Chinatown the walkway resumes its riverside course, just missing the shadow cast by the Brooklyn Bridge and its ramps high overhead. To catch the sun, steel benches, set close to the railing, are spaced along this half-mile straightaway that leads to another detour where you must go either right to South Street again, or left through the remains of the Fulton Fish Market. Either choice brings you to a pier crowded with shops and restaurants, a brace of tall-masted nineteenth-century ships preserved as floating museums, and, beyond this touristy patch, a series of terminals for ferries and sightseeing boats, then a helicopter pad, then the Staten Island ferry dock, a subway station, and finally Battery Park.

Whether you've been attentive or not to longer vistas of the East River opening here and there as you proceeded downstream, the Statue of Liberty won't be seen again till you reach Battery Park, and rather than standing onshore or inches offshore as it seemed to stand a half-hour ago when you first sighted it, the statue, situated on its own small, private island, has drifted away from Manhattan, separating itself from the war memorials, souvenir kiosks, and Senegalese vendors of Battery Park by a good half-mile of water you must line up and pay a fee to traverse by boat if you wish to get closer.

To view the Statue of Liberty from the original point on the river walkway I directed you to earlier, you don't need a perfect day. Unless fog or rain is unusually thick, it's easy to pick out the statue's distinctive silhouette, its imitation of a sprinter wearing a floor-length gown on the victory stand of the 1968 Olympics, fist thrust to the sky in a Black Power salute. The Statue of Liberty pokes up darker, taller than rows of skyhook loading cranes beyond it, a forest of cranes I once imagined as masts of slaving ships, though I knew better. Seen from that vantage point where we began our trip along the walkway, a tiny Statue of Liberty seems to be located directly underneath the Brooklyn Bridge and the Brooklyn Bridge itself appears small, spanning the East River much lower, closer to the water than the Manhattan Bridge, which frames your gaze downriver. Your eyes not exactly deceiving you, just performing the painter's classic trick of rendering perspective by shrinking and stacking things to signify depth and distance, time and space on a flat canvas. I read the language of stacking and shrinking, believe and disbelieve what it says, fully aware that appearances will alter drastically when, for instance, I reverse direction and retrace my steps to the place I started. Walking from Battery Park back to my apartment, if I stop beside one of the Brooklyn Bridge's stone piers and look upriver, I'll see a tiny, distant Manhattan Bridge crossing the river miles lower, closer to the water than the mammoth Brooklyn Bridge I stand beneath. Things once seen above are under and things once seen under are above, just as you predicted, Fanon.

You know the guys in here say they short after they done half they bit, say they're short, don't care how much time they got to do — it's short time, my brother in prison explained, *cause they know they already done that much time once and it ain't killed them so they know they can do that much again. So they short, you know, like running downhill, bro, after running uphill.*

Any plan, any tour is full of holes no matter how carefully organized. No reason to reverse direction now, no reason to overturn the truth my eyes privilege for this moment, a truth allowing me to feel

I'm not simply passing through but belong here, and here belongs to me, my senses dependably tapping out a code, tap-tap-tapping a version of the world like a blind person sounds the pavement with a cane. Surprisingly, when I'm lucky, I can manage, more or less, to guide myself through vast stretches of utter darkness by drawing imaginary maps, like this one I'm sketching for you, Fanon, connecting the dots, *tap, tap, tap,* connecting the emptinesses between dots, to get us from my apartment near the Williamsburg Bridge to Battery Park.

Given the construction work complicating and rerouting the walkway beside the East River, evidently someone has big plans. Thomas believes the area is being divided, impounded, locked up within a honeycomb of newly erected fences, gates, walls, and soon will be accessible only to those with keys or permission. One day when the many stout enclosures of chainlink fencing scattered along the walkway are employed routinely not to protect freshly planted trees or grass but to cage dissidents swept up from street riots, a day when police patrols deny access to the East River because it's a highway that could carry deadly cargoes from the sea to the city's heart, I wonder, Fanon, who will remember that this locked-down no man's land began as a proposal for a public park.

Every morning the helicopters come, the infernal racket of them every morning patrolling, attacking or guarding us, who knows anymore, all Thomas can say is that they arrive at dawn, rain or shine, and perform ear-shattering circles in the air above his building, friend or enemy how can he tell, they are so high, so tiny even when it sounds like they're crashing into his bedroom. Choppers impossibly loud in spite of the mosquito look of them, their bodies half eyeball, half string of trailing drool, bearing no markings he can see. Far away, calmly circling at first, then exploding *whomp-whomp* closer and closer, till he wants to scream, clamp his hands over his ears, throw an arm across his face as the walls buckle. He listens to sirens echoing in the street, hears the firing of air-to-air missiles, hears flaming bugs sizzling down out of the sky, ours, theirs, who knows, who knows who's winning the air war over the city, who knows whose city this is, whose war, except each morning sirens and choppers chop-chopping, but so far, thank goodness, no enemy has broken through rings of spinning steel blades, volleys of laser-guided darts to drop the weapon that will end everybody's troubles.

THE HEAD DEVOURS THOMAS

THOMAS DOES NOT REMEMBER when he began to think of the severed head as a message in a bottle. Old metaphor, but he liked it. Kept it around to play with. The metaphor, not the head, stupid. Then one morning he's certain the head not a message intended for him. It had been delivered by mistake. The package meant for somebody not Thomas. Not his head. No problem if he had refused the box. No return address visible, but somebody paid to have it delivered. UPS would have a record. Unless the brown uniform stolen and the brown guy wearing it a terrorist. If the brown person an innocent bystander like Thomas, he would have returned the refused package to the UPS depot. Dumped it in the limbo of dead packages and dead letters UPS must maintain. Thomas off the hook. The incident erased like the naked ladies on his magic slate.

But the meaning of a message doesn't alter necessarily if the recipient isn't the person the sender intended. A newish book about the black diaspora and internationalism Thomas is reading points out that W.E.B. Du Bois addressed his now famous words "the problem of the twentieth century is the problem of the color line" not to an American readership of *The Souls of Black Folk* but to a select international audience of distinguished black artists and intellectuals convening in London in 1900. When chasing the meaning of a message, it doesn't make sense to push the notion of an intended, targeted audience too far. Messages and their meanings wind up where Freud contends all writing commences — in silence. And end there. Where writers end. In a black hole big and bad enough to swallow time and space, the chamberpot where everybody does their dirt. You can't escape, Thomas. Your head's there too, waiting for you to claim it, rotting, smelling up the joint.

The head all gaping mouth now, circled by fat, white, rubbery minstrel lips that momentarily spare Thomas a view of its battered features. The mouth hole's laughing, chortling — yuk-yuk-yukkedy-yuk. I ain't going nowhere, bro.

This business of communication, of messages sent and received, of meaning and not meaning, of books written and unwritten, ruled by the same law of the jungle ruling the universe from bottom up and top down, Thomas fears. Eat or be eaten. Same circle, same simple principle — an appetite of one magnitude of power consuming until it's consumed by an appetite of a greater magnitude of power. Simple and neat. Figured by the ancient metaphor of a serpent swallowing its tail, or tail swallowing its head, old ouroboros the ultimate black hole, all existence ending and beginning as the greedy python, looking for a meal, whips back upon itself and plunges into its own guts.

Still, Thomas can't surrender the idea of words making a world. Billions upon trillions of brown UPS guys gathering every morning to receive and distribute messages to every nook and cranny of all forty acres of the universe. Each word delivered becomes real and worlds become real. Except the brown messengers like to play African games. Occasionally they trade messages, exchange routes, lie, steal, scramble messages, shake messages in their fists and shoot crap with them till it's dark and too late for delivery. Eat some. Misplace some. Squat and squeeze out new messages from the ingredients of old ones they've gulped down. Words never exactly say what someone intends because the messengers can't help misbehaving, Thomas thinks, a little bit like the people back home in Homewood. Wiggle room even when words seem to bring a mandate directly, irreversibly from on high. Words not meaningless but fickle. Grand plans fickle. Fate fickle. Just one slip — a head misdirected to Thomas's door — sabotages the entire scheme. The same words or different words, who knows, will be entrusted next morning to the assembled delivery persons in their brown uniforms. Words will try again and that's the part Thomas clings to, the part keeping his head above water. The part making him laugh, on good days. Words delivering messages over and over again, scripts for plans doomed to fail.

AFRICA

When thomas writes his Fanon book he'll borrow many voices to disguise his voice, speak from behind masks the way Fanon composed *Black Skin, White Masks*. A simple plan like Fanon's plan for saving Algeria. As simple as Hannibal crossing the Alps with terrorizing elephants to surprise attack Rome's back door. Or an American president dropping a fleet of helicopters at night into the desert of a hostile country to rescue hostages. Or Columbus sailing west to go east. Or terrorists chopping off heads to liberate bodies. As simple as accepting a face in the mirror as real. Simple if you don't ask who is gazing into the glass or who's inside staring back, simple if you don't insist that it's impossible for a face in a mirror to be real unless the one who gazes fabricates a history for it, a story no face in the mirror can take shape without.

We granted this meeting in spite of our better judgment, Comrade Fanon. Who knows whether a thousand-year-old trading route you discovered in a book about the ancient kingdom of Mali remains passable today. A reverse Ho Chi Minh Trail, you say. A lifeline up from the south to supply freedom fighters in the north. A second front, you say. As if one quick blow could sever the Gordian knot of bloody struggle with the French. Get serious, Comrade Fanon. The risks are unjustifiable. We're engaged in a struggle for Algerian independence, not a crusade to liberate the African continent. In this war we must count bullets as carefully as we count soldiers. No room for error. Treason to squander resources on fanciful notions. *An African Legion. Ethiop's dark hand stretching forth to aid the Algerian revolution.* Romantic nonsense at best. At worst an insult to the Algerian people who are starving and dying daily for freedom.

So it's just an eight-man commando in two Range Rovers traversing terrain rugged and treacherous as the worst on his island home. Fanon recalls the night he'd descended alone from Morne Rouge, sliding, stumbling, crawling down Mount Pelée's steep, ravine-crisscrossed slope to a beach where a rumored boat to Dominica might wait. Stealing away in darkness, stealing his father's suit to pay for a boat ticket, stealing himself to go off and fight for France, stealing his presence from his brother's wedding. Fanon and Comandante Chawkwi in the lead Rover rattle like seeds in a dried gourd. The ride's shaking their vehicle to pieces. More than once Fanon's helmet saves his skull from being split wide open when he's jolted to the roof of the cab. Less a matter of following a road across Mali than of doggedly pursuing a meager possibility that beyond the next flooded plain or blockade of boulders or thicket of impenetrable growth a merciful trace might appear, not of paved road but any encouraging sign that once upon a time a caravan of camels, mules, and horses might have squeezed a bit farther north by following this route. Easier now for Fanon to swallow the bitter pill of being refused the seriousness of a light plane or chopper for reconnaissance of the supply line he'd proposed. Mali's close-mouthed hills and forests wouldn't have divulged their secrets to anyone spying from the air. Doesn't the invisibility of the ancient passage prove his point, strengthen his argument. You can see the path only if you're on the ground, only if you shape-shift and become a lizard crawling over the rocks, a gazelle warily fording a swamp, a beetle scuttling this way and that. The Range Rover scrapes ahead into an opening that seems a tunnel through tangled foliage but leads nowhere, except to a precipice beckoning them over an edge. You proceed by reversals, by default. Unsure of your next move. In fact lost, always lost. To free a patient from the labyrinth of illness, a healer must become the patient. Become the map. Live in an alien world, live with unfamiliar rules for choosing right or left, up or down. Physician, heal thyself. Risk the step that may crack the ice of a frozen will. Rumbling down from piggybacked hills, speeding along clear stretches of road, this mission, this cure only as real as each inch, each kilometer the Range Rovers log.

Riding shotgun, bouncing, shaking in the lead truck driven by Comandante Chawkwi, Frantz Fanon is thinking the thoughts above or similar thoughts it's my duty, my mission, my folly to represent. I'm observing Fanon's vehicle from a low-flying, camouflage-painted Cessna he couldn't convince the FLN to beg, borrow, or steal for his mission. For convenience's sake, let's say my x-ray vision can penetrate the plane's belly, the Range Rover's roof, the helmet, hair, skin, and bone of Fanon shielding the brain brewing the thoughts I seek to translate into words or preferably visual images since my goal is to write a script a famous filmmaker can't refuse about Fanon's life, or to be more precise the last years of his life (occasional flashbacks permitted when appropriate), or to be even more exact and cut to the quick, a film script bringing a dead Fanon back to life.

It's 1961. Fanon's last year on earth, the year in whose first month, January, Fanon's new acquaintance Patrice Lumumba, first prime minister of a brand-spanking-new Republic of Congo, will be kidnapped, tortured, executed by Belgians and Congolese, his body burned in an oil drum, the year in whose last month, December, Fanon will succumb to leukemia in a hospital in Bethesda, Maryland, 1961 the year of this journey we're shadowing that begins in a Guinean town, Kankan, crosses the border to Bamako in Mali, then goes to Ségou to Mopti to Gao and north, always pushing north toward Algeria's war of independence from France, following the North Star or whichever star shining in the firmament above this hemisphere in the fall of 1961 directs pilgrims to the promised land, whichever star's luminosity and lustrosity beams hope, a beacon and benediction, Uh-huh, oh yeah, don't yeh hear me talkin to yeh, chillen, don't youall just adore that star shinin bright, oh, oh, oh, you are my shining star, the old, new star leading Frantz and his crew in SUVs humping north across Mali. Good golly, Miss Mali, you sure love to ball. Blasts from the past in my earphones, not Fanon's. Before his short life ended, will end just a few months from this moment we're imagining together, did Fanon hear our Manhattans, our Mr. Penniman, our glossy-topped star Little Richard sing "Tutti Frutti" or "Send Me Some Lovin" or "Good Golly," etc., or are these tunes anachronisms inserted into Fanon's stream of consciousness in a Range Rover in late September, early October of 1961. You can look it up. Google the songs' release dates in France or give me the benefit of the doubt. Let the beat roll on. Anachronisms galore sprinkle this story. If that sort of thing bothers you, you're in trouble. The boy can't help it. Fanon lay moldering in his grave (wherever it is) by the time Jimmy Carter's flotilla of choppers on a mission to rescue hostages got chopped in the Iranian desert. And the Ho Chi Minh Trail cutting through what was once French Indochina doesn't become famous until years after Dien Bien Phu and the Algerian revolution. Who knows whether or not Fanon ever devoted a single, solitary thought to Hannibal's sneaky conquest of Rome. And what about Fanon's presence in a future he apparently did not survive to see.

This present moment of haves and have-nots slugging it out in the torrid Middle East and Africa. Does Fanon still occupy a ringside seat as the bell rings for another round of a bout that can't end with a knockdown, only a knockout — arena, everything and everybody in it, *poof*, gone with the wind.

Good golly. No fun, Thomas, to think too much about Fanon's story or what you think you're going to make of it. No rules for scoring a life. Are there rules for scoring a movie. Who wrote them. Who's allowed to break them. Why not put everything in a soundtrack. Cantatas, garage bands, a DJ scratching, marching bands, shawms and bombards, traveling music, water music. Fanon beside a campfire in the African wilderness chews on a KFC chicken wing while *Eine kleine Nachtmusik* tinkles in the background. Audio a different story, different language from video. Another country with different coordinates of time and space. No death. No dates. No beginning nor end, a love match if the mix works the way it's spozed to work, Miss Molly.

Fanon's simple idea. A second front. Black blood flowing north like black gold once flowed from Mali to enrich Europe. When freedom achieved in Algeria the flow will reverse, north to south, inundate the Sahara, the dunes turning green, flowers blossoming, showers of petals, of seeds and fertile rain transforming desiccated land, reviving dusty cities baking in the sun. Africa rained upon, wet and newborn, slick with black blood, black gold, the continent astir, shaking off eons of sleep, a fresh new being who rises, roars. Erect finally, Africa sheds its fear of nakedness, then sheds the myths of gender, the chimerical skins of race and class and privilege, those blankets humankind has been cowering beneath, hiding, sucking its thumb for centuries. A simple idea. Why not.

What music should play in the background while Fanon dreams his simple idea. If not Little Richard, maybe Otis on the dock of the bay. Or a thumb piano playing picture-postcard Africa on the soundtrack. Smiling giraffes and zebras framed through a Range Rover's window. Then play music to make the frame jiggle like an old film about to go bad on the screen. Play the jeep exploded by a mine. Play the camera fleeing. Play Africa's stillness and immensity surrounding, shrinking the viewer. Africa stretching the frame, like an ocean or snow-capped mountains on the horizon, a reminder that your life ends in the blink of an eye but lasts as long as trips people take when they imagine themselves not alive anymore.

No music perhaps. Perhaps natural sound — assembly-line ratcheting of the Range Rover's engine, the thump, clatter, whine, bash of its tires on questionable tarmac. Modulate the noise. Play it like a kid playing with a TV's volume. Sound erratic and perverse, barely audible, then the ear-splitting crescendo of a chopper bursting into the Range Rover's cab. Fanon imperturbable. Impervious to tsunamis of sound. Not hearing what we hear. To guess what soundtrack he's listening to, follow his eyes. They're fixed on Comandante Chawkwi. We're a bobbing good luck ornament fastened to the dashboard and receive a full frontal view of the driver's face and Fanon's eyes absorbed by it. Jumpy, hand-held realism reestablishes the bumpety-bump ride over a corduroy surface juggling the Range Rover's wheels. Tighten the closeup of Chawkwi's face. Allow the engine's roar to recede, the shaking to diminish as the driver's face fills the screen, implacable as Africa a minute ago after we flew through the window. The stillness, the rugged serenity of the driver's features holds only long enough to register, then Chawkwi blinks, animating the wooden mask. He's simply a man intent on negotiating a dangerous, primitive road very much like back roads on Martinique, Fanon thinks. Chawkwi's ebony brow knotted by concentration, a possessed, almost crazy glint in his small eyes. Is he high on drugs. No. Absolutely not. It's not that movie. Revolution the only drug permitted. He's weary and dazed. He's been driving too long but cannot afford to relax. Past exhaustion, Chawkwi fights to keep an edge, determined not to lose his grip on an opponent he's been wrestling for hours, years, a sly, unrelenting opponent who feigns submission, ropadoping, winking at the ring of spectators that includes every single soul from both villages the two champions represent. Desperate wariness in the driver's eyes, dreading the next sudden lunge or thrashing explosion of the body wrapped in his arms, the opponent who seems drained of resistance till the second you forget his power and then he breaks free again, circling you again, grinning, his orangutan arms dangling, feinting, cuffing you off-balance, beast eyes glowing.

Fanon can't take his eyes off Chawkwi's fierce scowl. Reads the raw truth inscribed therein: no fighter will exit the ring alive. He studies the indwelling silence and discipline of the driver's stare. Is he dead already Fanon asks himself, a casualty whatever the struggle's outcome. In his journal of the mission, Fanon scores his vision of Chawkwi: *Eyes like this do not lie. They say quite openly that they have seen terrible things: repression, torture, shellings, pursuits, liquidations . . . You see a sort of haughtiness in such eyes, and an almost murderous hardness. And intimidation. You quickly get into the habit of being careful in dealing with men like this . . . Very difficult to deceive, to get around or to infiltrate.*

Impossible to write more on a jostling, washed-out segment of road, an absence of road, a wish for more road to open mercifully ahead so the jeeps can accelerate, regain lost time, give chattering teeth, leapfrogging bellies a rest. If I don't write now, will I ever get it down, Fanon asks. Reluctantly he wedges his journal into the unzipped bulk of canvas duffel bag his boots pin to the Range Rover's floor. Retrieves a book. Like the driver gripping the steering wheel with both hands, Doctor Fanon uses both his to steady the book he reads when he can't write. Never enough hours in a day. Dozens of wounded tasks stuffed into the dispensary's waiting room, a line of ailing, crippled tasks out the door, into the corridor, down the stairs, straggling into the street, around the block on which the clinic sits. Only ten minutes of office hours remain. And counting down. He spreads a large folio across his knees, pressing down the edges, nearly cracking its spine, cracking a knee when the Range Rover bucks and rams his legs into the dash. The words bounce, helpless as his body flying up and thumping down on the seat. Words unanchored from the page, launched into random flights and formations, new sentences bumped aside by newer sentences disappearing too fast to read. The stately pageant of medieval Mali disintegrates into carnival. The antique empire's dignified history, its orderly dynasties of rulers a hodgepodge bricolage of hyphenated Arabic names, dates, invasions, prophets, migrations, assassinations, dancing to a syncopated fast jook from home, his green island across the sea. No matter how hard he grips and attempts to concentrate, the bouncing words of Mali's story escape. A narrative typed in the air by as many flying monkeys as there are pages, as there are words, as there are riffs and verses and ways to move your feet, your swaying shoulders and dreamy head to the beat of a single island tune.

Strangely, after a day of intense, withering African heat, a desire for fire the first night in Mali. Desiring fire as much as they'd wanted each tepid sip from their canteens to become a crisp, cool, rushing torrent they could plunge into up to their thighs and splash and swim in as they drank. Fanon had sensed a slight chill descending as the sun dropped toward the horizon, an unexpected chill to match the abrupt, absolute blackness of nightfall. Just the opposite of home, where night doesn't fall, where darkness, as old sharp-eyed chronicler of Martinique Lafcadio Hearn wrote, lazily rises from the land to embrace the sky. Chawkwi, second in command, knows the tricks of this Africa and Fanon is learning to defer to his judgment. Earlier that day Chawkwi had sent three men to gather firewood, extending what Fanon had intended as a five-minute rest stop. Fanon had been a bit annoyed. Why waste precious daylight hours scavenging for firewood. The Range Rover an oven all morning. How much colder at night on a plateau that seemed only slightly elevated above the plains. They'd packed canned rations. Awful, heated or not.

While he was jotting notes in his journal and the men foraging for wood in a blighted gray patch of forest nearby, a shot rang out. Fanon jumped to his feet. From nomads they'd heard that French soldiers appeared unpredictably, a column of dust on the horizon or sealed in the armored halftracks they called rhinos suddenly crashing through the bush. He seemed the only one concerned by the shot. The others must have understood it was just Chawkwi buying dinner with his antique Mauser — one night a gazelle, another night bustards. Later, when a skinny, dog-sized gazelle roasts over a fire, Fanon alarmed again. Why risk a fire. Even in this desolate wilderness, they'd encountered signs of patrols. No telling whose patrols. The French and their Malian mercenaries used the same equipment. Bluster, Malian uniforms procured in Guinea, donned before crossing the border, sufficient thus far to speed the commando through the only government checkpoint. Proof of his plan's feasibility, more evidence of the accessibility of Algeria's soft underbelly. Still, why alert the enemy with an unnecessary campfire. He chose not to second-guess Chawkwi nor air his misgivings. Fanon wished to instill in the men under his command an impression of coolness, confidence, steadiness. None of them knew Fanon a veteran, that he'd been wounded fighting for the country he treats now as an enemy. Always a foreigner, an outsider, permanently on trial. Even here in Africa the color of his skin not quite right. Nor his perfect French. Always tests to be passed. A few yards from the fire, back turned to the others to piss and the African night drops over his head like a sack. He can't see the hand he passes in front of his face nor his pee striking the grass, a miniature fire crackling, echoing the blaze crackling over his shoulder.

Away from the fire, the sky's blacker, full of stars. For some reason he's remembering Paris. Its hostility and honeycomb ghettos. The cruelty of white gazes that excluded him yet followed him with an unbroken, calculating attentiveness to his every gesture, every word and breath. Some days his brown skin prickled, beaded by a literal rash. He remembered the indifference and invisibility he enforced upon himself to relieve the tension of constantly being seen, and worse, seen as something not quite human, a creature he couldn't prevent others from believing they saw. He'd given up the struggle. Too frustrating, too debilitating. He refused to allow their eyes to distract him from his goals, disappeared inside himself, left the dark mask of his skin on view, rendered the rest unreachable. Better to let the others think what they wished to believe. If they busied themselves with what they thought they saw, it opened more room for him to maneuver. Why should he help them search for answers to their questions, their ugly questions that could transform a crowded room into a cell, him under a harsh light, alone, roped to a stool, interrogated by loudspeakers screaming through the walls.

Still, he could love that cold, distant city. Love and pity it. Night the only time he relaxed in Paris, deep night, the almost daylight hours when whores began deserting their posts at windows in the clubs of Montmartre. Late at night he'd close the medical text he'd been memorizing all day, exit the cliché of his attic room, and stroll the dark streets. Cross deserted bridges over the Seine. Alone. Precious solitude and quiet in a teeming city. Alone, hunkering down with a glass of vin rouge in a postage-stamp-sized café or just walking, wandering alone, his body relaxing, no raucous soundtrack of daytime traffic, no muttering, shouting pedestrians on crowded boulevards and avenues, just the night pulse of hidden generators supplying the city's energy, the muted hum of the metropole consuming itself, shrinking into itself, retracting till it fit in the palm of his hand, small and warm and tame as his sex after he squeezes it empty. Paris a glowing crystal ball, a miracle of contracted, compressed force swirling within transparent walls, countless bright particles swirling, colliding, crackling, and just loud enough to hear at the sphere's icy core, if he holds his breath and listens closely, a heart like his pumps. The city his equal. A perfect match. Equally fragile. Equally abandoned. Equally doomed. A glorious city of a million times million lights carving a space in the night no larger than the flickering wedge of flame behind him on an African plateau.

On the first night of the journey north through Mali, did Fanon dream. My answer is no. My answer is that in spite of an exhausting day, he lies awake for hours listening to the tropical forest, his mind retreating, recalling birds, frogs, insects, monsters, and ghosts of his childhood, sounds so familiar, so embedded they must be memories of Martinique, recycled in this primeval setting. But the sounds neither begin nor end in Martinique. He hears the hum of Paris. Paris burning and disappearing and the Seine's lonely murmuring, waiting for Paris to be born once more on its empty banks. The night sounds of Mali are memories older than Martinique, older than Paris, older than memory — how could this be so, he asks himself, even as he thinks the thought — memories older than the first time his eyes and ears opened and his mind began listening. Sounds he hears his first night in Mali convince him they are older than anything. Older than ears and eyes. Old as silence. The Mali sounds drop him onto a dark, damp forest floor. He can't tell from what height, or if he's fallen down or fallen up or jumped or been pushed. No memory of an elsewhere — no nest, no wings, no leafy crotch of branches, no cradling arms or warm breast — only the thump of his heart, the thump of his feet landing, shattering the stillness, his body shaped by waves of silence breaking over him, waves crashing again and again, the same and different each time, and with each blow and between blows he learns himself, his gasps, whines, his coughs and grunts, his breath pushing at the darkness, opening it, sealing it, one more creature in the mix, learning to hear what he is, fear what he's not.

Alerted by the forest sounds, alerted and thrilled by them as high-tension cables bringing power to a New Africa will be thrilled by the passage of enormous voltage. And soothed too. Deeply calmed. Beyond sleep. Emptied of himself. Remembering whomever and wherever he'd been when his feet first thumped against the earth. Falling also rising, weightless as the forest noises he recalls now as he rides beside a driver who scowls at a road which intermittently crumbles to a sandpit or fills with water or skitters off in many directions at once, a fan of game trails, take your pick, the pages turning, skipping ahead, flipping backward. Inhabiting his own story like trying to construct a dam with water. His life never entirely believable. A morning sky opens after a night, Fanon, in which perhaps you had dreamed you'd never awaken. Maybe it's another person's dream you're living. You're only an extra, a bit player. Wouldn't you willingly give up your flimsy role for the solid world of darkness, the reality of creatures you can't see surrounding you, their hunting cries, death wails, scent of their shit and blood, their slithering and wings beating, their fear.

Whether Fanon slept that night or dreamed his dream of Algerian independence or didn't sleeps with him in one of his contested graves. Why do I need to go there. To sleep. To dream with him. Through a three-inch-wide feeding slot in a solid concrete wall I ask my keeper questions. Will a little bit of conversation soften up the guard. Will he respond to my pleading. Or despise me. Lead me on. He enters the cell and appears to listen, letting me run my mouth, write my book — blah, blah, blah — till he's bored and points to the floor. I drop to my knees and beg. He readies the gag, twisting it thicker between the cogs of his fists.

Doctor Fanon. Please free me. Release me from angers and fears that consume me. Heal the divisions within me my enemies exploit to keep me in a place I despise. Myself cut up, separated into bloody pieces, doctor. Like you. Fractured, dispersed, in death as in life. Help me, doc.

Come then, comrades, Doctor Fanon says, *it would be as well to de-cide at once to change our ways. We must shake off the heavy darkness in which we were plunged, and leave it behind. The new day which is already at hand must find us firm, prudent, and resolute.*

PITTSBURGH — A PRISON

THE WHEELCHAIR FOLDS UP easily once you empty it. The backrest and seat are wide leather straps and if I stick my fist under the seat strap and punch up, the chair's braces unlock, its metal sides collapse inward. Mash the metal wings together and I have a compact package that fits conveniently into the trunk of the car I rented at the airport for this visit home. Emptying the wheelchair's not so easy. Whether I lift my mother out of it or help her leverage herself from the wheelchair into the rental car's front seat, emptying the chair's an ordeal. My mother's not heavy, the wheelchair neither heavy nor unwieldy; the difficulty stems from the chair's existence and the truth that there's no way around it, the chair a simple, evil fact we didn't expect, didn't plan for, and when it's sitting there waiting to be emptied or waiting to be filled, we hate the wheelchair's implacability, the necessity to deal with it, work around it, include it in our activities. The chair's existence spites us, hurts us like the hateful fact of the prison's stone walls incarcerating my brother these last twenty-eight years. The prison also folds up when prison visits end. Folds up for us, the visitors, anyway, though my brother remains behind, locked in a steel cage. The prison emptied of us folds up for storage in whatever compartment we allot for it, shrinking smaller and smaller once we're outside its walls, so small finally we don't see it except we're always aware that the prison sits like a wheelchair waiting to be filled or emptied, waiting for us to arrive again, lift or squeeze my brother in again, ourselves in, a process far more difficult for him than for us, we come and go but with his legs cut out from under him, like my mother confined in her jail on wheels, he must depend on others.

For the price of an airline ticket I can reduce the four hundred miles between New York City and Pittsburgh to three quarters of an hour, not counting driving time to and from airports. Hours saved, it seems. A magic erasure of space, it seems. Except while I'm beamed at *Star Trek* speed from one place to another, my brother's clock ticks at its usual pace, minutes, hours, days bearing good news — more time served, therefore less time remaining to serve, and bad news — more time passed in jail, therefore less time for a life after prison. As both of us age and the years register on our faces, on the face of the good news/bad news clock, I understand a little better what my brother feels when he thinks about time in prison. Inside prison it's hard to ignore how little time there is, how each beginning, if not exactly an ending, is also a diminishment. The hand giving also busy taking away. My life sentence not spelled out like my brother's, but like him I've become increasingly aware that each day alive is one day less of whatever time's coming to me. My brother's prison time not my time, no one can do his time for him, no one can begin to understand the meaning of time the state subtracts from his portion, but on my island I've learned to count like him, learned the weight of minutes that accumulate and exhaust themselves simultaneously. Never one truth without the other. The count's the count. Stretching. Contracting. Counting up, counting down. Unforgivingly less, always less, even as more appears.

So what's the damned hurry. My brother ain't going nowhere. My flying carpet saves neither his time nor mine. I carry around the penitentiary walls everywhere I go, like a family snapshot in my wallet, those grimy, unmoving ramparts planted over a century ago alongside water that never stops flowing. What message did the state wish to send by siting the prison on a riverbank. What does a river mean to an inmate who glimpses it through stone walls enclosing the island on which he's trapped. Thick, towering walls built to look like forever and last forever. I didn't know how to react when I heard the prison's going to be closed, maybe razed or maybe converted to a casino.

How many black men in America's prisons. How many angels fit on the head of a pin. I once kept track of the number of prisoners — black, white, brown, male, female. Now I've lost count. Lots. Lots too many of us serving sentences lots too long, especially when one of the prisoners is your brother beside you, year after year, in the visiting room of the same facility where he's been locked up over a quarter century and counting, a count adding years, subtracting years, depending on where you start, how you figure what he owes the state, what the state owes him, time remaining, good time, suspended time, double time, you could get caught up in numbers, in reckoning, how many angels can dance on a pinhead, how many black men in prison for how long, you could get confused by numbers, staggeringly large numbers, outraged by dire probabilities and obvious disproportions. Ugly masses of brute statistics impossible to make sense of, but some days a single possibility's enough to overwhelm me — how likely, how easy, after all, it would be to be my brother. Our fortunes exchanged, his portion mine, mine his. I recall all those meals at the same table, sleeping for years under the same roof, sharing the same parents and siblings (almost), same grandparents uncles aunts nieces cousins nephews, the point being, the point the numbers reveal: it would be a less than startling outcome to find myself incarcerated. This scene I'm writing could be my brother visiting me, the two of us side by side just as we sit today, myself, my brother, one declared guilty, one declared innocent, variables in an invariant formula, but me in his place, him in mine, our fates switched, each of us nailed in our separate compartment of this hardass bench.

The length of these bolted-to-the-floor, orangish benches varies. They are staggered in uneven rows, separate islands of seats with plastic cushioned backs, shared wooden armrests, rigid seats affixed to one another, aligned so they all open in the same direction, and in order to speak face to face with the person next to you, you must twist sideways in your slot, talk across the hard armrest, or if you wish to say anything to someone two places away, you must scoot to the front of your compartment and lean past the person next to you to meet the eyes of the person you're addressing, prisoners and visitors tilting up and back as if davening before an invisible Wailing Wall. You must work even harder to have a conversation including more than one person at a time. Shout past the person next to you to be heard up and down the line of seats your group occupies.

In this case the group consists of me, my brother, and our mother, whom I've positioned as close as I can to my brother, angling her wheelchair at the end of our four-holer bench. The mobility of her wheelchair could serve as an advantage, but it doesn't. Each unmovable orange bench fronted by a low table that poses as a convenience for holding snacks purchased from the vending machines, and since there's a rule against moving tables, they also function as barricades, so I must plant my mom's wheelchair at the end of a unit of bench and table, stranding her as each bench is stranded and isolated yet also an intrusion upon the others, all visitors in each other's way, a perverse outcome so finely, successfully calibrated it must be intentional, perhaps computer generated to maximize exposure of every seat in the room to the raised platform where a guard oversees the visiting area, but also an arrangement designed to minimize intimacy between prisoner and visitor, preventing comfort, touching, privacy. No room for maneuver down at the end of our module, where I angle the wheels of my mother's chair as best I can to achieve a feeling of closeness, and there she is, stuck for the duration of our stay though her seat's the only one in the house, besides the guard's tall stool, not fastened to the floor. The clever floor plan has anticipated the variable of a visitor confined to a wheelchair and renders my mother's chair as useless as her flesh-and-blood limbs. Technology trumping technology. Her wheels immobilized, her poor hearing worse in this low-ceilinged, concrete-walled airplane hangar space where sound eats itself, everybody's words slamming into unforgiving surfaces, messages chewed up and spit out, mangled, transformed to a harsh, deafening collective din that frustrates listening or speaking when the visiting room crowds up on weekends. I doubt my brother hears much of what my mother says, and I catch almost none of his words when his back's to me. I can't tell if he's addressing her or both of us and that's probably much more sense than she can make out of my attempts to speak to her and I wonder if my mother actually hears Rob, though his mouth is only a couple feet from her ear.

Almost thirty years ago I tried to write a book I hoped might free my brother from a life sentence in the penitentiary. It didn't work. Everything written after that book worked even less. Now my brother's face is turned away from me because the three of us, me, him, our mother, sit lined up side by side in that order inside the State Correctional Institution of Pittsburgh (SCIP) and in order to speak to our mother parked at the end of this compartmentalized bench constructed of wood and molded, indestructible, orangish beige synthetic, he must turn his back to me. His polished bald skull a marvel — a shiny hive of buzzing busy invisible business. Many colors and textures on a canvas stretched tautly to define each ridge of bone, each phrenological knot and bump, his brown skin thinned nearly to transparency. If you had no knowledge of a skull's hardness and durability you'd think you could crack this bright shell with a single flick of a finger the way your fingertip could shatter a crystal goblet, the way I popped my brother Rob's hard bean-head *Gotcha* when we were kids to remind him I was Big Brother and merciless when I wanted to be, pop-pop-pop, hurtful, stinging to tears forget-me-knots upside his big head or playful teasing flicks and pings, presumptive strikes, punishment, revenge, affection, nuisance — pop — *Got you, little brother, and you better not never forget, boy, you better not even think about trying to change who's on top and always will be.* I'm fascinated by the innocence of his gleaming skull, shaved clean or almost clean, a bluish five o'clock shadow here and there, and on closer inspection nicks, dents, blemishes, scrapes, healing scratches and scars, rough patches of chicken skin where the razor's worked too hard, too often, and I look away, embarrassed like I am by those telltale raw, prickly stripes where a woman's cleaned up her crotch for a bikini, embarrassed that I'm looking, ashamed for her sitting with her thighs cocked exposing her not very skillful, not very beautiful grooming, her not very secret secrets I don't desire to share on display and I avert my eyes, sorry for both of us, trying to think of something nice about her, something unprivate so next time our eyes meet, mine won't hold shame or pity, or any detectable trace of my spying or of what I noticed, what caused me to wince inside at the hopelessness and sadness of all the small vanities and disguises I cultivate, just like my brother, like the woman, like everybody, wasting time to keep other folks from seeing us the way we see ourselves, as if my cheeks freshly scraped each morning or clothes covering my nakedness convince anyone I'm not what they know I am beneath whatever cover story I piece together for the public. My brother's bare skull admonishes me. A rock fragile as breath. Beyond judgment or blame as any breath any person sucks in to remain alive.

My strongest desire after passing into the visiting area through the last remote-controlled sliding steel gate is to see my brother's face appear in the little window of the door next to the guard's platform.

The next strongest wish is to leave, get the hell out. I want the visit to be over, a good visit concluded with a big hug like the bear hugs of greeting. I want to be freed by the steel gate clanging shut behind me. No one wants to be here. But the alternative of not visiting my brother would be worse. Much worse. So the instant I arrive I would leave — flee — if I could, but I can't, don't, not so far anyway. The visit's oppressed by contradiction, squeezed between conflicting desires. Is the visit actually happening. Will I be able to handle it. This familiar turf. These terms out of my control. This prison reality forcing its rules on me. Unreal and irresistible. A woman you love hopelessly who announces she doesn't love you any longer and opens her arms for one last embrace.

In spite of my need to visit I bring the cold distance and detachment of the streets into the prison with me. I'm an outsider inside for a minute. An imposter, a traitor. Nobody can be in two places at once. Who am I. Where do I belong. Why am I here one minute, gone the next.

Rob's told me more than once he doesn't think he could make it without visits. Another time near the end of a visit, leaning back, legs shot out straight from his seat, speaking quietly with his head bowed, eyes front, addressing the emptiness the benches address, he said, *You know something, man,* he said, *I just about made up my mind last week to call Mom and tell her to tell everybody to stop coming here. Believe me,* he said, *I understand how hard it is for anybody to visit this goddamn place, especially Mom now she's old and crippled up and I hate to think about all the trouble I'm still causing all youall. Tell the truth though, man, it ain't about youall. It's about me. I made up my mind to stop visits for me, for my benefit. To save me, bro. Great to see Mom and you when you're in town and everybody else who goes through the hell of getting here. Ain't no words for the good feelings when I see my people. And looking forward to visits, hey, almost good as the real thing. But see, that's the problem. Cause visits and looking for-*

ward to visits ain't the real thing. The real thing's the time I got to do. And I got to do it alone. Nobody, nothing I can depend on besides myself. In here you got to fight every minute of every day to survive. I ain't just talking about watching your back with all these fools and the games and the evil guards round here. You got to stay strong inside yourself. And the truth is nobody can help. You got to stay strong inside. Fight every minute of every day. Awake and asleep cause your dreams fuck with you too. What I'm trying to tell you, he went on to tell me, *visits make me weak.* And suddenly he was the elder brother and the deep lines in his face made me think, Damn, mine must be deeper than his.

Everybody leaves, he said, *then I got to start all over again, working myself up to deal with being alone. The stopping and starting's too hard. Better to let visits go. Keep it real or I'll lose my grip and die in here. And I don't want to die in here. No. No. No. I ain't gon let them kill me in here. If visits break me down, then visits got to go. That's what I decided laying in my cell, tossing and turning instead of sleeping one night last week. Give up visits, just like I gave up jailhouse hooch and reefer in here. I love everybody as much as ever, more than ever, believe me, man, but surviving comes first. Then, maybe, maybe I can do my time and git back in the world and git with my people,* my brother said to me and meant it, though he didn't phone our mother because here we are. He meant what he said that day no more or less than he means it when he says he couldn't survive without visits.

A rectangular space, maybe thirty feet by twenty feet, serves as a waiting area or bullpen at the front end of the SCIP visiting room. It's bound by cinderblock walls on three sides, its other side a waist-high iron fence open at one corner so there's a small entrance into the main area. Visitors are supposed to remain inside this enclosure until the inmate they've come to see emerges from a door adjacent to the guard's platform and is cleared for a visit. Sometimes a visitor spends a long time in this bullpen. Maybe the guards can't locate your inmate or maybe they don't choose to look. Maybe he's hiding.

Or dead. If you're unlucky and your arrival coincides with a botched inmate count, you can cool your heels an hour or more. Even on the best days it can seem forever before a familiar face appears in the slot at the top of the door beside the guard station. Another eternity some days before a guard glances up at the slot and decides to punch the button that permits an inmate entry into the visiting area.

A few visits ago I'd been stuck in the bullpen over forty minutes, no word of explanation from the guards, enough time for low-grade paranoia to kick in — had I been duped — am I a prisoner too. I knew better than to show up at count time, so a misfired count not the problem. I also knew better than to ask questions. Just sit tight and keep your goddamned mouth shut. Be grateful you're granted those privileges. Remember, the prison says, the state says, it could get a lot worse. For instance, as bad as the prison yard or those cells full of dangerous animals. So shut up. Mind your own business. Who the fuck do you think you are anyway. I'd heard it all before, the very clear message the prison, the state beam to citizens who ask questions. That stalled day a bulky woman, *heavyset,* my mom would say, sat on a bench catty-corner to mine, her small feet in white sneakers planted wide apart on the stone floor. She hadn't raised her eyes when I joined her in the bullpen and we hadn't spoken during nearly an hour of waiting. She probably resented my presence just as I resented hers, shared misery bad company for us both. She had fidgeted at first, a wedge of dark flesh stuffed into a baby-blue jogging suit at the periphery of my vision, conducting a busy, silent conversation with her hands before she went still. Dozing off, perhaps. I was surprised how quickly she stood, how light on her feet after the guard barked an inmate's name and she stepped toward the opening in the black fence. At the threshold of the visiting area proper she hesitated, scanning back over her shoulder as if she'd forgotten something in the bullpen. When she started up again, she took her

own sweet time. Well, not sweet exactly — steps dripping with atti-
tude, the reluctant steps of a balky child nudged on by an adult.
Noncommittal, random little up and back and sideways shuffles,
then a full stop, hands on mountains of hips, her body telling anyone
who cared to watch that she was tired of this shit, of dealing with a
half-assed, good-for-nothing black man got hisself jammed up in
this sorry slam. Bosom thrust out, shoulders swaggering, head wag-
ging, sighing audibly, she took minutes to cross a few yards of floor
between the bench where she'd been slumped and the inmate standing beside the guard who'd hollered his name. When she's almost
close enough for the inmate to touch, she jerks back, poses again, hip
cocked, daring him to cross the last couple feet separating them. The
man stares at her as she mumbles, cuts her eyes, jabs her fingers at
him. He leans away, letting her shit fly past, then steps toward her,
soft-talking, copping a plea, his body bent and swaying *Baby, baby,*
reaching out while she bobs and weaves, agile as a boxer avoiding his
hands. The man stops, retreats one large soap-opera step. Hisses
loud enough to be heard in the far corner of the visiting area, *Fuck
you, bitch,* before spinning sharply on his heel and pimp-strutting
without a backward glance to the door beside the guard's platform,
waiting there to be buzzed out as he'd been buzzed in a few minutes
before.

I resist the urge to flick my finger against my brother's naked head.
Instead rest my hand on his shoulder, lightly, so he doesn't think I'm
demanding his attention. When he finishes speaking to Mom, I'll tell
him how I let him slide. Didn't take my big brother's prerogative to
pop him upside his noggin. He'll probably cut his eyes at me: *Watch
out now. I don't play that dumb old shit no more,* smiling cold gangster
menace from back in the good old bad days, the days I bet he's sharing with our mother right now so I don't want to distract him, pop
him or lay my hand too heavily on the orange jumpsuit pumped up

by the bulk of his weightlifter's shoulders. Would the chalky color come off on my fingers. The cotton cloth smells freshly laundered, soft to the touch, and I wonder if jumpsuits are personal property — as much as anything can be personal in prison — or if the men dirty them and toss them into a massive, funky pile to be washed, dried, folded, and stacked, distributed the next week willy-nilly.

Rob twenty-four years old, twenty-eight years ago when the cops picked him up and never let him go. When Mom and Rob get together, sooner or later they go back to this beginning, or end you might say, almost thirty years ago, when they last lived in the same house, Robby just barely maintaining himself on the civilian side of prison walls. Back to those days when she knew him like a book, Mom claims, and also admits he knew precisely how to squeeze her heartstrings and play her for whatever he wanted.

Oh, that boy always could make me feel sorry for him. Don't care what he did, he knew how to come up to me looking all puppy-dog sad like his world's about to end . . . Mom, Mom . . . I'm sorry, Mom, he'd whine, and I'd give the rascal whatever I had. Forget about how mad at him I was and dig down in my purse for the dollar rolled up and hid down in there.

Just before he turns slowly in my direction I overhear my brother repeating the mantra he depends on to keep our mother alive. *Remember, Mom. You promised me you ain't going nowhere before I get outta here. Don't forget, old lady. You promised me.*

Mom looks good today, don't she, bro. You gon stay around a good long while, ain't you, Mom. Lots of mileage in the old girl's tank.

Your hair's grown back nicely since the chemo. The way it's styled really does look pretty.

This old gray stuff. Your sister dragged me along last time she went to the hairdresser. I told the girl, Cut it short. Cut it all off, for all I care. A wig would do just fine. Or bald. Child looked at me like I was crazy, a poor, crazy old lady. Thought she might cry. So I said cut it short, dear. And she did a pretty good job, I guess. Trimmed it up neat and even, anyway. Stuff more white than gray now.

Hey, it's nice. Hairdresser did good. Short makes you look younger.

Girl'd need a hot comb to straighten out the wrinkles in this tired old face. Enough of this silly talk. You two can leave my hair and looks alone now.

Maybe the prison barber fix you up like chrome-dome Rob here.

Better ask the barber to take a turn on that toilet seat of yours, older brother. Grandpa and Daddy and now all my brothers be wearing that fuzzy toilet seat on top they heads, don't they, Mom.

That's when I sneak in a pop. Pop. One finger snapped on his bald head but Rob's laughing too hard to care, floating way up high somewhere looking down on his dead grandfather, dead father, his live brothers, all except him branded with that semicircular crown of hair inside which nothing grows, the ring of hair he fired before it quit.

Running out of hair, running out of time, running out of quarters for vending machines, running out of things to say because the floor of the visiting area is steeply pitched and as soon as you enter and sit down everything starts running away, draining away, running out, racing down a slope so steep it takes your breath away sometimes, your eyes tear up, you fear shortages, a crash, everything speeding, no turning back or slowing down, everything in the visiting room slip-sliding away, including you and your mother and brother strapped in your seats, everything rushing by, you thought you were safe on your little island, believed you were sitting still while you teased and talked at each other, but the sea's carrying you with it, slipping, sliding down the slippery tilted floor, no way to stop, nowhere to grab and cling, things running out, running down, out of time, out of all the missing things you can name and can't name, things running down and out, spilling over the edge.

You hungry, man. You want me to get you something from the machines.

They changed the rules. We can put in quarters now. Same ole shit in the machines, but they changed the rules about inmates handling money. Always changing the rules, you know, so guys fuck up and they can take away privileges.

Mom, let Rob wheel you over so you can pick out something to eat.

No, no. Fine right here. You two go on.

Want us to bring you anything.

Huh-uh. Thank you, baby. Not hungry right now.

Ima bring you a soda. You know you can't sit empty-handed and watch us eat.

Don't have the appetite I once did. Appetite gets old and tired like everything else.

She didn't have any trouble last night with the smothered chicken, gravy, greens, and yams I brought from the soul-food joint across the street.

G'wan out of here boy and get your food. Good days and bad days for my bones and my appetite. Today not a good one for neither.

Bringing you a pop and a bag of Fritos. Know you like Pepsi but Coke's the kind of Pepsi here so Coke will have to do, okay.

At the row of vending machines I wind up with two bags of popcorn I don't want because I'm too vain to put on my glasses to read the tiny printed instructions. Seventy-five cents apiece for two little bags of air, salt, and grease probably cost five cents to produce. Rob notices me squinting and bashing on a machine, stops me before I commit the same mistake a third time. He's grinning when he says the popcorn won't go to waste, he's always hungry he tells me and popcorn a good snack after his two packages of chicken wings, two orange juices, two packets of fries. *Motherfuckers brought in a private company for the food service,* Rob had said once. *They hired nutrition experts they say to figure how much a grown man needs to eat to stay alive. Of course the company's paying them so-called experts and you better believe rations round here got real slim real fast. Little stuff you hustle from the canteen — you know, peanut butter and crackers, candy bars, cookies and shit — used to be extra. A treat, you know. Now on a good day hardly nothing on the canteen shelves and you got to bid for it to keep yourself from starving. Ain't nobody I know starved to death yet, but they keeping us lean, bro, mighty lean.*

The two of us, my brother and I, make good use of the table that owns the spot in front of our bench. *Wings ain't half bad,* Rob tells us. My mother manages — corn chips open in her lap, a can of Coke steadied by her hand on the arm of the bench.

Your oldest son about to be jammed up in here with me, Mom. Ready to tear up the man's machine cause he wouldn't put on his glasses to see which button for Fritos.

Do youall remember Miss Morris. Esther Morris from over on Kelly Street. An old friend of mine. You would have seen her at church when you were children. Her kids about youall's age. I bet you know the kids if you don't know Esther. Anyway, you've heard me say her name I'm sure. A nice woman. Not one of my close friends but I liked Esther and she was always nice with me. Her kids, Laureen and Catherine, Tank and another boy, Lawrence they called Sonny, I think, Sonny, it doesn't matter, they were near youall's ages so you must remember them. Doesn't matter one way or the other, does it. Nothing to do with the point I'm trying to make about Esther Morris and Fritos. Esther loved fried pork rinds with hot sauce. Every time I see a bag of pork rinds, or Fritos cause they remind me of pork rinds, first thing I think of is poor Esther Morris dead with her hand in an open bag of pork rinds. Found her sitting dead in her chair just like that, after the doctor warned her with her pressure she better leave fried, salty things alone. Pork rinds not salty enough for Esther. Huh-uh. She'd salt them down and sprinkle on salty red hot sauce. Couldn't help herself, you know what I mean. Had a stroke year after her husband Earl died. Crippled up in a wheelchair just like your mother is now, and the doctor warned poor Esther, told her, Esther you're gon kill yourself if you don't stop eating pork rinds. But pork rinds all she had at the end. Earl gone. No children at home. Couldn't go nowhere unless a kind soul drove her. Found her dead doing what she couldn't help herself from doing. I think of poor Esther Morris every time I see a pork rind or corn curl. Esther dead and reaching for more. Wonder who kept bringing those things to her.

Mom, that's a helluva tale to tell while you're munching on Fritos. I won't be supplying you any more. Huh-uh.

Don't get too smart for your britches. I'm not Esther Morris. Esther barely seventy when she passed. Had her children young. A young woman. She just overdid it. I'm way past killing myself with bacon rinds and hot sauce. With everything that's wrong with me, a few Fritos more or less no big thing. Won't touch a pork rind, though. Haven't touched one in years, not since I heard about Esther with her dead hand in a bagful.

If I said to my mother, *There's a war going on, a war being waged against people like us all over the world and this prison visiting room one of the battlefields and Esther Morris one of its millions of casualties,* my mother who gives human beings the benefit of the doubt would say, *Didn't I just tell you the doctor warned Esther she better leave those things alone.* My mother would point out the doctor's warning as evidence of no war waged on Esther Morris, proof Esther Morris to blame for her own death, use that fact and other facts, the hand of god for instance, to dismiss my idea of a war waged by an enemy most of us don't think of as an enemy, a total war waged by an implacable foe. Invisible war, an unseen enemy with Esther Morris's hand in its grip, dipping her grasping fingers again and again into poison, the ghost hand of the enemy guiding Esther's hand wrapped in its unseen hand, the brown hand rising again and again full of poison to the old woman's mouth.

My mother's catnapping when Rob asks, How's your Fanon book coming. Can't wait to read it, he says. Been reading the *Black Skin, White Mask* book you sent, bro. Wow. Some deep shit. Soon's I finish, be ready for another one his books. You don't know this, but I kinda looked at one of his books way back when I was a junior-high militant. Didn't read it, but I stole it, carried it around with his name sticking up in my back pocket. You still writing about him. Or is it the other one about the head.

I assure Rob it's Fanon. Assure myself. Oh, yeah, Fanon for sure. Slowly, and not as surely as I'd like, but I'm working at the Fanon book just about every day. I don't mention the dead head project. Thomas's project. Thomas's head.

Guess what. Your mother over there claims she met Fanon during one of her stays in the hospital.

What.

Told me she got to know him a little bit. Friends in a way.

Naw, man. That's too much. Mom's flipping. When was Fanon in Pittsburgh. You never told me nothing about Fanon coming to Pittsburgh and I know damn well Mom ain't never crossed no ocean.

Well, I hadn't heard anything about a meeting either, till Mom told me the other day.

I thought Fanon died a long time ago.

He did. In 1961, according to the books. But Mom's Mom. She doesn't lie. So who knows.

You jiving me, bro. Is we talking about Mom getting to know a real sure-nuff live guy or a dead man.

She got indignant real quick when I asked her the same question.

Said the man sure wasn't dead when she talked to him. And I sure wasn't going to try to tell her he was. No. No. What I said was, Mom, tell me about meeting Frantz Fanon, please. And she did and it's going in the book.

Bro, I got to hand it to you, man. You keep writing those buggy books. Always fussing cause you say nobody reads them, but you keep writing them. I dig it.

Being locked up, you know, I got nothing but time, plenty of time to read. Pick up your weird shit and whoa, sometimes it makes perfect sense to me. Probably because you're my brother. Plenty times I don't agree with them knucklehead ideas I been hearing from you my whole life, but I like to hear your bullshit anyway. Funny, you know, the craziest shit's what I like best. When you get off on words and get to rapping and signifying and shit. Getting off on shit like we do in the yard. Just to hear our ownselves talking sometimes, just to say goddamn words we ain't gon hear less we say em. Guys hanging in the yard talking crazy stories. Know what I mean.

Mom's the storyteller in the family. Wish I had half her gift. I said you're the best storyteller in the family, Mom, and I see you over there pretending to sleep so you can eavesdrop and get more stories to tell on us.

Those words or those words more or less are what I address to my mother, raising my voice louder when I say them than it had been while I spoke with Robby. My mother doesn't take the bait, her ears may be pricked but I believe her eyelids remain shut, hard to see from here with her head slightly bowed the way it is and it's the softness of her pale skin I think of, the freckles I can't see from this distance with my failing-fast eyesight, and strangely it stops there, the map of her face I'm trying to draw, familiar as I am with her face I can't sharpen the image of it, of her, can't bring her more clearly into focus than to think the words *softness, freckles, pale* and I know better than to worry her image past the peace offered by these few words said to myself into the space between us, the peace for this moment in these brutal, war-torn surroundings.

NEW YORK

IT HAS BEEN RAINING this morning. They are working on a rooftop nearby. Stop. Not *it*, not *they*. *It* and *they* are me. I am the weather, the workers. I drive the toy cars nine floors below, gliding silently past on Essex Street. I am the guy wearing a silver-and-black Oakland Raiders jacket, a baseball cap assbackwards, and climbing a scaffold to add a new story to a building across the way. I am diffuse, saturate everything, like the grayness coloring the sky, gray weather passing that will leave behind no mark, a mood hanging over the city, using the city to paint itself, a painting gradually unpainting itself, the city colored while the gray presence lasts, disguising the city as something else it might be or could be. Streets dark-skinned from rain last night. The familiar clutter of tall buildings out my window fades as the buildings recede, row after row, last row a silhouette framed against gray distance, pale through a curtain of mist. If I let my eyes follow one of the rain-slick parallel streets running toward the skyline — Hester, for instance — it appears to slant upward and narrow before it disappears, squeezed to death between rows of buildings it no longer can hold apart. Hester and the other streets like it are exposed strips of a giant carpet, soaked and ruined, upon which a roomful of ponderous furniture rests. Hidden below the horizon are hands tugging the carpet inch by inch, lifting its edge slowly, carefully, without prematurely destabilizing the buildings balanced on the black rug, allowing them to tilt without dumping them until the final grand yank that will remove the ruined rug, send the whole city tumbling down or leave it standing magically intact.

Does a fine rain still fall. Rain would chase workers off the rooftop, wouldn't it. Or would wet weather concern them any more than the fact today is a Sunday, the day of rest. I pilot a helicopter across the sky. I push a shopping cart heaped with everything I possess past steel-shuttered, graffitied storefronts on Essex. If all the above is true, shouldn't I be able to decide whether it's raining or not. Maybe none of the above's true. I give myself too much credit when I announce that I am everything, create everything I look around myself and see. But if what's out there is not me, not inside me, where is *it, they.* Where am I. Everything one thing, everything one and the same thing only and always, the world I make of myself, the self the world makes of me. What else could be outside my window this morning pretending to be a city.

After I write and read for several hours in the morning, my habit most mornings, I turn on the news channel for five minutes, precisely at the hour or half-hour when major events are recycled. In the company of other viewers I'm reminded how narrowly we've escaped disaster. Only a few minutes of viewing required to learn that many others on the crowded planet didn't get through the night. I need the encouragement imparted by the bright yellow lines the news draws between victims and survivors, oppressed and oppressors, jailers and prisoners, executioners and executed, right and wrong. Without the yellow lines how would I keep track of who's who. Who I am. Who I'm not. Unless the lines are clearly demarcated and I can stand tall on the side I'm told I occupy, unless I belong squarely in one group so I can speak confidently on behalf of my group or speak against the other group, nothing transpiring in the big world of affairs makes much sense. When I watch headline news, I'm not forced to sort out endless conflicts and overwhelming ambiguities. East is East and West is West and the rest consists of reams of details I needn't concern myself about — plus an occasional human interest feature to remind us viewers we're human — details the news represents and summarizes with numbers, graphs, polls, statistics. After all, the point of watching the news is to verify the single fact that counts: survival. The flood, car bombing, drought, AIDS, train wreck, cancer, death in all its menacing, spectacularly repeatable forms didn't zap me. Those terrible things happen to other people. I'm still safely sealed in my citadel, a viewer above, beyond the fray. Not immune, of course, I'm not dumb enough to think that, but who knows. I'm still peering through my window, still watching the news. For a minute or two after 9/11, my viewing habits, along with my fellow countrymen's viewing habits, may have altered a bit, but we've settled back onto our sofas, watch like NASCAR fans numbed by the noise and power of super turbo-charged cars racing around and around an oval track, secretly hoping against hope a fiery crash will lift us out of our seats again.

COUNTING

AFTER THE EARTHQUAKE and tsunami in Southeast Asia, the number of dead uncountable. We understand this simple fact, but count anyway. New totals hourly, daily, weekly, counting though we know that sooner or later the count must include the one counting.

It's almost funny, Thomas thinks. Counting up the countless number of chickens humankind has consumed. In that war of attrition between species, we must be way, way ahead of the birds. No contest, he guesses. How many chickens wiped out just yesterday by the smiling Colonel's legions or troops marching under the banner of the fabulously rich chicken farmer who ran for president a couple campaigns ago. Birds may never even the score. But they keep on pecking. If chickens destroy every single human person this time around with the flu arrows grasped in their scaly feet, will the birds still be far behind. Who's counting. Who keeps score. What's funny or almost funny anyway is that we know and knew all along no matter how many battles won, how many we fried roasted broiled plucked eviscerated boiled chopped penned in coops fricasseed barbecued crushed and pulped for sausages or ground into mealie meal so they could make a Happy Meal of themselves, no matter how many of their eggs we sunny-sided up or scrambled or sucked or deviled or painted on Easter, we know that sooner or later, just as Malcolm X famously warned — though Malcolm's words were quoted out of context to seem as if he approved of the president's murder — we know those motherfucking chickens are coming home to roost.

On counting days like this one Thomas keeps looking up, Chicken Little searching for signs the sky's falling. Not exactly hoping for his life to be over. Just ready for the relief of the end. Not scared exactly, not exactly paranoid either because he's not making shit up. He distinctly recalls the flutter of something he saw out of the corner of his left eye, something drifting down, white, ruffled, what could it be if not a speck of sky, the ceiling cracking, plaster starting to leak, a dusty trickle before tons and tons let go and the weight of the entire universe collapses on our heads. How long can a thin blue partition keep all that heaviness at bay. And why. No good reason or perhaps a very good reason beyond his understanding, the same reason Thomas understands he won't understand any better when the dike fails.

I'm walking the Williamsburg Bridge with Thomas, end to end, from the Lower East Side of Manhattan to Brooklyn and back again. We spy on the sky through crossties overhead that stabilize the two sidewalls of the pedestrian ramp. Peering straight up you see boundless blue sky between one steel beam and the next. If you lower your eyes and look ahead, perspective gradually erases gaps between the red girders and they fit together snugly, a seamless roof you assume you will pass beneath if you continue to advance. Illusion of open sky above. An illusion of red tunnel ahead. One certainty exchanged for the other as your gaze shifts. Illusions like the illusion of peace with the birds. The illusion of victory and dominion. The illusion doom's not always on its way.

Some say if the birds had not manufactured the scourge of flu with their bodies, humans would have invented it. To correct miscalculations. Crop an explosively expanding human population. Like the precaution of not curing AIDS until it removes swarming undesirables. Or experiments to develop toxins that spare one race and obliterate another. Humans toying with science fictions, refining the power of words, word by word, to inflict suffering, death, extinction. At a vast distance an observer from another planet might mistake us for a nasty species of bird, Thomas thinks. Our birdlike insouciance. Chirping at daybreak. Serenading night. Our bird brains. Our chicken-shit schemes. Our easily ruffled feathers. Restless flocks and flocks of us. Stinking islands of guano wherever we land and roost. The predictable patterns and destinations of our migrations. Predators of our own kind. Clipping each other's wings. Shitting in our nests. How many omelets would a woman need to consume before she lays an egg. What kind of creature would emerge when the shell cracks.

Was she loved at first sight, Thomas wonders on the bridge when a pigeon-toed Chinese woman passes slowly in the opposite direction. Eyes lowered, she keeps to her far edge of the pedestrian ramp though the walkway relatively empty at this early morning hour. Thomas flashes on chicken egg foo yung, his favorite from a neighborhood takeout joint. Accepts a pang of guilt. Chicken and eggs. Eggs and chicken. Chickens and Chinese. The woman supports a very pregnant belly by tilting slightly backward, weight on the heels of her tiny canvas shoes so the baby rides more comfortably on her pelvis. The ostrich-sized egg bulges under her short-sleeved shirt that's a drab style and color no young sister of Thomas or mine willingly would wear in public. The count never ceases. More always on the way. More and more others to account for and worry about. Chinese. Chickens. Chinese. He envies them. Their busy sex lives. Boundless fertility. What else is there to do cooped up all day in their ghettos. Thomas knows better. Apologizes. Suffers another bite of guilt. Egg foo yung. Why do chickens' crinkly-lidded eyes blink incessantly. Do they tilt their little heads so their beaks don't block the view of what's in front of them. We twist, twist the night away, twist their necks, scald off their feathers, chop off their heads, toss them naked in piles. Creatures not us. Never, never us. How long does the image of the killer remain frozen in their dead eyes. Thomas counts on love to swoop down one day and seize him in her beak. Tear him with her talons and feed him to her scrawny-necked, beady-eyed, nappy-head chicks who cheep-cheep-cheep, jostling for position in the nest like rebounders under the hoop.

I'm beside Thomas, up high in a giant metal cage. With our elbows resting on a steel railing, we're catching a breath after the steep climb to this point where the Williamsburg Bridge walkway peaks and mellows. Comfortable to lean here, the view superb, opening like a storybook where the river broadens and divides, its banks so overwhelmed by gray piles of skyscrapers you wonder why the land doesn't sink. Helping to frame the view, other bridges arc gracefully over the water and planes inch slowly, slowly across the screen, some gliding high above the skyline, others vanishing into the emptiness between the tallest towers. We can't see passengers inside the planes and the passengers can't distinguish us from the bridge upon which we've stopped. Like millions of our fellow citizens we stare up anyway. The passengers believe in us, stare down at our invisible shapes immaculate within muddles of concrete, glass, and steel or racing along highways in strings of cars or lying in green parks along the riverside. Everyone certain someone, somewhere is staring back. A city, after all, isn't it. Fabricated of eye exchanges. Living and dead.

Open and shut. The feathery wake of a long, slow barge plows the glittery water, an arrow pointed at the bulk of Oz silhouetted against hazy distance.

Thomas has learned that Fanon and Malcolm X, aka Malcolm Little (coincidentally, a surname he shares with Chicken Little), share, by coincidence, the same year of birth, 1925, and that Patrice Lumumba dies, by coincidence, in 1961, the year Fanon dies. Fanon, Malcolm, Lumumba, three men of color born separated by oceans, two of whom spoke French, the other English, men who invent a new language, unheard till they begin conversing with each other.

Was Fanon a third, silent other on the Williamsburg Bridge gazing at the river, the island, with us. Was Fanon grieving, recalling the murder of his birthmate, Malcolm, the murder of his deathmate, Lumumba, Fanon's words visible on invisible pages the silence turns . . . *Europe now lives at such a mad reckless pace . . . let us try to create the whole man whom Europe has been incapable of bringing to triumphant birth.* Fanon on the bridge that morning admonishing us, Fanon addressing us as comrades, saying, Don't jump.

PITTSBURGH — A HOSPITAL

MY MOTHER STUDIES her Bible after her coffee and morning paper. She's sure these are the Last Days. No doubt in her mind signs of the Last Days all around and about us. Uncanny correspondences daily between what the Bible foretold about the end and what she watches on TV, she says. A shudder of pain deep in the Earth's bowels sending a skyscraper-tall, mile-wide glacier of deadly water moving fast as the speed of light to drown islands in the South Seas. Three-headed turtles, civil wars, a giant asteroid on a collision course with the Earth, boys killing boys in Homewood's streets, fires, floods, plagues, cops handcuffing and arresting an unruly seven-year-old colored girl misbehaving in her elementary school. Topsy-turvy, pell-mell, no center holds, things falling apart — the Last Days sure enough and she nods gravely as I recite lines from a somber Yeats poem written on the eve of World War II. Meanwhile, in these last days, I'm trying to imagine with her help, her witness, Fanon's last days. Numbing waves of pain blurring his nights and days. Do I ever fall asleep, Fanon might have asked himself during a lucid instant, or am I always sleeping. Consciousness, identity experienced as degrees of pain, as drifting, the boat, the sea, the passenger merging, the island of his destination no longer separated by time or distance from the island that he departed from. Fanon a name like a beacon blinking on then off, found, lost again in a fog of pain. An endless tossing and turning passes for sleep or could be sleep roiled by constant, nagging dreams, his body, what's left of his body, a banner flapping in the wind, ripped and shredded, fragments of meat and bone, bloody waves, the body eating itself, screaming from a mouth that may be his or a mouth he dreams screaming silently, choked, gagging on the tail end of himself he swallows. His last days, ours, these, my mother's wheelchair parked beside Fanon's high-railed, high-tech hospital bed, my mother's hand on Fanon's chilly shoulder that also somehow sweats. She's squeezing it, the rhythm of her stroking fingers calming shudders and heaving of his flesh. In her other hand a remote controlling the TV suspended from the ceiling at the foot of the bed. She clicks from scene to scene, Bedouins on camels crossing a desert, masked skiers, snow that looks like sand, sand dunes drifted like snow, talking heads speaking foreign languages, a man in a chef's hat chopping a red lump of something into tiny bits with a huge cleaver, a woman who sings and dances as she scrubs an oven, a naked man and woman in bed, tonguing each other's fashion-model faces, a helicopter's-eye view of roofs burning, a posse of galloping cowboys, a plump baby circled by a tire, etc., and on and on and so forth as if the flow of pictures might soothe like Muzak soothes, as if the eyes of the man in bed, shut now, might pop open and be seized by an image flashing on the screen, distracted from pain for a split second by a lucky coincidence of worlds bumping and overlapping so he can beam from one spaceship into another, escape his flaming berth, his anguish, long enough to catch a breath, gear up for another breath, saved by an image he takes as real. She clicks, instantly weaving and dissolving worlds with her nimble touch, hoping to seduce his eyes, to fool him or awaken him or relax him to sleep. Who knows which is better or which is which. Awake or asleep. Does it matter in these last days. Either one, either way, any way, just so the pain quiets. She asks this peace in her god's name before she dozes off, clicking, watching with him.

Never forget this simple fact, he warned her one day: always some person or persons at the controls monitoring what you read, hear, see. Never underestimate the power or ruthlessness of those at the controls, Fanon had taught himself and instructed his patients, as he's instructing her. He sees a split-screen submarine view. Submarine-split screen. Two underwater scenes, one on each half of the screen — one day, one night. One side the other side's nightmare. Screen half in color, half the colorless black, white, and gray of scorched earth. Brightly painted plants and fish busy on half the screen, the other half a wasteland of wiggly gray fingers, their bones crushed to jelly, tens of thousands of wiggly gray fingers all you can see, soft rippling fingers the current animates so they seem to be waving slow, sad goodbyes. After the counts of drownings and deaths, cameras pan the ocean floor in Southeast Asia to reveal long-term ecological damage. A telling submarine view of a coral reef before and after tsunami devastation, Fanon understands, in spite of the babble he doesn't understand coming from the TV. Then later, another submarine story on TV, not connected, not displayed split screen with the tsunami story. Unrelated it seems because numerous stories in between and more ads than stories in between the stories in between ads. Submarine, nuclear, the woman in the wheelchair tells him, a submarine belonging to the USA, operating in Pacific waters when it runs aground. On a sandbar not there pre-tsunami. An accident. Not nuclear, thank god. Everyone's relieved. Hasn't god been flogging us enough lately. Yes, Fanon replies, though he doesn't speak her language and she doesn't speak his. Time out. Take a day off, old murderous god. Have mercy, Mr. Percy, she amens. Submarine/split screen. It rhymes, she says, like rap and nap and gap. And therefore the words go together. And therefore related. Therefore, how, why. Who's in charge of this juxtaposition, this submarine mission. The bright versus dark side. Peace and war. The split screen. Fanon sees a nuclear device implanted. Sees it detonated. The floor of the ocean rising like a rocket ship. Like lava from Mount Pelée. Overnight the seabed's fourteen fathoms below the surface instead of a thousand. Something wants out. Who opened the door. Who exploded something deep, deep within the deep.

After the tsunami story, the second submarine story. Comes too late. The sub not guilty. No. No. Heavens, no. No split screen mourning our mutilation of our world. Nobody asks questions. We've already swallowed the old natural-disaster story and forgotten we've swallowed it — so many stories so many ads ago. We blame the tsunami, nature's bloody tooth and claw, god's will. The new story admits there was nearly a manmade disaster after the natural disaster, but thank goodness for those heroes in charge of the nuclear submarine and its nuclear weapons, thanks to them a tragedy of epic proportions averted at the last instant. Split-screen submarine. The sub's radar, the story goes — a story she translates into her language and he understands in his — the sub's radar picked up at the last split second the unexpected, uncharted, post-tsunami mountain of heaved-up sea floor so rather than ramming it full speed, the craft full-throttled its engines in full reverse, as close to slamming on brakes as you can manage underwater, plowing a deep furrow with its steel beak into the mushy heap of erupted seabed, a rough landing that flipped the sub on its side but didn't split its steel skin, the accident an embarrassment with a full nonpartisan inquiry to follow but thankfully no fatalities reported so far, just a long, sleek submarine drydocked beneath the ocean, radioing S-O-S-O-S-O-S, while gray wiggly fingers comb the sea, zombie fingers, blades of gray grass rippling where acres of coral of many colors once bloomed, the seascape an evil twin of the lost world we saw just yesterday on the split screen, a scene so Edenesque, Disneyesque you half expected cute talking fish to swim by any second, a pair of them, identifiably female by their miniskirts and painted cupid's-bow lips emitting bubble-pipe bubbles of gossip. If these fishies survived and crossed the split-screen divide, what would they say about the big steel shark stuck in the mud. Would they recall its shadow gliding above them the day of the tsunami.

Was the submarine accident accidental or part of a plan or cover story for a failed plan. Who knows. Who would tell us if they knew. Gentle stroking soothes Fanon's sweaty splitting brow. How many seconds required for an image to burn into the TV screen. How long after the tsunami's shockwave does news of the submarine wait its turn, submerged no one knows where before it begins its ascent to the surface, toward the news, toward the accident waiting to happen as reported on a sandbar, nature intervening again to rain on man's parade. SOS — Same Ole Shit. Nature flexing its muscles, indulging its mysterious ways. In this corner Man. In the other corner Nature. A mismatch some promoter has dreamed up and hyped and sold to the gullible public. Clever and simple as three-card monte. A simple matter of distracting the player's eye while you work. Pity the poor sub. Pity injured sailors trapped in a metal prison. A hero will emerge to save the day. A good story to seize the public's attention as the tsunami story recedes. Who remembers the tsunami. The disconnect rolls on, the fog rolls in. Fanon's mind skips off to other pastures, different sleeps, different islands. Mom mopping his brow like she used to mop mine when I had a fever.

THOMAS TEACHES HIS LAST CLASS

GOOD MORNING, BOYS and girls, sisters and brothers, my likenesses, good morning. Thomas smiles. The sixty-four-thousand-dollar question this morning — are your stories more than words.

Since stories, whatever else they may or may not be, are composed of words, let's ratchet back and begin with a more fundamental question — are words more than words. If we're able to answer this question, then perhaps we can go forward, or back if you will, and examine stories as a particular case of words governed by the logic or illogic we uncover after we determine whether or not words are more than words.

Words. There's one. Thomas mimes grabbing it. Gotcha, he says. This specimen, *words*, will serve as well as any other word to establish (a) the inherent nature of words (b) the emergent capacities of words that might enable them to transcend the qualities defining them as words, in other words, their potential to become more than words. *Words.* Employing *words* or any other word to determine what words are and also what they might become limits from the outset the seriousness of this endeavor. Like cronies of the president appointed to investigate the president's conduct. The circularity, the slippery slope of our enterprise this morning girls and boys becomes even more apparent if we pose a parallel question — what is a human being. Who decides who's qualified to serve on that board of inquiry. The dog-chasing-its-own-tail aspect of our investigation can be mitigated, if not entirely overcome, as long as we decide beforehand we won't bite down on our tails if we capture them. We should always be as gentle with ourselves as circumstances allow, especially since no one else in this world, except perhaps good ole Mom, will be gentle and forgiving toward us when we fail, and if we consider those ever-present, nonhuman dimensions of our environment — fire, flood, plague, etc. — in these Last Days, gentleness is obviously a nonexistent concept in whatever wordless language those forces of nature speak. So let's be easy on ourselves.

Gentleness. Remember Mom, remember the tear in the corner of her eye when you do wrong, Thomas. Her gentleness the good news. The bad news, boys and girls, it don't get no better. Huh-uh. So don't make things any harder on yourself than necessary. *Words.* If you choose to write, words are a necessary evil. And if necessary means *no way round it,* then we have the answer to our original question: yes. Your stories are more than words. They are evil.

NYC-PARIS-NYC

TWO OR THREE TIMES a week for the past three or four years, usually in the early morning, I've walked or jogged along the East River from the Williamsburg Bridge to Battery Park and back. The apartment-for-rent sign I noticed on one of my first trips along the river still sits in a second-story window above the Paris Café. Given the Paris Café's location (since 1873) on a street corner about two hundred yards from the river's edge, just beyond the overarching shadows of the FDR parkway and Brooklyn Bridge, near the eye of a foul storm of loading and unloading tons of fish that used to occur in the Fulton Fish Market every morning except Sunday, it's no wonder no one wanted to live over the Paris Café. Either the noise or stink alone enough to dissuade any sane person from renting the vacant apartment, so why some mornings do I imagine myself its tenant, hope the sign will greet me when I pass. Would I enjoy being awakened by the clamor of trucks, vans, forklifts, the odor of rotting fish clawing at my window. Perhaps the perfect awfulness outside would sink me deeper into the nest of comfort and safety pitched inside a tiny room above the Paris. Or maybe I'm attracted by the idea of disciplining myself to be unaware, if I choose, of whatever mayhem the city produces. Proud of my acquired immunity, my eccentricity. Undisturbed by crashing pallets overloaded with boxes of iced fish, the *beep-beep-beep-beep* warning of trucks backing up, vendors hollering, doors slammed, tailgates banged, the braying, honking, and wailing of way too many vehicles crowding a limited space, tires crunching mounds of spilled ice, hoses spraying, hissing streams of slimy runoff from the tarmac into South Street. Ignoring this chaos even if it's rife in my hair, my clothes, inside me. Body and mind impervious as the Paris apartment, welcoming more stink, wallowing in it. Pleased to have discovered a hiding place where none exists.

When I imagine living over the Paris Café, I guess I'm actually daydreaming about living under it. A mile deep where the East River licks and sucks the fill that long-dead workmen once dumped in to tame its flow, the river engaged in a continuous, nibbling assault, hollowing out more space, reclaiming its ancient precincts. Corrosive grains of sea salt pushed inland by tidal swells, then swept back downstream by the current are efficient as sandpaper, deepening the wound beneath the Paris where black water laps in mile-deep darkness and my little yellow submarine swims, its fuzzy, disintegrating finger of light checking out what's down there, groping live fish, suicides, dead kittens and babies, all the unexpected creations of drifting cast-off debris and muck that wind up in a scooped-out pocket of water a mile deep below the edge of Manhattan. A soundless, etherized realm exerting unimaginable pressure as I bob there alone, hidden from view, or if I get lucky, with a lover beside me in my bed each morning, fellow sailor, mermaid, fellow ship-wrecked isolato sealed like me in our bungalow, denizens of an immortal city beneath the mortal one, marveling at the quiet, the air of our two breaths, our two fleshes quietly mingling, nuzzling, sour and sweet as measureless tons of water at bay just beyond the porthole.

NEW YORK–PARIS–PITTSBURGH

THOMAS WATCHES THE CURTAIN pretending spring. One of four matching, semitransparent goldish curtains with a darker gold floral pattern veining them. The panel lifts, no, dances in the draft from a window he'd cracked, not because it was spring but because the apartment had overheated during the night, its thermostat predictably unresponsive to changes in temperature outside or inside his old building. Inadequate boilers, clogged radiators, broken traps. Heat on warm days, then AWOL when the city's arctic. A frigid wind agitates the curtain, gropes its folds, and pleats with icy fingers, but the poor pale thing, a colorless rag in the harsh winter light streaming through it, quivers, shudders, would girlishly sigh if it could speak.

Was he concentrating on the problem of representation. Shouldn't he admit to himself at least — who the fuck else is paying any attention — that his mind's as idle as the diddled curtain he watches when he isn't watching for the newly resident mouse to dart from under the stove and skitter across the tiles. Was Thomas contemplating distinctions between literary and cinematic representations of reality or was he speculating on the mouse's next move, stalking the beast, formulating a strategy for killing it. Who knew the French director he'd chosen to rescue Fanon's story from the sorry-assed inadequacy of words would turn out to be fed up with images, falling in love with literature. Did the filmmaker quote writers more and more in his films because he believed images had lost their tongues. Or spoke too much. Working out to the same thing. A global commerce in images usurping, colonizing, lobotomizing, digitizing, roboticizing thought. Instead of being alive, instead of, you know, possessing agency and unscripted, unpredictable possibilities, images are slaves, prisoners. Images kidnapped, copyrighted, archived, cloned. Property. Images serving power, speaking the master's language, saying and doing what the master orders.

Or maybe he's disappointed less by the slavishness of images than by their refusal to be his slaves. Prospero snapping his wand. Appalled by his career's tail end, the gathering darkness of any career winding down. All those pretty candles lit one by one with so much care and hopefulness, then one by one they gutter out, and when you peek over your shoulder, the room's just as black as when you started.

Stupid to choose a director as betrayed by images as I find myself betrayed by writing, thinks Thomas. Wouldn't our collaboration produce an invisible Fanon, white mask, white skin, white screen, white silence on blank sheets of paper. C'mon. Don't you guys see the albino cows moving about in the snowstorm. Can't you almost hear them mooing.

He hated the mouse, would stomp it, kill it if he could ambush it crossing the kitchen floor because the mouse, not much larger than Thomas's thumb, had scared him. Not housewife-jumping-up-on-a-chair-and-shrieking-for-help fear. A recoil, a shudder of profound disgust and needle-prick of terror before anger took over and he cursed the stupid twit trespassing on his turf. A quick pinch of vulnerability, unexpected and ridiculous given the mouse's size relative to his. Not about size, of course. The mouse had reminded Thomas he's not alone. Countless other creatures inhabit the planet, creatures unlike Thomas, not enemies exactly, just radically different, as different and chilling as touching feathers or scales or the scraggly brown fur of a hamster when he was a boy. Touches he'd always declined. Unthinkable difference he thought he'd finished thinking about, grown up now, armed with adult fairy tales that cartooned and marginalized beasts who would eat him as nonchalantly as he gnawed on a spicy chicken wing from KFC. The mouse kin to wolf, to sabertooth cat, to grizzly bear, and if Thomas didn't maintain constant vigilance, wouldn't one of his ancient enemies rip him from guzzle to zorch, feed on his steaming guts. Good riddance, maybe. Time maybe.

Thomas's crossed legs terminate in brown bare feet, one planted on the floorboards, the other aloft. The airborne foot in respect to the floor repeats the angle of Thomas's frozen ballpoint pen relative to the plane of a yellow tablet. Foot and pen mismatched wings of a *V* that exists nowhere except in Thomas's fancy, like the foraging mouse he probably only thought he saw when his eyes jumped from the daydreaming curtain to the tile floor and found nothing there.

Film unsettles him almost as much as the idea of fierce man-eaters lurking just outside his range of vision. Holding up a negative or a strip of motion-picture film to light was like staring into a cave, Thomas thought, a voluminous darkness also strangely depthless, all mouth, all surface, yet infinitely deep, as deep as travelers' tales reported the ancient African city of Wagadu to be, a cave with uncountable layers of silvery black and white hunkered down in there, compressed, compacted, each layer invisible as the mouse under the stove until thirst or hunger or curiosity — who knows what it's like under there — drives it across the kitchen tiles. When light streams through the film's dark skin, Thomas sees ghosts. They wait for him to enter their icy cave, wait for his warm breath. Thomas huffing and puffing with all his might, turning himself inside out, reversed like a glove snatched off his fingers, his insides out, outsides in. The film a balloon inflating till it's large as the earth, all the tiny frozen figures scurrying like roaches from my grandmother's oven when she lit it in the morning, scurrying here, there, everywhere across the planet's sticky surface, a story unfolding while Thomas uncrosses his legs, closes the yellow tablet, kicks back into the cushions of the couch to watch instead of write the movie he's making.

On the TGV Thomas second-guesses his bright idea of asking a Frenchman to direct a film about Fanon and the Algerian revolution. A bit like putting a Georgia cracker in charge of a flick about Nat Turner (the sound *flick* = *film* in English = *cop* in French). To be fair, not all Frenchmen or Frenchwomen or French persons alike. Not all crackers alike. Maybe. There are French Algerians and Algerian French. *Pieds-noirs.* Harbis. Grown-up mixed babies and mongrel kids in the process of growing up in France who don't know what the fuck they are. French Muslims born in Europe. French Jews born in Ethiopia, Lebanon, Chicago. Senegalese, Indochinese, and Moroccan French who fought for and against the empire at Dien Bien Phu. Brown French Tunisian guerrillas who fought beside Palestinians against Israel. French Israelis. French African Arabs who served in the FLN before they emigrated and settled in the outskirts of Paris or in Mayenne, falling in love perhaps and raising a French family that produced a generation of Senegalese/Swiss, Guadeloupean/Filipinos, Viet/Bretons, etc., and what about the mulatto *martiniquaise* arriving in Nice after ten years of French civil service in Togo where she wed a Congolese and their son marries a blond *niçoise* with one Swiss German parent, one from Russia with Afghan ancestors, what kind of French person would that union produce.

After all, Thomas, you're only choosing someone to direct a film, not save the world, right. Judge not by the color of skin or content of character but by the size of the talent, size of the wallet. Promote equal opportunity or affirmative action or ethnic cleansing or hire the handicapped, fashions come and go, don't they, and shame on us all, so what's wrong with choosing a Frenchman to direct the Fanon film, a filmmaker who push, push, pushes past the point of good taste or logic or obscurity or complicity with any audience but his own wandering eye. Collaborating only with whomever he imagines himself to be. Or not to be. Or pretends to be. One truth for a minute exchanged halfway through a scene for another, more or less, if the narrative, the flippity-flop of the frames slows down to less instead of expanding to more than meets the eye, you know, a guy who doesn't really seem convinced of the content of nobody's character, black brown yellow red. Or loves/hates them all, indifferent to different colors unless they paint a scene. Use value. Surplus value. Marx or Marx Brothers. Who cares. *Sauve qui peut.* Just a movie, ain't it. A lie. Just play.

In his essay about the Swiss-French *maître*'s films he would expand the riff above if he ever got around to writing the essay. A writer once. And now. Now he talks to himself, composes notes to himself each morning on long walks and runs beside the East River or across the Williamsburg Bridge, entertains himself with invented selves, free-style, free-forming them, allotting each persona enough rope to lynch itself, herself, himself, as if gender mattered any more than color to the dead. He worries about his idea of importuning a foreign director but also likes the quixotic naiveté of traveling to France. A sentimental journey to find the Swiss-French director and coax him out of his what — lair, lethargy, business, retreat, mourning, last days, resting in peace. Pressing into an old comrade's callused, workingman's hands a Fanon script he can't refuse. Then what. The promise of resurrection. Eternal life in cinematheques, film society screenings, video stores, luxury DVD editions, the film dissected, analyzed in university classrooms, memorized and memorialized, reissued for late-night showings on pay-per-view, immortality guaranteed by the few but fit, who will not willingly let him die. Who die. Whom.

Recently, accompanied by an actual woman, a precious woman I won't name so as not to jinx a new love, I attended a lecture by a French literary critic whose training in psychoanalytic theory gave her plenty to say about chopping off heads. Though decapitation not the announced subject of the lecture, the topic emerged as a recurrent theme in her presentation and during the course of her remarks she alluded more than once to an encyclopedic-sounding tome she was compiling on beheading. I could barely sit still in my seat. The scholar a star. She'd packed the joint and here she was generating a buzz about the novel I was writing. All these excited, restless, poorly dressed folk around me on the edge of their seats — her distinguished colleagues, the throng of starry-eyed undergrads, the super-serious junior faculty and doctoral candidates researching dissertations and articles they wouldn't dare publish without citing, pro or con, the visitor's writings — were hearing from the horse's mouth the archetypal, overarching significance of my central trope. *Man has escaped from his head as the condemned man from prison,* she said Bataille said in his journal *Acéphale.* I wanted to rush home and get back to work. Shoot both arms into the air and holler, Tell it. Tell the truth, girl. I wanted to sneak onstage and sit at her feet. Wanted to gag her. Pimp her. You sitting on a goldmine, sugar. Don't be giving up that good shit for free. Of course if you've been paying attention to how it works around here, you've probably guessed I did none of the above, just melted down in my seat, listening intently until my attention wandered to the cul-de-sac I'd written myself into. My enthusiasm about the talk waned to low-grade depression. The weight of her learning oppressed me. I felt a headache coming on. Like my skull was being squeezed into one of the medieval reliquaries she described, the miniature busts of queens and kings with painted eyes, a tiny hole in the head, a crystal window through which the faithful could check out a saint's bones preserved inside. Gleaming metal spheres *celebrating the head's status as intersection of material and spirit, human and divine.*

Though the language of her multidisciplinary rap dazzled me at first — a bling-bling parade of fashion models sashaying across the stage in bizarre costumes — quickly the gaudy models got bumped off the runway, morphing into a funeral cortege, a lugubrious procession of mostly dead men's dead thoughts quoted, paraphrased, and seconded, all gray and rained on, moldering in heavy caskets borne on the shoulders of stoop-shouldered, gray-coveralled workers. Antsy, trapped in my seat, I realized I was hearing a kind of obscure, complicated report on weather anybody with eyes could check out for themselves if the goddamned windows weren't set so high in the cathedral-like auditorium's walls.

We didn't share a subject — we shared a tooth in an overworked mouth and the tooth was cracking. The distance between what she knew and what I knew about the subject widened as she lectured on. Heads rolling since the beginning of recorded history. Rolling at history's end. *Theriocephalous representations of Gnostic archons and astrological decans sitting at the Messiah's banquet of the righteous on the Last Day.* Rolling before recorded history — masks and painted faces of primitive ritual the borrowed heads of animals or gods. Heads detached, stolen, appropriated. Heads on platters, heads of state, head-hunting, talking heads, heads on stakes at the entrance of medieval cities, heads on billboards, maidenheads excised, circumcision, clitoridectomy, the headsman, axeman, the guillotine, taking heads, giving head, shrunken heads, decapitation as emasculation, castration, sex change, regime change, bundles of heads delivered to terrorize and destabilize a nation, beheading a booby prize if you don't pay your ransom. Nothing new under the sun. She outed my new fiction as old fact. Me whispering to her, *Look at the beautiful star, the incredible snowflake.* Ho-hum, she replies. The sky's full of them.

On the way home from the lecture, walking New York's mean streets again, I felt cheated. Couldn't tell my new love why. Undeniably the speaker had radiated a glow. Who wouldn't dig the swirl of

Jean-Paul Gautier silk around her neck when she tipped on stage like an adolescent in her first pair of heels. Cheated because she performed a kind of reverse striptease, spinning an opaque cloud of words, silencing the beautiful music we could have made together. My story of receiving a head in the mail yesterday's news. DOA. Too late to earn a footnote in her comprehensive survey.

Never say die. Fanon to the rescue. I accepted the fact that fact had overtaken my fiction. Waylaid my story. Wasted it. On the other hand, Fanon's story remains relatively untouched, forgotten like novels on the bestseller list the year he died. Or the list from twenty years ago. Five years. Two years ago. Who could name one of those fabulously reviewed, avidly purchased books. Who reads them now. Who will recall today's list tomorrow. Is the list always the same list. I spring Fanon's name on unsuspecting suspects. A few of my contemporaries smile wistfully. Young people generally puzzled. A blank look from just about everybody. Some ask me to repeat the name and on a second hearing, shake their heads, no, definitely, no. So maybe with Fanon a chance to start fresh. Start at the beginning — paint Fanon on my face, wear the mask of him. Pretend he's real because I am. Pretend I'm real because he is. Or was once. Behind a mask he might become real again. Better than crying over spilled milk.

And speaking of my new woman, the real one I won't name for fear of jinxing our love, I decided the morning after Fanon saved my life that Thomas needed love and I needed a love hook to jazz up the story of going to France to peddle the Fanon script. Autumnal love, a bit like mine. Part mellow and wise, part scared, obsessional, and torrid, you know, like the amours of seventy- and eighty-year-olds in *Love in the Time of Cholera*. The guy on his way to France with a Fanon manuscript in his suitcase will be a decade younger than the Marquez characters, a little younger than I am. Not much. Let's say sixty. Sixty a good round number, easy to remember. Sixty also for many readers a bright yellow line on the far side of which a person is definitely old, definitely on the way out, if not quite numb yet. Our hero sixty and on his way south, stopping for a week or so in Paris, a city familiar from his student days when, like me, he used to spend lost weekends on the Left Bank, playing hooky from stiff grad school across the channel at Oxford University. And like me, once upon a time in Paris he meets a beautiful woman, one whose sprawling headful of blond, curly hair wouldn't fit easily into the box delivered once upon a time to Thomas's door, a woman approximately ten years younger than Thomas and who, like him and me, is compounded of fickle flesh and blood so she, like us, will stop speaking in the not-too-distant future and vanish, never seen again on the earth, yet after two weeks, one of them stolen from time budgeted for tracking down the film director, Thomas tells her and believes in his heart he means it that he has no desire to outlive her, that life without her company would lose its appeal.

If you're crazy enough to fall head over heels in love at sixty-odd, why not in a captivating place like Paris. In spite of the fact you know better. Forget Paris is a city as full of enemies as any other city and love's only a game, willed blindness, wishful thinking. Forget the fact you're close enough to your grave to smell death in your sweat, see death yawning on the other side of doors you hesitate to open and walk through for no good reason, unless being tired is good reason, and it's not that simple. Forget disappointments too numerous to count. Forget the peace of mind you've learned to maintain by lowering drastically your expectations of what's possible between two people who discover a mutual attraction. It's spring in Paris. Fall in love, Thomas. Forget the season of discontent sure to follow.

So let it be the City of Lights and Thomas sixty, eager as a colt for love, even though getting out of bed some mornings he feels like a condemned prisoner mustering for roll call. Well, maybe aging's not quite as bad as all that but you do get tired, awfully tired of sharing a tiny cell with a dying stranger whose stink and noises you abhor, whose whining, constant neediness and selfish demands appall you. Who could love anybody like him, the drool dried on his chin, the earwax, toe jam, wild hairs in his nostrils and ears, the leaks and nasty stains, nasty habits. Who wants to listen to his nattering. This twin who either grumps around belligerently silent or chatters way too much in a language more and more opaque each day whether someone's willing to listen or not. Your cellmate.

Enough about growing old, Thomas complains. You could just say old's a rerun of youth, of feeling ignorant, sidelined, inadequate. Reexperiencing childish terrors you spent a lifetime trying to put behind you. Painfully eager and willing to please, unable to comprehend why no one seems interested in what you have to offer. Except, back when you were a kid, you believed in time. Believed you had time to grow. Time to prove yourself. Time to hurt others who hurt you. Believed time on your side and the world would change if you just hang on, keep pushing.

The lovers meet in line at a Paris theater where the latest American hit's showing, dubbed in French or French subtitles, Thomas can't recall which, nor remember who joined the line first, followed by the other, or who smiled first, only recalls that initially neither spoke, except with looks, polite, respectful, casual looks, two strangers acknowledging each other as markers to identify a place in line, glances traded, quickly dropped, then their gazes bumping again, perhaps accidentally, then the next time not an accident, was it, and it's okay, fine, I see you too and approve of what I see and return your glance's positive appraisal of me with my positive appraisal of you. I'm pleased by the exchange as you seem pleased by it, thank you, you're welcome, time to look away, and it could end easily here, a look away, never a look back. Thomas studies posters on the walls under the marquee — lots of naked flesh, men brandishing oversized weaponry, buildings burning, weird helicopter-like vehicles — looking away from her and then back too soon, both pairs of eyes instantly averted after they bump, a bit embarrassing, except also almost funny, who's pretending they're new at this old business. But it requires practice either way, doesn't it, requires time and luck to get the timing right. Thomas stares over his shoulder at the line that's lengthened nearly to the street. Pedestrians framed by the marquee's glitter and running lights bustle past. As he turns back he widens his eyes and nods, his gaze brushing hers, letting her share if she chooses the information his eyes carry about how rapidly the crowd's growing for this matinee performance in dismal weather and somewhere in there between glances and glances away he says hi or says hello, an English greeting in France, and she responds with the same English word and he repeats it, the echoing maybe a bit too cute, more playful than cute he hopes, aren't adults allowed to be playful, though there's a chance someone standing in this line or in the crowd streaming by on the boulevard would, if given the opportunity, torture you, chop off your head, stuff your carcass in a freezer, or bury you in a backyard pit except for certain delicate tidbits of choice cannibalized before bidding you farewell, sayonara, darling, a person perhaps not very unlike the villain starring in the movie you're about to watch — *Silence of the Lambs,* wasn't it, Thomas can't say for sure, it seems right, he'll ask her later and ask what else she recalls of their swift courtship or flirtation, whatever, a very unlikely happening whatever you choose to call it, given their different personalities, their different colors, nationalities, the ten-year age gap between them, but eye conversation and a single word spoken three times enough to persuade whichever one of them — Thomas probably — who purchases a ticket first to step aside and wait just beyond the booth for the other, the unknown person addressed only once, only minutes before, enough conversation to convince them both that it makes perfectly good sense to stroll into the darkness of a movie house together and sit side by side, both guessing — who knows to whom the guess occurred first — that it might also be okay when the movie's over to risk leaving the theater together, risk what comes next.

Growing old mostly a pain in the ass, so why not perform love's rites one last time in Paris, in spring, in spite of drenching rain when you exit the movie house with her, torrents, geysers, flying columns of rain, loud, splattering, sluicing rain spilling from gutters and eaves onto sidewalks, flooding the streets. Rain he welcomes like the ancient Greeks welcomed it on wedding days because they believed rain augured a fruitful union. Pouring rain a backhanded, assbackwards gift in this Paris case too, because sheets of rain obscure the corny, buffed-up city Thomas's x-ray eyes, sixty and counting, had been straining, without success, to penetrate, searching for the old city's hiding place beneath a new Paris he didn't recognize. A stalled reunion. The city invisible in this downpour not the old Paris he'd crossed the ocean for the first time in twenty-two years to find. Getting soaked not exactly the kind of fun he'd anticipated either till he realizes how tightly she squeezes the hand squeezing hers and he smiles out loud, echoing her laughter, and just as quick as that, with one hit of the magic wand, zingo, there it is, instantly visible, in spite of the blinding rain, his old Paris solid and real around him, risen in the blink of an eye, like Venus on her half-shell from the sea or like a movie flashed on a screen, the whole remembered city intact, remembering Thomas, the old Paris shimmering, its golden stones, bridges, spires, cobbled alleys, rows of buildings lining the Seine like shelf after shelf of elegantly bound books.

A surprising number of people caught outdoors in the storm, dashing here and there, you know, like water's not wet if they hurry. Thank goodness it's not a cold day, at least not cold unless you're totally soaked as she is, lips blue, teeth chattering, chilled from head to toe. Her feet might as well be bare in those silver harem sandals splashing along beside him through the drowned streets, little sprints from one bit of cover to the next — the theater marquee, a hotel balcony, porticoed entrance of a restaurant, an awning, a cloister scalloping the façade of a grand apartment building — *clack, clack, clack,* a torn silver strap clacking as she runs. Thomas sees a rain parka in a shop window, cheap, and she lets him buy it for her. They pause under the shop's canopy to get their bearings and her eyes are closer to green than blue when she looks up at him from beneath the canary-yellow plastic hood, lifting her face nearer to his so they can hear each other over noisy rain. Is it okay to kiss her cheek. Yes. Yes. Yes. The yes in her eyes tastes so good Thomas savors it, saves the first kiss for later, for her lips. Shapely, full lips, dark against skin that's washed unnaturally white and bright by rain, skin glowing like marble, he thinks. It's marble Thomas thinks of again when he rubs her chilled feet, later, out of the weather, snug in her sister's apartment on Rue Blomet, alone with her for a couple of hours until her sister arrives with Vietnamese takeout she called and asked her sister to pick up on the way home from work. *Delicious,* she promised. My, my. Yum-yum. Thomas sixty and counting on this day he's met a shiny new woman, enjoyed a movie, found the old Paris, slogged through it in the rain, and it's barely five, no company expected before seven-thirty at the earliest, so he rubs slowly, each icy lump of foot in turn, chaffed, squeezed in both hands, blowing his breath on those snow-white feet, perfect, Thomas thinks, as a marble statue's.

If he ever returns to the novel that begins with the delivery of a head, Thomas will be much younger in it. A teacher of creative writing at a university. Newly married, maybe one or two very young kids, maybe, a professor of color adrift in a hostile sea of colleagues and students, a writer afflicted by writer's block, beset by lots of issues, personal and political. Decades younger than the character in the Paris romance (the Paris *Romance*? — see Hawthorne's preface to *The House of the Seven Gables* for distinction between Novel and Romance). In Paris no choice about age. Or rather he chooses to give himself no choice. His age is what it is. No choice. No sweat. Sixty plus and counting. In the other story he intends to shed decades. A young man in his prime will receive a head from a delivery person one morning and, like the life fate has delivered to him, he won't know what to do with it. Not like the old fool in Paris who pretends to know precisely what he's doing: who arranges his balding head on a platter and offers it to love.

Riding the bullet train from Paris south I wonder what she's thinking. If I'll ever see her again. Rub her bare feet. Kiss her painted toes again. If she were beside him she'd probably be reading. Reading a kind of narcolepsy, a disappearing act she performs. With a book in her lap, she can be talking or staring out a train window and if he looks away from her a minute, *poof*, she's gone when his eyes return, dropped off the edge of the planet into whatever she's reading. A few words, a sentence or two enough to capture her. If no book of her own available, she might lean over and peek at what he's reading. The pages disappear behind her sprawl of hair. She's gone, caught up in the writing's spell. He'll have to pinch her, tickle her ear to remind her the book where she's hiding belongs to him. A cute habit he teases her about but sometimes a stupid sting of jealousy. Whose writing has smitten her, stolen her. Would his words on a page do the same trick. And so what if they do. Why believe his writing's a special treat for her if somebody else's words will do.

Thomas daydreams about the pleasure of dreaming about her. Wonders if people dream less as they age, if the dreaming faculty wears out like everything else wears out. He seldom remembers his dreams. Not much practice in dealing with dreams. When he tries to retrieve dreams they fray. He worries rather than remembers the few dreams he recalls, even though worrying them — trying to find words for them — shreds the original.

On the TGV south Thomas practices dreaming. Imagines making

up a dream for Fanon. How would Fanon see himself in his dreams. Wouldn't he disguise himself. Who might he choose to be. Do we choose. A good disguise maybe the key to dreaming. A dose of deception administered to ourselves to cure disbelief. Experiencing alternative possibilities, living other lives too threatening to imagine unless we wear the mask of another's face, unless we inhabit another's body. A taste of being who you can't be so it's easier to be who you are. Or are not. Or wanna be. Or who you were once. After studying all the required theorists and interpreters of dreams and listening to his patients recite their dreams, how would Fanon respond to his own. Would he be skeptical, condescending, amused. Touched perhaps by naive images sallying up from his unconscious, as if he didn't know better, as if their crude, insinuating costumes not transparent to his expert's eye.

The dream screen's bright as an operating room. A bearded giant in a surgeon's green smock perches on a high stool or throne and appears to be grooming or perhaps patching up wounded jungle animals he props on his lap. Lots of rubbing or first aid, stroking the creatures' tummies, their fur, feathers, hide. A kangaroo, chimp, wildebeest, gazelle, an elephant tilted back against the doctor's chest, its ivory-toed foot grasped in the doc's sure hand, his other hand extracting black quills. A man who looks like Thomas waits next in line, Thomas with his bloody, detached head in his hands, staring down at it like he's gazing into a crystal ball.

It's not working. He gives up on fabricating a dream for Fanon. Impossible with a made-up Thomas always lurking, always butting in. The screen dims, fades. No more god or Dr. Doolittle tending to his flock. Daylight twists, diamond by diamond, into his eyes. He squeezes his lids shut again, turns away from the burning window, sinks lower in his hard seat, and there, unannounced, a view of her naked from behind, padding on her hands and knees, a lioness, though she's allowed to keep her sprawling mane of hair. Sinuously dangerous, cuddly, she glides in a tropical forest, Thomas standing enthralled, just beyond the picture's frame, watching the syncopated cheeks of her ass squeeze the darkness between them, her sleek haunches, tick-tock-tick, regular as a metronome until she disappears into tall black grass. Be careful, Thomas. Don't embarrass yourself on this French train. Tell your blind, not-too-smart buddy to be cool, be patient. Remind yourself she's not leaving, not gone forever, she's just not here now, at this moment, on this particular train, so cool it, he whispers to himself and doesn't waste breath on his clueless companion who will swell up anyway and aches anyway imagining himself personally addressed by any random breeze, as if the universe is organized solely for the purpose of delivering each blow or caress upside his bald head. And Thomas asks again, addressing no one in particular, where do dreams come from — where do they go — will this one return — will she . . .

Why Fanon. I'm disappointed when my brother asks the question. The answer's obvious, isn't it. Given the facts of Fanon's life, my brother's life, my life, the decades in prison, the besieged lives of the people we love and who love us, the lives and deaths shared with them, why wouldn't my brother, of all people, understand my need to write about Fanon. Mom not well enough to visit the prison, so only me and Rob, our longest talk alone together in years. I'd just finished sketching Fanon's life — born brown and French on apartheid Martinique, boy soldier running away to Europe to fight for France in World War II, psychiatrist in a North African clinic where he treats French torturers and their Arab victims, then fighting against France in the Algerian war of independence, writing books that helped destabilize Europe's colonial empires, a visionary philosopher who argued that humankind must liberate itself from the shackles of race to become truly human. After all that, my brother Robby, aka Farouk, had asked, *Why Fanon.* What else could I say. I felt impatient, upset, even betrayed by my brother's question. He knows better than I do time's running out. Too many of us locked down in places where we desperately don't want to be. Every choice urgent. A matter of life or death.

The world needs Fanon, not some tale about a dead head in a box. I recalled old black-as-a-bowling-ball, roly-poly Reverend Frank Felder strutting the pulpit of Homewood AME Zion, preaching himself into a sweat. Had my brother nodded off during my sermon. Is he still on square one. Does he expect me to go all the way back and start over. *Why Fanon.* C'mon, bro, I said to myself. Mize well ask, *Why me. Why you. Why these goddamn fucking stone-cold-ass walls.*

Shit, man, I said out loud, then answered him with something more like a fingerpop upside his shiny bald head than an explanation.

Fanon because no way out of this goddamn mess, I said to my brother, and Fanon found it.

PART II

Discovering more about Fanon as I continue this project of writing a life, it becomes clear that Fanon is not about stepping back, standing apart, analyzing, and instructing others but about identifying with others, plunging into the vexing, mysterious otherness of them, taking risks of heart and mind, falling head over heels in love whether or not there's a chance in the world love will be requited or redeemed. At least I think that's what my mother understands about Frantz Fanon, what she shares with him, something like that anyway expressed in her own words, in the actions of her life.

❖ ❖ ❖ ❖ ❖ ❖ ❖

I want to take you back, way back, show you around the neighborhood where I grew up, Mr. Godard. Where my mother and other folks raised me. Show you this place from one end to the other. From the end that ends in prison, to the end that has no end (of shame, for instance), to the end that is here, now, this dwelling place where we stand I want to show you around. Let me be clear from the outset. We didn't do this neighborhood to ourselves. Neither we negroes who inhabit the dead end where we're stuck nor we Americans doomed to undertake the task of saving a world we fear by destroying it first.

Here the shelves are mostly bare and where not bare crowded with shit. Bottom-of-the-barrel shit, unhealthy, overpriced, past the expiration date, dumped here on these empty shelves in these bare streets my mother watches day after day for miracles, watches reruns of the usual suspects strolling up and down, watches for holes to open in the sidewalk or the sky to fall, watches from the top of the neighborhood's tallest residential building, on her sixth-floor balcony of the K. LeRoy Irvis senior citizens' mini-high-rise, watches people going in and out of this store we stand outside looking up at the concrete wall enclosing her perch, hiding her unless she leans up to peer over it.

Exiting the double-locked-down double doors of my mother's building you can turn right, walk a half-block on Frankstown to the corner of Homewood Avenue, look right, and sometimes not see a single goddamn soul on the entire three-, four-block stretch that once served a busy community as main stroll and commercial heart, no one, nothing, no car or cat till Homewood Avenue disappears under an overpass that carries railroad tracks and a busway to and from downtown Pittsburgh. I won't even attempt to convey to you, Mr. G., how this emptiness shocks me. Shocks. Yes. A dramatic word, an obsolete word you may think, after the numbing horrors we witness daily. *Shock* a word you may consider dead, dead and empty as these bare shelves, as bareass dead as dead Homewood Avenue appears some days when I view it from the corner of Frankstown, a kind of stranger returning to my mother's house to finish my ailing book and gaze down at a body I made love to many years before but that was then and now is different, the lover's gone, gone, and yes it's one kind of shock dead, and another kind when this lifeless thing quickens and courses through my body, busy groping inside me, touching, arousing me again, shocking, yes, a palpable thrilling current. What's living. What's dead. Who knows which is which here, my friend.

I know I won't find anything I want on the bare shelves, probably not even the one or two staples — fresh milk, bread — my mother and I need to get by till the next two-mile trek to the nearest decent supermarket can be arranged, but here we go anyway doing what we do every time I'm in town, me stepping up the awkward step backward through the entrance of this store, bumping the wheelchair with my mother in it up and over the paving-stone threshold, her riding in backward too, past the man whose name I've never asked or did ask then promptly forgot, who's outside smoking, tipped back on a busted-up wooden kitchen chair propped alongside the narrow doorway and he doesn't budge to hold the screen door open for us till a voice inside the store hollers at him, *Help the people, man. What's wrong wit you, man,* the voice of the youngish entrepreneur behind the cash register eager to please the public with his shop full of nothing, full of sugar and spice and everything not good for them that people love anyway, his shelves stocked with products he can afford, staking his cash on bad risks, on the unlikely chance that he might be able to squeeze blood from a turnip, a figure of speech I have been hearing since my earliest days growing up in this community, my Homewood grandmother saying it first I think, squeeze blood from a turnip, and me with not the slightest idea of what a turnip might be and recognizing blood as something that drips or seeps or runs from a bloody nose if you pick at it too much or get punched in the face in the schoolyard I understood blood in that sense and worse if people got hurt in car accidents, but not as a warm fluid filling me up and keeping me alive, binding me forever to certain faces, certain places, and as I think back on the impression made upon me by my grandmother saying *squeeze blood from a turnip,* I guess the clearest image it evoked was her or my mother, her daughter, squeezing clothes, twisting water from rolled-up shirts or pants or towels when they washed clothes in the double metal sink in my grandmother's moldy cave of a cellar or on their knees scrubbing a floor and squeezing a scrub rag into a bucket to rinse and then dry a patch of linoleum they had just washed with soapy water, and thinking of the women in my grandmother's house, her and whichever daughters happened to be living at home or never left home and the endless chores, the women's work they shared, I probably understood as much as I needed to understand at the time about what my grandmother meant about hopeless endeavors, about needing something badly you're not going to get no matter how hard you squeeze, about people and situations hard-pressed and wrung dry, about foolishly hoping that something that has never worked might work this once, even though I didn't understand then the fact that it was my blood she was talking about nor understand that the problem was the fact that one person or a group of persons could somehow get invisible hands around another person's neck and choke and choke that other person past the point of fighting back, past the point of seeing themselves anything much like a human person, more like an article of clothing rolled, twisted, squeezed as dry as hands could squeeze, then fed through the rolling-pin wringers of the washtub wedged inside one sink of the double sink, the washtub's handle cranked till the flattened, stiff thing that might have been someone's shirt or housedress is squeezed lifeless as a run-over pigeon dried up bloodless along the curb, enough meaning squeezed out of my grandmother's metaphor enough history squeezed up in the words to keep me thinking about them to this day, to this usage and recycling when my mother and I roll in assbackwards through the needle's eye of a neighborhood store the man behind the register squeezes and squeezes waiting for blood that ain't coming, squeezing himself, these bare streets, these bare shelves full of stuff even tackier than what the previous owners stocked, this emptiness greeting us as we pass the half-asleep cook outside the door, the cook the one who keeps us coming back, a dark-skinned guy with godawful teeth, in a white undershirt and a painter's bibbed overalls who only speaks sometimes when spoken to or speaks with his eyes when he sees something he cares to address, the dumb things done or said by customers who sidle in casing the joint or sweep in as if they own it though he or she, lost in space, has not slept indoors for days, who do they think they're fooling with not as much as two thin dimes to rub together in the deep pockets of baggy-assed pants, the cook who always dresses in white or off-white if you will, his measured stares and silences and raised eyebrows keeping account of who comes and goes, nodding if he's greeted, if he chooses to raise his gaze from where it's permanently slunk down at the level of aluminum pans he tends when he's standing behind the steam table, everything heard and seen inside the store, everybody in it something he's cooking, sampling now and then while it steeps, a tiny bit of the broth or sauce from the tip of his big spoon, just enough to fire up the messages that flash through his eyes after he observes people's words and gestures, this cook in white who hadn't stirred to help us through the door till the owner hollered at him is the main reason my mom and I come here every time I'm in town and I wind up scanning these empty shelves for some item worth buying, a purchase for the store's sake, the owner's sake, for the sake of Homewood, any little trickle-down contribution or reparation I could make for the sake of all of us, Mr. Godard, while we're waiting for the cook to ladle out the lunches or dinners Mom and I have ordered into compartmentalized Styrofoam containers whose lids he battens down with Scotch tape before swaddling our meals in tinfoil, that guy in his spattered whites can flat-out cook his ass off I tell anyone who asks and tell them that's why we keep coming back here no matter how dead the place appears from outside, the cook steady takes care of business inside, a compliment I know I ought to pay directly to him and hope I have, and maybe I did or at least tried but he'd be gone before I got the words out of my mouth, too busy doing whatever he's doing to be bothered with listening to what I have to say, not rude exactly, he's just not there, so much not there I'm not certain whether I ever complimented him out loud or if I simply carry around in my head the words I say occasionally to other people but probably haven't said to him since I know better than to waste words on a man past words who cooks for the same reason you make movies and I write, because, you know, who cares about the bullshit, the Hollywood hype and so-called fame. Don't you prefer a bare exchange, bare as shelves I want to knock the crap from with a swipe of my fist, bare as the streets we walked to get here if you sweep away the pomp and circumstance. Who gives a fuck really about the mise en scène, the gleaming church that used to be black before the congregation paid to sandblast its stones, Too Sweets barbershop, the pizza joint, the new cell phone shop, the regal cars parked shining along the curb, all the stuff squeezed out of people who live here, lorded over by the smiling Colonel whose greasy breath you can smell a block away, sweep away all the Hollywood murders drawing real blood, flowing rivers of blood you'd think you could wade in it, wade in the bloody gushing water but not a drop really or droplet if you're the entrepreneur behind the cash register waiting for rain, squeezing a pinkish vegetable shaped like a Christmas tree bulb or is a turnip the gray, weird, wrinkled one with a hair growing out of its eye.

And I guess I've about squeezed all the juice out of that metaphor, squeezed it dry, right, Jean Luc, what's in a metaphor anyway, what's in an image. What language does it speak. Is it what it is because it fakes being something else. Can it exist. Be. Like a stone exists or does a metaphor only represent. Both. Neither. And if a metaphor points out something real, in which direction does it point — ahead or behind. Or circle every which way at once. Which direction does language point — past or future. Are words and stones equally unquiet, restless, swirling, bloodstained and dangerous even when they seem to be asleep. Like those Sumerian stones in the next-to-last movie of yours I saw, *Our Music,* maybe, the camera panning silent acres of stones archeologists were identifying and classifying to decode an ancient Middle Eastern kingdom's past or unfold its future. I really got off on your idea of stones as a metaphor for language.

Words written in stone. By stones. Stone writing. Stoned writer. Stones so notoriously associated with lack of speech: stony silence, mute as stones, stone-faced, etc. . . . Word. A vast field of stones scattered in the desert, meaningless fragments and fragments of fragments, indecipherable signs of disorder, waiting for someone to imagine what they once were, what they might become. Stones disappearing as fast as dreams if you step closer and try to touch, count, weigh and measure, Magic Marker them, examine them for clues. Flying stones that can knock your head off.

Anyway, I often think of the future as something that has already happened, something I'm struggling to forget and remember so I can believe I'm inventing it. My way. My dream sleeping within the stones. Not something I lost I happen to stumble across. Not like when I imagine my lover's erotic history, her sexual encounters with others before I met her, irrelevant maybe, but also terrorizing because in some form the others may still be present in her body — her secrets, traces of the others she misses, denies, seeks — as my previous lovers may be present in my body, like it or not, the desires and pleasures we're pursuing in each other's flesh are also a continuation of those former episodes, a playing out of remembering and forgetting, a coverup and recovery of old stories, a kind of perpetual archeological dig. I can't win for losing, Mr. G. Always more stones, a deeper hole, you know what I mean. The stones don't just sit there waiting for me to figure out some past or future for them. They slip out the back door when I run to answer a knock on the front door. They start flying around, screaming, falling down again. Like when you attempt to picture love in your *In Praise of Love,* like me trying to get words to speak in my fiction.

Hello, how you doing. Good to see you again [I shake the owner's hand]. And thanks again for the pretty purple umbrella you loaned us. Kept my mom nice and dry in her chair on our way back home.

Mom sends her best. Oh, yeah, she's doing just fine. Doesn't like being stuck in a damned wheelchair, of course, but hey. That's the way it is. I'ma get your umbrella back to you next trip. Mom probably be with me. You know we'll be coming round like we always do when I'm in town. Like we been coming even before you took over. Bet Mom's up there now, out on her terrace checking to make sure Homewood's running the way it should. I'll get her a lunch to go when we finish here. Brought you a little business as you can see. These folks stone hungry and I've been bragging on your food.

This is Mr. Godard. Jean Luc Godard. A very famous filmmaker from France. Famous over here too. And these other folks are his fans, come all the way from across the pond to see what Mr. Godard's up to in Homewood. (Maybe they thought he said he was going to *Holly*wood. Ha-ha.) They're newspaper, magazine people, you know. Kind of people who tell other people what's good. Critics, you know. They love Mr. Godard. And love to hate him too, don't you folks. They make fun of his black sunglasses. Laugh at his seriousness and seriously resent his lack of seriousness. A good bunch really. They don't mean no harm. I enjoyed getting to know them this way, guiding them through my old home place and telling them gritty Homewood tall tales so they'll have something to write about besides Mr. Godard's movies which, no offense, are kind of a pain in the ass to watch and make sense of. They could write about Mr. Godard himself but that's not very much fun either since not much juicy gossip for years, and in interviews, with him hidden behind his shades, they can't tell whether he's laughing with them or at them, so I'm hauling them around, helping them cop quotes from the locals, you know, authentic bullshit from the mouths of the people to pump up their articles with what's real. Then the story won't look exactly like the story they brought over here with them, you know, the story their readers pay to hear and they get paid to write. I volunteered to handcarry them around a day or two, tour the happenings up close and personal so they'll be experts and can fuss at whatever Mr. G. comes up with in the film it's rumored he just might direct here, on location, you know. A rumor about Mr. Godard enough to bring all these folks to Homewood. Not only from France. You got your Dutch and Italians, Spaniards, Germans, Swiss, and comrades from the former Eastern bloc and a couple from godforsaken countries I never heard of before they applied for membership in the European Union. Told you Mr. Godard was famous, didn't I. And if you feed these good folks good, they just might make you famous. Put this sorry joint on the map. That's how it works. Ask Mr. Godard if you don't believe me. He sprechens very good English. Better than me or your mama probably. Lotta these white folks speech good English. I could tell by their eyes when I bragged on your grit. Warned everybody your place ain't fancy. But see, they don't seem to mind. They look happy to me. Just a plain swarm of nice hungry white folks no different from you or me when we're hungry under our skins. Hey, my friends. No table service. Just step right up to the steam table over there and order from the man. You don't need to speak English. Just point. The cook sure don't speak your languages but I guarantee his food does. Man can cook his ass off, folks. Step right up.

[Dissolve to . . .]

To me and Mr. Jean Luc Godard side by side on a mourner's bench with a bare shelf serving as our tabletop in a corner of a local mom-and-pop grocery store just north I think of the intersection of Homewood and Frankstown Avenues enjoying heaped plates of soul food and casually discussing our respective crafts while Jean Luc Godard, in another language in another conversation to which I'm not privy, considers the possibility of shooting a film in Homewood or perhaps shooting himself in the head in the spirit of all the shootings of one young person by another around here and I consider, in my language in another conversation I'm not absolutely certain Jean Luc Godard doesn't overhear, various means of impressing him with my knowledge of cinema, writing, and life in general, hoping he'll be tempted to request a copy of *Fanon,* the script I have yet to write in any language, and turn it into a movie.

Can Homewood's language be reduced one-on-one to another language — film for instance. What's the point of language if another language renders it transparently, disappears it. Why pretend anything can be established by words except other words, either in the same language or different, and if different and they establish the same thing, how and why are they different, except arbitrarily, *they* being the two languages reduced, elided, identified, passing away, redundant, the words of both languages pointing to the same referents, a verifiable reality that finally strips away each language's pretensions to difference, any language a slow boat to China, groaning under the weight of its slowness, inconsequence, its inadequacy because what everybody really wants is China.

Enough scene setting, props and marks on the floor, scenery, greasepaint, costumes. *Lights — action.* Dialogue's needed to animate this obviously fake establishing shot. It's always obvious isn't it, Mr. G., the transition from one fake reality to another fake reality. Always requires the benefit of the doubt — active resignation, suspension of disbelief. The suspended sentence in one language ending in air before it takes off again in another language, or doesn't . . .

JLG: (whose English is excellent) Very good grit.
JEW: (whose English is heavily accented) Blah-blah-blah.
JLG: *Bien sûr.*
JEW: There are some advantages to balance the disadvantages of being from the hood. Especially when I'm in the hood. Like a seat at the closest thing to a table in this joint, for instance. Or like the way these reporters, your fans, Mr. G., fawn over me, hang on my every word. Clingy as starlets. They desire more than anything access to

the top, and for a minute while we're here in the hood, I'm the top. Observing their behavior you'd assume, if you didn't know better, each of them is my best friend. They all want to eat and drink and rap with me. The men want to hoop and hang out afterwards all funky getting high. Women want to braid their hair, take off their clothes, shake their booties. All them, men and women, want me to take off my clothes. Each one would murder for a little extra smidgen of precious, chimerical, one-on-one access. Power feels good, Mr. G. You know. Even reflected power. Especially in the hood after all the shit some us underdogs must eat to gain a little power. Fifteen seconds' worth. And that fifteen seconds more than most people, particularly the ones stuck in this bareass ghetto, get. Here you better go ahead no questions asked and snatch what you can snatch when the snatching's good. Do you have that word in French: *snatch*. Have it so it's noun and verb and can mean *pussy* and *to grab*. France is an old country, very much older than the US of A, of course, so youall gotta have a word for grab, like when you snatched those beautiful islands from the sea and those big hunks of Africa and Southeast Asia, you know, and naturally like every other country youall got a long list of nasty words for a woman's private parts, but does French have one word like *snatch* that stands for both. Not important really. Just a sound check, so to speak. Me, I'm always getting off on language. Weird words, taletelling words like *rapture* and *rupture*. You know. Bet you get off on images the way I groove on words. Like when you see something you always also see something else, right. A sous-conversation as your Ms. Sarraute puts it, me and the language having this private conversation, underground, offstage, off-color, off the track, just plain off sometimes (do you have the word *off* in French so it's as multipurpose as *motherfucker*, a noun, verb, adjective, preposition, proposition, *off* meaning just about anything, from *crazy* to *insect repellent* to *ejaculating* to *murdering somebody* all in one word).

Anyways, me and the language have these conversations going on between us, between the cracks, so to speak (*crack,* we won't even go there, Mr. G.), conversations in my head cracking me up sometimes, crackling below the surface of what's being said out loud, a tête-à-tête, two invisible old heads nodding and exchanging words nobody else can hear, except strangely enough on occasion somebody else does overhear and jumps in giggling or frowning, surprised as I am, and I wonder which conversation is which, who's talking and who's listening and maybe it's never me but the language always in charge, willy-nilly sort of anyway cause it talks to itself too and gets confused: you know like I can't speak French worth beans but now and then I find myself speaking bits of it inside-my-head, French sneaks in without me knowing and it feels natural, you know, like *merci,* like a spot on the dial bleeding into another spot, I'm picking up a sous-conversation between the English-language station and the French-language station that's been going on time out of mind and sometimes I think I'm just plain going out of my mind but it ain't all bad, no it isn't, Mr. G., but I've strayed far afield, as my mom complains age strays her, and all I really wish to say is there are advantages hidden in the disadvantages of being from around here, for example the two of us seated one-on-one in this space you could say resembles a restaurant booth though it's a church pew if you study it closer and god knows how it wound up in this store, maybe the same guys stole it who ripped off the stained glass windows from my mom's church, Homewood AME Zion, cause the thieves around here are some desperate, shameless motherfuckers, man, and maybe they offed them as much of a pew as they could snatch and stick in their pickup, if the trifling motherfuckers had a pickup the night they robbed the pretty colored glass from the back end windows of the church, and maybe they swapped the pew for a meal or two, who knows, the point is, here we are, Mr. G., receiving a bit of special homeboy treatment, seated regally one-on-one with good food and a measure of privacy within a homely but authentic wooden parenthesis that used to rest in peace in church.

And speaking of how shockingly empty and bone-dry Homewood Avenue appears sometimes, do you think there will be a flood one day, Mr. G. You know, like rain, rain, rain. Rain not stopping till everybody drowns. Our Mr. Baldwin's fire didn't finish the job so the flood's turn again. Everybody, including us, floating around bloated, mouths full of smelly shit we shat in our pants when we saw death by drowning bearing down fast as a tsunami. If the flood happens, one consolation in my view is that for a while it will be quiet round here. At least people won't be making noise with their stopped-up mouths. So a flood wouldn't be all bad, would it. What do you think.

Do you think the meaning of life evolves in one direction toward a future like your spooled films running from reel to reel, unwinding, gathering momentum as they roll on from the snapshot that is the first take the audience sees and hears. Does meaning accumulate from what comes next and next. Or is meaning in place, fully articulated in the first snapshot before the film advances a single frame and then swallowed when the film's over and the lights come on, meaning drowned in the same darkness the first frame's light seemed to interrupt.

When you make movies do you know what you're doing, where the film's headed, or is the making of a movie a gradual revealing, nilly-willy, of shit the camera just happened to catch. Not the narration of a story you had in mind from day one of the film's inception but a kind of *Damn, what the fuck do we have here* discovery of shit you never thought of till it's on the screen, in your face. Does meaning reside within images and words, meaning released as a sentence or scene unspools, or is meaning a regression. Meaning a film running backward we experience as if it's progressing, because our eyes fool us like they do when they reverse upside-down images on the retina and turn them right side up so we don't think we're pitter-pattering along in the world on our heads propelled by tiny dready feet growing out of the top of our skulls. You know. Like your Mr. Sartre said life's a train ride going one way and we sit on seats facing the other way, so everything we see from our pew done been here and long gone.

Nothing stands still, does it, my friend. Including meaning. The light beam interrupting the darkness of the theater, the darkness of the screen only appears to break a stillness. The world never stops, never slows down for us to catch up. During the split second when darkness becomes light, the audience pretends to slip into a movie's flow, riding the light that propels the camera's gaze, then our restless gaze, across a moving field of images. We focus on the first frame and the next and next, as if we're being born again, born innocent of meaning, but the first frame's full, not empty of meaning. Too much meaning erupts. The meaning for instance of you, your person, your history, your culture, Mr. G., your language and ideas at a given moment all packed up into the first frame, a frame drowned, saturated with meaning, like a cell containing invisible prisoners, an unruly mob of prisoners, scrambling madly to escape through one tiny porthole of light.

Have you ever considered what you'd do if someone stole the only copy of a film you'd just completed and chopped your movie into single frames, piled the celluloid chips on a table in a closed room, and turned on a powerful fan. You know. Let it blow, let it blow, let it blow. Till there's a mess worse than the Sumerian stones scattered in the desert. What would you do after the fan hit your shit. Would you call the janitor to shovel the pieces out the door. Would you gather up the humpty-dumpty pieces and begin again. Would you try to reassemble the frames in their original sequence so your film would appear onscreen intact. As if the shitstorm never happened. Or would you remake your film so it tells the story of its destruction, recounts the brutal scissors and knives dismembering it, the howling tempest, swirling chaos. What would the film mean if it carried no memory of its history, if you skipped its history and showed your film unmarked by its death and resurrection. With the modern advantages of digital remastering, who'd know what you left out or what you slipped in. I don't expect you to answer my dumb questions. I mean everybody lies, right. I mean imposing order also preserves disorder, and etc. Blah-blah. Or vice versa. Or something like that. I mean people get caught lying because the first lie leads to another and another and the lies start tripping over each other. Down you go. Like our Mr. Pryor's grandma says, "Everybody got roaches, Richard." And everybody acts like they don't.

Hey, folks, don't study your plates too hard. Eat up, youall. It's true grit. Bon appetit.

[Dissolve to . . .]

Exterior: The corner of Frankstown and Homewood Avenues, quiet in a photograph taken at dawn from the sixth floor of the K. LeRoy Irvis senior citizens' residence. Shot should include the shops on the north side of Frankstown across Homewood from Mason's bar. No people in picture. A kind of postcard of the neighborhood before its residents hit the street. The screen's divided to accommodate below this frozen image a string of words subtitling French spoken by offscreen voices, words passing like the crawl at the bottom of a TV newscast. As the crawl of words from invisible speakers — English words translating French words taken from a case study Frantz Fanon appended to *The Wretched of the Earth* — moves across the screen, the photograph of Homewood blurs and darkens, gradually disappearing altogether, the screen black finally as the interrogations below end.

Voiceover

Today in the trial of two Algerian boys aged thirteen and fourteen accused of murdering their European playmate, transcriptions were read in court of conversations between expert witness psychiatrist Dr. Frantz Fanon and the two accused. Because they are minors, the accused boys are designated in the following excerpts as Thirteen-Year-Old and Fourteen-Year-Old.

The Crawl

THE THIRTEEN-YEAR-OLD

We weren't a bit cross with him. We used to go and play together on the hill outside the village. He was a good friend of ours. One day we decided to kill him because Europeans kill all the Arabs. We can't kill big people. But we could kill ones like him, because he was the same age as us. We didn't know how to kill him. We wanted to throw him in a ditch, but he'd only be hurt. So we got the knife from home and killed him.

And yet you were pals?
Well then, why do they want to kill us.
You know he is dead now.
Yes.
What does that mean?
When it's all finished, you go to heaven.
Does having killed somebody worry you?
No, since they want to kill us . . .

THE FOURTEEN-YEAR-OLD

At home everybody said that the French had sworn to kill us all one after the other. Two of my family were killed. And did they arrest a single Frenchman for all those Algerians who were killed.

I don't know.

Well, nobody at all was arrested. I wanted to take to the mountains, but I was too young. So my friend and I said we'd kill a European.

Why?

In your opinion, what should we have done?

I don't know. But you are a child and what is happening concerns grown-up people.

But they kill children too.

That is no reason for killing your friend.

Well, I did kill him.

Had your friend done anything to harm you.

Not a thing.

Well.

Well, there you are . . .

[Dissolve to . . .]

To a young man of African descent standing on the corner of Frankstown and Homewood. Around ten-thirty at night. Summer. He's about fifteen or sixteen, the age of my dead nephew Omar, my jailed brother's murdered son, when I took him once upon a time to buy a black-and-gold Pittsburgh Steelers winter parka his mother couldn't afford at Sears on Hiland Avenue, a department store that's since disappeared from East Liberty, a section of town to the west adjoining this part of town, Homewood, whose chain stores have also disappeared as my nephew disappeared from these streets, though the kid my nephew's size and age on the dark corner, from the distance we're shooting, could be Omar, his familiar man-sized shape in a fat T-shirt and droopy pants, a silhouette cut out distinctly then unresolved again, merging into shadows draping the corner on which he stands fidgeting, a figure partially visible in patches of fire thrown by passing cars or light cast by a streetlamp or shed by the gleam of a cell phone store's neon lights and Too Sweets barbershop sign on the opposite corner and I wonder if my nephew Omar, alive again in my thought about the boy on the corner, had ever thought of me dead. I had thought about him dead often, a victim of Homewood's dangerous streets. Wouldn't it have been more natural once upon a time for him to think that thought about me, his elder by three decades, than for me to have thought it about him. Natural for Omar to have imagined me, if not dead exactly, removed. Out of the picture. Out of the goddamn way. Me and everybody else my age and older moving aside to give him room to breathe, give him some room for himself, room to make something of himself. King for a minute of these streets with next to nothing in them. What happens to you. Where do you go if someone thinks of you as dead. To be in someone's thoughts or stories keeps the dead alive, the Igbo say. But what if a person thinks of you as dead. Or you think of someone as dead. If you think yourself alive, does your thinking protect you, change the power of the other's thought to remove you to wherever a person goes when someone thinks of them as dead. When anyone thinks of someone else as dead, are they also with this thought returning that other person to life, a sort of life or imitation life at least since life is all we know, all we've experienced and continue to experience till the end, so if we hold another in our imagination even if we think of them as dead, do we grant them a chance, however slim, however temporary, however inconclusive and inconsequential, a chance, something like a reprieve, to be in the alive state we are, since any other state, anywhere else is beyond our power to conceive, the state of being dead for instance, though dead we may be in another's thoughts, but is that too a kind of life, like the Igbo say, though we might be remote, out of the picture, beyond our power to recall ourselves, as it seems the case might be if we are dead.

The young guy on the corner, for all his fidgeting, stares intently at Mason's bar, even with his back turned toward Mason's, he stares at Mason's. Mason's an eyesore, Mr. Godard. From this distance, in the poor light, you can't see how looking at Mason's damages the boy's face, how it fucks with him, but it does, it does. My mom could tell you about the shenanigans going on outside and inside Mason's twenty-four-seven. People inside drinking and shooting up, people outside pissing, shitting, turning tricks, sleeping, eating golden nuggets of Kentucky Fried Chicken in the mess of weeds and rubbish just beyond the bar. Mason's a doorway into one of the few structures left over from neighborhood renewal of the block of Frankstown across from the senior citizens' residence on whose sixth and topmost floor my mother rents an apartment subsidized by the city of Pittsburgh. Mason's occupies the ground floor of an otherwise empty two-story brick rowhouse, and next comes its boarded-up Siamese twin, empty except for vermin, and next the toilet of weedy vacant lot and next more rowhouses, some partially occupied, then a fenced, carefully tended green space advertising itself as the future site of the Homewood Bruston African-American Cultural Museum and finally, blessing the block, recessed and elevated from the street to separate it from the Velvet Slipper Lounge on the corner, a large Baptist church set in immaculate grounds, looking dazed and brand-new after the congregation paid to sandblast away a century's worth of steel-mill soot and grime blackening its stones. You can see this entire block of Frankstown and beyond disposed as I've sketched it in what you could call a bird's-eye view from my mother's terrace, but that's not the perspective of the young man on the corner, his wings have been clipped, when he comes and goes he hip-hops low to the ground or glides along permanent grooves in the sidewalk. He hustles, flees, perpetrates, pinned down by something that never permits him to stretch up to his full height of over six feet and breathe deeply. He leans in at a stylized slant so as my mom peers down at him he appears to be going about his business pressed down by a transparent slab of glass, thick enough to reach from his head and shoulders to the sky, a blue sky some days, framing Homewood's highest hilltops, blue sky plotted for flight paths into Allegheny County airport, so the sky's crowded at certain hours by planes my mother watches, and though she'd miss him, miss him terribly if he left and didn't return, my mother tries to think of the boy on the corner elsewhere, on a plane headed to someplace where he is not dead so soon so often and she wonders who decides where those planes fly and who decides who rides them and who decided that her old frail body, locked down in a wheelchair, will outlast the boy's.

The young man can't take his eyes — eyes we can't see, only imagine — off Mason's. We watch him like my mom watches, reading his posture, his motions, for any sign we can gather at this remove of what intention or errand might have brought him here, stalled him here. She can guess. She could whisper his story to us and probably get much of it right. She prefers to give him, as her father, my grandfather John French, used to say, the benefit of the doubt. She observes meticulously. Reads the signs of what he's doing in the dim light of that shadowy corner, wondering if he's one of her daylight regulars she tracks up and back, up and back on Frankstown or Homewood Avenue, her folks working the grid of streets as if the streets have walls, are tunnels and chutes and corridors allowing no slack, no escape as her people go about their business. Her regulars instantly recognizable when they enter the maze visible from where she sits six floors above the sidewalk and each regular also for an instant could be a stranger or could be a grandchild, a grandniece, a great-grandnephew, could be herself down there strolling or slouched on a shadowy corner at night smoking a cigarette. Does smoke warm your mouth, your lungs, the smoke inside you and outside, is it nasty or nice with a burning stick squeezed in your lips, how would she know, how could she guess unless she watches, watches him staring at Mason's as if he belongs inside the door, longing for it to open or shut, for someone to enter or leave so he can tag along unnoticed where he wants to be so badly she guesses his mind's already inside, trapped inside as he's trapped outside, the lungs one place, the smoke in another, wishing to mix, to slink into Mason's or slink outside and down to the corner and be whole she guesses as she watches him send messages of himself to somebody inside Mason's door, the door not closed, a black hole sealed at this hour by night and she guesses the young man would need more than the strength he possesses in both arms, both legs to push into the bar or push himself back out into the street if he's inside, need every ounce of strength in his body, more power than he can muster for the moment to brush the curtain of night aside so he waits on the corner, sends messages down the block into the black entrance. Someone with something the young man needs sits on a barstool or stands inside Mason's. Or someone outside Mason's waits for him to arrive with something badly needed. For unknown reasons the exchange stalled. Is it impossible or dangerous or what. Or who. Why. How could she know for sure what keeps the young man standing where he is, his eyes fixed on Mason's, feet shuffling like he's chilly and can't get warm in all this July heat. A million little tiny going-nowhere dance steps. Why doesn't he begin walking the . . . what, twenty, thirty steps from the corner to Mason's or better yet why not go in the opposite direction, any other direction, go the twenty or thirty steps across Homewood Avenue, go, go, go young man, go that way please, please run, run away please she begs grandson or great-niece or great-grandnephew whom the streets make strangers for that instant when they first appear and the shape at a distance could be anyone coming or going down there in the street till the next instant a heartbeat, heart burp, or sigh away when the miracle she's watching for is something else again, not a lost one returning, not one saved, but the same old regular thing again happening.

*

When it's the next frame of the movie and after it the next and next and next, enough frames per second to restore an illusion of motion, of life to a scene that for an instant seemed neither old nor new, seemed outside time as if time sleeps when we sleep as if time slows down when motion slows and somehow we inhabit a slowed-down seamless space outside time, disembodied in the stoptime of a snapshot or perfect word until we return to ourselves and the movie that never stops seems to start up again because we're watching again and our attention's seized again by what appears to move across the screen, but something's wrong, the next frame, next scene can't possibly be the next, it doesn't follow, we've missed something, something has intervened, the boy has moved from the corner and is lying shot to death in the vacant lot next to Mason's. Where have we been.

[Dissolve to a woman in a wheelchair on a balcony of a six-story public housing facility for the elderly. The recessed balcony, guarded by a solid, waist-high metal wall, is long and narrow, a space in which two and a half coffins lined up head to foot or assbackwards, foot to head, would fit snugly. The woman is approximately eighty years old. Depending on the light, the distance, and the angle from which you shoot, she can seem decades younger, decades older. Retain a tight focus on her face the entire time she delivers her monologue. Her features should more or less fill the screen, unnaturally large at first, monstrously oversized features, a wasteland of skin so the viewer doesn't feel comfortable, confronted on an exaggerated scale by the mix of familiarity and strangeness any human face expresses. The closeups of elderly faces in In Praise of Love could serve as a guide here.]

The Woman: Well, I was outside, you know, like I like to be if the weather's decent, sitting up here in this chair, minding my own business (you mean minding everybody's business, don't you, Mother dear), a hot day in a hot spell, middle of the afternoon I remember because they said on the noon news expect thundershowers or thunderstorms later today breaking up the heat and cooler tomorrow the man promised but you know how changeable the weather is and they get it wrong it seems to me as often as they get it right but I listen anyway and to give credit where credit's due they did warn people about the terrible winds and the flooding this spring and it's a good thing too they got that right because the storm tore up Pittsburgh, big trees down everywhere and roads closed, people's basements full of water and I saw on TV the whole insides of some of those houses out in the suburbs floating away but nobody hurt bad or killed thank goodness and thanks to the weather people too I guess, to give credit its due, anyway no sign of rain on that afternoon the news had promised rain the heat still laying like a wool blanket down there in the streets and I'm up here a little sleepy the way I get some afternoons, tired, though it seems I don't do much of anything these days except sleep, sitting here dozing off, then trying to wake myself up by thinking about what I might fix for my dinner and nothing I can think of sounds like much I don't know some days why I bother to eat just don't have the appetite I once did but you know the eating habit not a good one to break so this afternoon I'm telling you about it's around time to start thinking about fixing some little thing or another for my dinner but I'm not coming up with much with nothing really I have a taste for because I'm never hungry the way I used to be hungry chasing all day after youall and it worries me some because you know your mother always loved to eat, that's where you got that big appetite of yours and I know it won't be me anymore, not myself anymore if I don't care about the food on my plate and it's late in the afternoon school-bus time but no school bus because it's summer I can't say the hour exactly, I hate to look at my watch, I love my watch because you bought it for me but I don't let myself get in the habit of checking the time all the time it just makes the hours go slower time gets heavy on your hands when you're always watching the clock you know like heat's worse when you think of heat so it's best not to think heat if you're trying to stay cool, best if you put your mind on something nice and cool and sometimes time flies if you leave it alone it used to fly anyway when I had no watch no time to myself not with all youall needing this or that or your father's table-waiting white shirts to iron, the food, food, food everybody looking for every hour of the day, mouths open, hands out, I'm hungry Mom my hands always busy and time seemed to fly but when you stop and really think about it, time doesn't change doesn't go fast or slow just goes on its own sweet time, it's the same time really going fast when youall were little and going slow now with me locked up in this chair still the same time it's always been, only me that's changing when I stop to think about it, me coming here a baby to this old earth and leaving here old and still the same time it's always been since long before I got here and long after I'm gone from here the same time, not slow, not fast the way people say it goes I have that thought sometimes and it doesn't go any further than I just said, just a dumb old woman's thought I think sitting here cause I don't have nothing better to do than sit in this wheelchair and think while I watch the people down there in the street doing whatever it is they think they're doing I bet you walk up to one with a microphone in your hand like on TV they wouldn't know what to say if you asked, What are you doing, ma'am. Why are you out here in these streets with the sun beating down on your nappy head. I wonder sometimes if anybody has the slightest idea of what they think they're doing except they're doing it, like me sitting up here in this chair, doing it because I did it yesterday and got used to doing it and now it's what I do, it's too late it's not really worth thinking about too much if you think about it. Listen to me going on. See, that's what happens when you're alone. You start to talking to your-self. Harebrained conversations don't stop, don't start or stop just come from nowhere and go nowhere you talking to yourself just to hear somebody talking, talk that wouldn't make the slightest bit of sense to anybody else besides you and as a matter of fact makes precious little sense to you sometimes, you're just talking to hear somebody talk and you're the only one listening so it don't matter start on one thing and jump to another thing without finishing what you started who cares just a way to pass the time and sometimes time goes faster that way or maybe slower you don't want to know either way so don't look at your watch, it might make a liar out of what you want the time to be and still a long way to go before it's time to get ready for bed not bedtime yet the sun's still up it's bright afternoon sleepy-head old fool, school's just out, school-bus time if the school bus had been running that July afternoon I'm talking about and I remember thinking there's a clock inside me with no hands on its face but I hear it tick-tock telling me the school bus taking the children home been here a couple minutes ago and stopped just down from the corner of Frankstown and Homewood to let the little boy lives cross the street off, stopped and he hopped down that last tall step and scoots across Frankstown Avenue, looking both ways up and down like I holler every time he better look, the bus stopped sure as if I'd seen it stop and seen him hopping down and crossing with my own two eyes, though I know good and well no school and no school bus in summer.

No school bus ever when I was a little girl. I walked to Homewood School. Walked Cassina Way to Dumferline up Susquehanna or up Tioga to Homewood Avenue and right on Homewood to Hamilton left on Hamilton you know the way as well as I do why am I telling you how to walk to Homewood School from Cassina Way it's just about the same way you walked from Finance Street to get to the same raggedy building I walked to when I was little and your children would go to school in the same building today if you had little children and the school was open today if you hadn't got yourself together and moved away from here, same old trifling building except they stuck a new brick front on it and parked some trailers for classrooms in the schoolyard where we used to play hopscotch and chase one another around like wild Indians I don't need to tell you how far I walked on which streets it wasn't really all that far but back then seemed like a long ways a long walk from home past other people's houses a long way because I didn't know the names of any of the people lived in those houses, not much of a walk when I think about it today you know as well as I do the school's not very far except in a little girl's mind who needed her mother to walk with her and hold her hand the first couple weeks of school and anytime after that she could blackmail her mama squeezing tears out my eyes there on the front step and Mama in the doorway Mama please, please that little hussy begging with her crocodile tears so her mama would walk her to school not really far except I couldn't take one step of the way today not put down one foot after the other and walk two steps if the pot at the end of the rainbow sitting on the pavement full of gold shining two steps away it's me and this chair that's how it is now the walk to Homewood School mize well be a million miles I'm done with walking but there was something I wanted to tell you and I'm trying to get out the words but I'm old and my tongue's starting to stumble and soon it's going to be just as hopeless as these useless legs where was I going I was walking on my way to Homewood School a little girl walking on Susquehanna Street in the empty morning early just me no mama with my hand in hers up Susquehanna just past where Dumferline cuts in and three cute houses set back from the street with fences out along the sidewalk, not rowhouses like the rest on Susquehanna and the other streets I walked to get to school these three houses separate small neat homes Italian people kept up nice, you know, the way they do, vegetable garden along the side green striped awnings and grass and flowers, rosebushes in front like Mama grew in the front yard when we moved to Finance Street from Cassina Way I think half the roses in Homewood from cuttings Mama gave people from her rosebushes everybody passing said those sure some beautiful red roses, Mrs. French. You sure do raise some beautiful roses. I used to daydream sometimes passing those three particular neat little set-back houses pretend I lived in one or pretend I had a dollhouse at home looked just like one of those houses I could play with full of tiny furniture and tiny people I'd move from room to room, sit them on chairs or lay them down on their tiny beds to sleep or *tack-tack-tack* walk one of those stiff-legged dolls up the steps for some reason I don't know now and probably didn't know then either just *tack-tack-tack* up steps and in and out of rooms busy you know for reasons I can't say and don't matter really just tiny people busy in their tiny homes just a little girl daydreaming how pretty and busy her house would be if she was grown up and had a house and next thing I know a big snarling dog so close it sprays slobber on my bare arm, big dog up on its hind legs barking and snapping, tearing around then it drops down off the fence and runs in circles then brams its mean self up on the fence again and I can't even say, grateful as I was for that fence, what kind of fence it was, wire I think, a strong fence thank goodness with steel posts and that twisted steel wire maybe so it don't go nowhere but my heart in my mouth I just knew no fence could hold in that wild animal jumping and barking and whipping around in crazy circles to get at me and eat me up steel and wire or could have been wood I think each set-back house had a different kind of fence. All I remember is running fast as I could cross the street and promising God if he saved me from that dog I'd never walk next to those fences again and never did, never even thought about trying again ever in life. After I got away from the nasty dog come running and biting at me that morning, I always crossed Susquehanna before I got to the place where those three houses set with their green grass and flowers and fences and painted all nice and clean, never ever let myself get caught over there where the dog hated me. I made sure to cross over and would cross today if God put me back on my feet and let me walk the sidewalks again. Funny thing is I kept crossing Susquehanna long after that dog, I started to say giant dog but to tell the truth I can't really say how big or what kind of dog it might have been, bigger than a timber wolf to me when it ran at me trying to bram down the fence to get me but that was then, those were a little scared child's eyes, the little girl I was then who didn't know any better but now here's what I really wanted to tell you. Once when I walked you to Homewood School I was holding your hand in mine and crossed you over to the other side of Susquehanna and then further up the block, near the corner, I marched you back across Susquehanna Street to the side we'd been on in the first place after we turned from Dumferline and you always were a smart little boy you looked up at me as if to say, What you doing, Mama, almost as if you knew we'd gone out of our way for no good reason crossing and crossing back and probably by that time after all the years it took for me to grow up, well, almost grow up, grown enough anyway to get married and have you and for you to be a boy old enough to start school and big enough to begin learning your alphabet and numbers and your own way so you could leave the house in the morning and walk to Homewood School by your own self, and after all those years if you would have asked me that day why we crossed, I would have been ashamed to say because after all those years I was showing you a way didn't really make a bit of sense, the dog long dead, the three cute separate houses all rundown, maybe not even sitting there any longer, maybe a dead vacant lot dead as the dog and I'm teaching you my fear, teaching you to cross, teaching you to look out for something bad not even there anymore.

And I said all that to say this. The spot right outside Mason's bar along the vacant lot where the weeds were high before the city came and cut them, where the boy they shot laid there and died and left the mark of his body in the mashed-down weeds, that very spot where the worst thing happened to their son, I saw a couple had to be the dead boy's mother and father who else could it be with the boy's little sister by the hand, standing there on Frankstown, all three of them staring down at the spot where the weeds had sprung up again after the boy's body lying there had mashed them down to its shape, the three of them staring and I wondered how in the world they knew the exact spot where he'd died. I was sitting outside right up here the night they shot him and I heard the shots and watched the boys shot him running down Frankstown and him lying so still in exactly that spot I will never forget, never, never forget, I could go right to it now if you pushed me over there and draw the spot and he'd fit in my drawing just like he fit the spot that night. I don't know how his people knew the spot because I watched and watched the carryings-on after the paramedics covered up the boy's face and took his body away on a stretcher, watched the detectives marching through the weeds, cops searching up and down the alley behind Frankstown, watched the ambulances and trucks with searchlights and paddywagons and a hook-and-ladder firetruck and one with big spools of hose for god knows what reason unless they had the good idea to burn Mason's to the ground and wanted fire engines sitting at the curb so the fire wouldn't spread, armies of men and machines and big lights all kinds of commotion after they carried the boy off in a black van and I watched it all, watched till everybody left and it was quiet again as it ever gets around here and I never saw the couple that night I'm sure I never saw them till I saw them in broad daylight the next afternoon the boy's mother and father I'm certain, the right age, right look, with a little girl by the hand must be the poor boy's sister, I said to myself, the three of them coming up Frankstown and stopping after they passed Mason's right beside the exact spot where I'd watched a boy lying so still I had no doubt from the first moment I saw a dark shape not moving down there in the weeds he was dead, and the three of them walked up like I just said and stood still a minute then they started moving, hugging one another and forgive me god for thinking and saying this they danced a kind of grief jig, the little girl watching, the two grownups moving jumpy like it hurt them to move and hurt too much not to move, like they had to shake their feet and hands in jerky little circles and shuffles, you know, because the air, the ground all the sudden too hot or too cold to touch, circling around each other, each one needing to fight that cold, that fire their own way, the best way they could and then all three hugging again and after that they dropped down on their knees, raising their arms, kissing the ground, swaying real slow, mashing down the weeds in the exact same spot the son's body had mashed them the night before and I thought of leading you by the hand to Homewood School and wondered if I remembered something terrible could I pass it on to you without saying a word and remembered your big eyes on me after I'd crossed you back and forth across Susquehanna for no good reason and I wondered if you saw in my eyes that nasty dog and if you'd always cross at the same spot I crossed you and now I'm asking myself and asking you too, could a person hold open in their mind the dead boy's place in those weeds for his people to find and drop down on it like I saw them drop. Could it have been me thinking of him lying there, right exactly there, me leading them, guiding them to him so they see him though nothing's there.

[Dissolve to JEW and JLG — interior of grocery store/restaurant]
I don't need you to remind me that getting my mother's stories on film next to impossible, Mr. G. I share your pessimism about the limits of cinema, about the lost cause of any made-up shit supposed to be representing real shit and I know my mother's old, her stories old stories and who gives a flying fuck these days about old folks' rambling stories, who's prepared to bankroll movies about grungy, smelly tail ends of lives when sexy, young-fleshed lives photograph so pretty, sell so well. I admit my mom's getting old but on the other hand she's not as old as the Sumerian culture you sample toward the end of your latest film *Our Music* to make your point about how

language (thus narrative and meaning in general) operates both forward and backward in what we call *time,* the bit about Sumerian grammar employing a future tense to describe the past. Never goes away, does it, the paradoxical old/new nature of time, so how old is old anyway or how young and who cares Mr. G. when you get down to the nitty-gritty, everybody just wants their own time and more of it, call it whatever you want to call it, past, present, future, who cares it's all the same, my mother's old stories, mine, yours, young again if we're alive to hear them, tell them, see them, act them, the ancient Sumerians singing about past glories as if their history's going to happen any day now, tomorrow, today, yesterday, centuries in the future and keep on happening forever and Sumeria a heap of old stones scattered in the desert in the vicinity of Iraq and Iran, time's stupid and indiscriminate whether it's measured by dynasties or by inflections of verbs or carved up by calendars into months and years and centuries or light-years or the half-lives of elementary particles decaying or annular rings of a tree or geological epochs or intervals on a musical scale, the same bullshit same wishful thinking, whatever talisman or computer program people set to divvy up time, rationalize it, tame it, chain it, preserve it whatever year of this dog or that snake or this bearded savior or that comet or shooting star or quark's rotation around an imaginary nucleus, time stays what it is, waves goody-bye, goody-bye, like runaway slaves wave to Old Massa, old names forgotten, old chains broken, no tick, no tock. Goody-bye.

On one hand, given the above, I understand your reluctance, Mr. Godard. On the other hand, the invisible hand that makes clapping with one hand possible, why not try to film my mother's stories. Why not try your luck, set down your bucket, here, where we sit, Jean Luc, Lucky John. What's to lose. Except time. And there's always plenty of time. It's all we have, right.

And speaking of the future, Mr. G., do you know that the dead talk like niggers. Which means the language of the dead may be nigger language or the dead may be imitating for whatever reasons the language we hear around us in this neighborhood I grew up in. Maybe the dead hang with niggers a lot. Or maybe niggers hang out a lot with the dead. Or it could be the fact that all the dead are niggers. Could be the fact only niggers die, but I don't think so. Shit, to be honest I can't explain why the dead speak like some of my people speak. A thought about why once crossed my mind but I didn't take it seriously. It made me laugh really. The gist of it goes something like this: so-called white people rule this world — who could dispute that, Mr. G., everybody knows white people on top even if it's only a very few really on top of the top and more and more so-called whites sinking down through the cracks into places basically indistinguishable in many ways from Homewood, and yellow people and brown people and purple people and beige people coming on fast, breathing down white people's necks but that's another humorous thought not so funny according to your Mr. Eminem and that's not the thought anyway that cracked me up when it flashed through my mind to explain why the dead speak the way niggers speak. Just grant me the obvious fact that white people or so-called white people because they call themselves white, run the world as we know it, the world striding out of our TVs every day bigger than life and upon that world they run they impose their language as the official language for doing business, for deciding who's famous, who's smart, who speaks intelligently, the language for writing history and the last word on what's good or bad, ugly or beautiful. Their language a sign of who's on top and why and also a way of identifying who ain't on top, who can't be and ain't spozed to be since they speak the wrong language, like nigger language, which is not to say that many languages don't have their places in the world the ones on top administer, the many languages have places just like many so-called non-white, colored people have places and some, a few anyway (even a few niggers), have places you could call significant or desirable, per-haps indispensable in the world they serve, but the point I've already belabored far too much since as I said it's such an obvious point is that at the end of the day and when the day begins too, *whites* or if you will "so-called whites" run things, and a few reap godlike profits from this bullshit called a world, or whatever they call it, profiting even from the bullshit cages you see in this place we're visiting today called Homewood, these cages you might think belong to the people you see caged in them but in fact belong to the ones who built them and got the keys in their deep pockets, and even here in this so-called ghetto white is spoken, whether or not you hear one word of it everybody understands who's in charge whose voice matters but back to my tickling thought which is this: maybe on the other side, the so-called dead side, the side that's located, you know, through the looking glass or just below the surface of water or on the other face of a coin you can't see when you're looking at one face, over there maybe the people whom/who the language ruling this side calls col-ored or negroes or whatever, maybe over there some of the so-called black people are the bosses. And over there where everybody winds up sooner or later or maybe never exactly leaves, over there maybe — ha-ha-ha — you better speak nigger or else.

[Dissolve to the woman's face on the balcony]

She's always wondered if she'd given him his taste for coffee. Her first son. From the beginning of the time he'd been inside her, every morning she'd splashed the island where he lived with a tide of strong hot coffee and the Carnation evaporated milk that served her as cream. Then him, at last, outside at her breast, coffee's flavor and color seeping from inside her into him as she rocked him while he suckled. A strangely full, ready-to-burst almost achy feeling lately takes her back to those early days in Washington, D.C., barely more than a child herself, bellyful of baby and nothing all day to do — how many times a day can you sweep and dust a one-room flat, how much cooking of the single meal two (three) share — too timid and tired to walk very far on streets lined with block-long stone buildings packed with strangers, learning to tie a scarf around her telltale hair and sneak into whites-only movies a few afternoons when there was a spare dime for sneaking, bearing a child, afraid of it, afraid of a new city, then the miracle finally, from her flesh comes flesh more precious than hers, yet her flesh too. After all, the simple truth is he had dropped out of her bottom, down there where she opens to pee and shit and bleed, opens for a man, yes, he'd dropped out from down there in a noisy, embarrassing shower *Goddammit, nurse, who fed this woman beans* so it's true and not true they are mother and son, coming and going, not exactly the same flesh, not exactly separate either, a hopelessly mixed-together oneness now and always with this "he" she named with his father's and her father's names *John Edgar.* She must feed and cradle and comfort him in her arms, sing to him not because anyone tells her she must, she has no choice, understood from the first instant that her arms, her legs belong to him, his puny limbs and blind fingers are hers, preciously, forever hers like certain expressions on his tiny face she sometimes coaxes from him are hers, expressions mirroring her huge face hovering, breathing into his, speaking to him without words in a language her body had learned from others to express with the muscles of her face, passing on family looks becoming his looks and though she understood she must be the source of much of what he saw then she saw spreading across his features, she also discovered new likenesses she had never perceived in herself. She was beginning to know herself in a different fashion, recognizing features she carried, looks taught by glances she exchanged with this baby. Not exactly as in a mirror. He was so different, far more precious than she was. Except watching those big eyes, small ears, that nose, that mouth, strangely she suffered his pains and pleasures deeper inside herself than the truth of her own sensations. But she couldn't pee for him or bleed for him, only mop up the damage, watch the hungers and aches inside him flow one to the next, relieved or not, tended to or not, pleasure or pain. His body would go on about its business, coping, thriving, or limping along as his flesh willed, while inside her, anything that had hurt or threatened him kept on terrorizing her flesh. She would see lifetimes of pain twisting across his face. Enough pain for many generations, the old people's pain from long ago, undreamed pain still to arrive — as real as her memories, as her perpetual fears of what might come to pass — all flickering in an instant across his features and after this unhappiness passes, he might smile, coo, fall asleep and there she'd sit, tears welling up in her eyes, a crew of phantom aches cruising through her body like they say you still feel in the space where an arm or leg used to be before a doctor cuts it off. His body, long gone from the nest inside hers, yet it's still eating her bones, her heart.

Her coffee inside him, wherever he's sipping his first cup this morning. Not really hers. Not from the cup in her hand, not from the pot she just brewed. From inside her. From those loneliest, fullest times in D.C. No. She'd never be that silly, silly little girl again but feels the vaguely familiar fullness again of carrying him inside, a heaviness and fullness puzzling, puzzling, with her helpless as a baby now in this womb of chair. No. The damned wheelchair not a womb. It's her chain, her steel-barred cell. The evil jailors starving her with a torture worse than withholding food. The apartment's stocked with frozen dinners, cans of beans, boxes of rice and macaroni, a two-day-old roast sealed in jellied gravy at the bottom of the CrockPot in the fridge, cold cuts, one stale-ish, two mostly fresh loaves of bread, milk, Maxwell House instant coffee, orange juice, Pepsi, cereal, bananas, and so forth, she can list to herself a couple weeks' worth of provisions because it's not about not having stuff to shovel in her mouth and load up her stomach it's about appetite and the torturers are killing it, deadening day by day inch by inch her will to fix and chew and digest a meal. A ghost heaviness balloons inside her while she wastes away in the chair. Nothing she eats will return strength to her twisted legs. No amount of food will help her rise up out of the chair and go on back to doing the things she's been doing day by day, all these hard years to keep herself alive.

Oh, pity, pity, poor me. One of my pity party days is how she tries to explain it to him and herself when he says her voice over the phone sounds like it's coming from a deep, dark pit. Oh yes, she's tempted to answer. Do you really want to hear how deep and dark, my son. A hole if somebody was digging it to find oil they'd have given up and put a cap on it long ago. Ha-ha. And you know how greedy those oil-drilling folks can be. You know cause a Texas one of them runs this country and he's drilling us dry, drilling down down till the greedy hole's all the way through to China and almost out the other end and this poor old world's gonna spring a leak, groan, cut one long hissing fart, and all the nasty air gon run out she'd like to say something silly like that and laugh with him, *hisssss, phew-weee* all their troubles, bad as they seem, bad as they are, trouble don't last always, my son, right, but no appetite for silly sayings or dumb stories she makes up from reading the news or watching TV when she talks with him on the phone to prove she's okay, that she's still fighting still following what's happening in the big world around her little squeezed up one shrinking shrinking to a greasy-looking stain and a bad smell, all that will be left of her in the chair one day, soon.

These are not precisely her words, of course. Not mine precisely either. A mix, we'll say. As everything turns out to be. I'm making up words. Exchanging words with her to teach myself whatever might remain to be said. At times anything's better than silence. Better than silently abiding her illness and loneliness, the slow, sure progress of losing touch. Better than the silence of sitting alone, crippled in a goddamn wheelchair above those bare streets watching for miracles. Anything's better. Fire. Flood. It's okay to knock her up, even. Have her a girl again, walking D.C. streets again. Expecting. Heavy and uncomfortable in June heat. Unwed. Baby's father unknown. Maybe the daddy's you, Mr. Sneaky Motherfucker Godard. You, Mr. Luc lucky John. Maybe she'll be sitting six floors up on her balcony one afternoon so big the dumb chair's bowlegged under her young girl's fully packed lushness miraculously recovered and she howls a bloodcurdling air-raid-siren howl everybody hears from one end of Homewood to the other, hears it all up and down and around the axis of Homewood and Frankstown Avenues, a ground-zero howl so loud even all the vanished folks can't stop up their ears against it when Mom pops wide open and surprise, surprise out comes Frantz goddamn Fanon, lips all bloody munching on the barbecued afterbirth. *I'm back.*

[Dissolve to me and Mr. Jean Luc Godard side by side on a mourners' bench with a bare shelf serving as our tabletop, etc. — you remember, the place where we were before. We're still sitting here waiting between one dissolve and the next.]

So what you're saying, Mr. G., or not saying since I been jabbering nonstop and you ain't squeezed out a mumbling word for hours, I guess what you're telling me bottomline is you'll be in touch, right. In the sous-conversation of things not said aloud, you're hipping me, aren't you, my man, saying, Don't hold your breath. Well, I hear you, bro. And I appreciate your candor. It takes the pressure off. Thanks. I can go on about my business now. Write my Fanon book without worrying about a shooting schedule, balky stars, budget overruns, guys in suits, censors, distribution rights, percentages, anxious banks, my poor French, and your good English. You know. Hey. There's just one last thing I need to tell you. I fell in love in Paris once. In spring. I love Paris in the spring, love spring everywhere it breaks between the cracks in your beautiful old country, even where those ferocious hedgerows grow they say men died like flies fighting through on D-Day. You've seen the movie, haven't you.

Dear Frantz Fanon:

As you've probably figured out for yourself, I'm reluctant to say whether my evolving project is fiction or nonfiction, novel or memoir, science fiction or romance, hello or goodbye. A little tweaking and maybe it would fit in one category or the other. On the other hand, the hand supposed to keep track of what the other's doing, that tweaking, those categories one might say, are what I've been writing about, or trying to write my way out of, not only the last few years, but since the beginning. Perhaps that's why I'm dazed now and subdued by a sense of bittersweet resignation when confronted by the necessity of tweaking, and the implacable either/or categories. Anyway, gotta go now. The doorbell's ringing. I'm expecting a package.

PART III

I WANT TO TELL YOU one last little story about why I need to tell your story, Frantz Fanon. I'm going to employ the license you often employ in your writing, narrating a story in the present tense as if it's happening as you speak. For the writer, writing's always in the present, isn't it, in a vanishing moment the writing attempts to communicate, to transform into something tangible, lasting, something not lost, not gone before it gets here, something not disappearing the instant it's set down in words, words that disappear too, like dreams, like the writer writing them. Remember me sitting on a deck one evening in a garden at the back of a small house in Brittany composing a letter to you, claiming I was trying to save a life. Remember. I promised to say more about the evening, and here's the more:

I'm sitting in a small garden. Dinner, an improvisation of whatever's at hand, about over. Me outside, quiet on the deck, finishing off the last of the wine, my wife inside, noisy at the sink, hurrying through dirty dishes, me outside, grateful inside for the simple rhythms of this day still ending, still some time to go, watching the light fade or rather sitting here thinking about how slowly light leaves the sky this far west and north in France, fades *reluctantly*, the word popping into mind not so much a word about the imponderable light's way of leaving, it's a word expressing my mood, my awareness of the simple back-and-forth between two people that can render a day's passage unspeakably more than satisfactory, create a feeling of regret almost, a reluctance to let the day go, melancholy threatening to settle in, though the day's still quite alive, dishes rattling, my nearly empty glass a mysterious thing delivering intimations of other dimensions of time and space, bouncing light, refracting light, light swallowed, sliced, pooling in a dark mirror as I slowly swirl the glass's contents, each configuration unpredictable, once and only once, only here and now, because there is no way to experience what I look at, what I see this moment, unless someone, a god, would start up a universe precisely in the manner some god had started this world I inhabit and give me or another person in that matching universe exactly the place I hold in this one and then wind up the parallel universe and let it play forward to precisely this instant, a silly idea all around, *god, starting up, precisely,* yet those words like the word *reluctantly* alive in the air and I need to say something, make something with them, because they say themselves to me, part of the give-and-take rhythm of this day at approximately 10:15 P.M., words like everything else nameable and unnameable, part of me and not me, not mine exactly, like the light outside and inside still strong enough to keep night at bay longer than anyone would have the patience to watch, really watch it slowly diminishing by imperceptible degrees, my wife inside at the sink with her back to the sky, and I can almost hear her thinking out loud. Can't wait to get upstairs and plop down in bed with my book, she's saying inside, water running, dishes clattering, not much mess really, she'll zip through it in minutes and quickly get her wish then take her time once she's upstairs in the bathroom, just like she took her own sweet time earlier rinsing salt from her skin, washing her hair, scrubbing her face, applying ointments, creams, oils, color after our swim in the ocean, busy upstairs till she was good and ready to come downstairs while I improvised dinner in the kitchen, set the table, opened wine, me busy downstairs while she takes her time upstairs and you get the point, I hope, we take turns, or more to the point, I'm beginning finally after sixty some years on the planet to understand how people are always in each other's way and not and both always and therefore when two people want to love one another they must be clear and lucky and learn bit by bit what either one can give or take, what either one's willing or able or chooses or chooses not to give or take and learn a comfort with the things living together allows them to change in each other or things they can't change, fabricating space, slack, turns taken not in order to earn credit on some blackboard keeping track of whose turn, who's in debt to whom, no, more like discovering you're turned on head over heels, learning to dance or screw or talk with somebody and the other person seems to be enjoying it at least as much as you are, happy doing whatever it is you're doing together and you don't even need to give it a name, don't want to give it a name that might jinx it, because whatever you're doing isn't like it was on other occasions, doing it with anybody else. These new sensations of being glad and being willing to give what it takes to improvise dinner, to wait, to relax into the doing of needful things or silly things, clean up the dishes, get to bed, stare at an almost empty wineglass I jiggle in my fingers. Soon I'll go up the stairs, find a woman waiting for me and not waiting, not locked up by my expectations, in sync rather with a mutual, unspoken rhythm, the woman I've always hoped I'd find and now she's here, for no particular reason, every possible reason required to unfold this piece of the world as it is, just so, her hair sprawling to bare shoulders, bare breasts, she's leaned back against two big pillows, a book resting on knees steepled under the sheet, a part of me up those stairs already, opening our bedroom door, seeing her skin's soft glow, its many hues shadowed, bathed in light from two hooded reading lamps, one on either side of the bed, I'm getting there, on my way, though first the business of this inch or so of wine in a long-stemmed goblet I doodle in my fingers, tilting it to catch glimpses of other possible worlds, night inching not falling and the Fanon book measurable in inches too, inches or note by note, since I prefer conceiving my project not as a mountain I must struggle up inch by inch but as music, finding it, playing it note by note, word by word, trying to teach myself to play and listen at the same time, as if I'm jamming with another player, listening and playing at the same time, listening for notes the other will play, listening to myself play in my mind the notes I'm guessing might sound good with what I guess I'll hear when the other's music rushes at me from the silence, listening to music nobody else hears, there and not there, inside and outside, beyond me, though the music fills me up and I'm playing before I know I'm playing, breaking silence already broken by the other's music not waiting for mine, searching for mine.

When I listen closely and listen well, what I hear when the best musicians are playing together at their best is give-and-take, the possibility of touching, of closing the space that separates each thing from every other; each player's solos remain just that, alone, solos reaching out, as if to say you can't go here, but listen and maybe you can taste a little bit of how it might feel if you could, and played by a master's hands that little is a lot, and hearing it means something is being made, being resolved out of nothing, out of the wish to touch, to play in the silent space enfolding another, the silence beyond words always separating one person from another, something's crossing the uncrossable space, a contradiction like the god I don't believe who's also real for me because my mother loves him with an enormous, unconditional love she mistakes as his love for her, and so it serves as such, she's sure her love's reciprocated, no, more than returned, magnified because she believes his love for her humbles her love for him, his love burning a million times brighter than her unbounded adoration, his love saving her in spite of her unworthiness, she believes, another proof of his bottomless compassion, a mystery she's content to worship without understanding and her mistake about him, her belief generates an appetite for love, a flickering presence around her and an abundant radiance within her she shines on me, and who needs, who comprehends more reality than that, I wonder, though it's also a reality I do not share, only observe, ponder, enjoy, envy, a reality crossing through the silence of these thoughts I play and listen to inside, filling in the blanks, reaching out with words like *reluctantly* to describe a sky darkening by the minute, by the millisecond, by inches, by notes, this wineglass reflecting, refracting, drinking light, infinite skins peeled one after the other, bright ellipses floating to the liquid surface, endless layers of what's possible, what's real only for this instant and no other, for no one else, anywhere, moments thinner than nothing where billions of us fit effortlessly as angels fit on a pinhead, each moment giving way, each one a kind of lifetime, a kind of eternity, each a world, like this solid, solid, solid world seizing my attention, this one breaking apart always as I watch, except it's more not less real as I reach out and attempt to cross the silence, reach out and nothing's there, falling short always of your music, if indeed your music's playing out there, Fanon.

Many thoughts like these, so many they must be flying faster than the speed of light, or at least fast enough for a replacement thought to quickly close the void and rescue me from the screaming despair of one particularly devastating thought: *this thinking all fine and dandy but it's not the book, where the fuck's the book,* because I'm able to think another thought and get quiet again inside, and then outside I see snow falling. A quiet rain of large, wet flakes as out of place in summer in Brittany as snow in Martinique. Still I see it and because snow doesn't belong here in this season I gaze with wonder, with almost an edge of fear, like you must have greeted your first snow in wintry France, the dying and killing of war surrounding you, the sky opening and white particles filling the air, disintegrating on contact with your uniform, skin, the armored vehicles, the frozen black ground. Snow in my garden lasts long enough, the white rain of it glowing against the dark wall of hedges enclosing the rear of the garden, to convince me of its presence, impossible as its presence is here on a summer night while I sit outdoors staring at a glass, twirling it in my fingers, powerful as a god conjuring other planets inside the wine's shimmering depths, stretching this long day I'm reluctant to surrender because it's been full of proofs of love and simple good living and promises more of the same still to come, if I can somehow move from my chair in the garden and walk up the stairs without disturbing the rhythm, without shattering the fragile truce — a truce easy as breathing, uncertain as the next breath — peace two people can enjoy together when it's their turn, when they work at the give-and-take of it and nothing too ugly, too large or overpowering works against them, this truce, while I'm enjoying it, that seems everlasting, invincibly secure, a full stomach, a bed to sleep in, someone to talk with and share the bed, no agonized screams, no bombs exploding or fires crackling, no collapses or shutdowns or excruciating pain inside my body, in other words, this peace a spectacularly lucky interval, a miracle outside, good luck I assume will be my portion always while I'm seduced, enraptured, blinded by the simple pleasures it materializes inside me, a miracle I'm most aware of when it ends or I'm waiting, or hoping, or sorry for myself because I've lost faith the good time will ever come again, all of which may or may not be an adequate explanation of why the light fades reluctantly, why I'm reluctant to breathe, to budge one inch from this quiet place which feels both outside and inside me, a place real as snow falling in summer, snow sinking into the blackness of a green fence of hedges, snow arriving like another person's music, not intruding, not changing my mood, not competing with the silence, blending instead, seamlessly as the coo-cooing of pigeons in thick foliage sealing the garden's perimeter, their call-and-response cries or call and no response except echoing silence suffused with longing and sadness, though they are the same sounds the birds warble to greet dawn, the difference being inside me because in one case I hear their coo-cooing affirming that light follows darkness and in the other case affirming that darkness follows light, so now for a moment I can't help hearing my fear of what's coming next, my fear of loss and mourning and I hold my breath until I also hear the law of give-and-take, the same law always cycling and recycling to reach out and almost touch the mirror image of itself, the pigeons are simply announcing that it's time, letting me know darkness has descended, the skies black enough for stars now, no snow visible now, it's done its work, imprinted a memory of you, Fanon, your presence, unexpected as snow in Martinique, snow in Brittany in July, the coo-cooing signaling it's night's turn now and if I raise my eyes I'll find the first star then more stars, stars, stars like fixed, glowing specks of snow, snow forever raining somewhere and there's nothing extraordinary about universes bumping, bleeding into one another, conversing, exchanging information like the mute axons and dendrites inside my body, the day changes, sky changes, I change, a give-and-take, whether I look or hear or believe or not, whether I wish for things to be different or not, whether or not I toss out words like *reluctantly* and *love,* skipping stones off water as if the game might reveal what the sea means and help me grasp what's happening to me as I float in my bubble inside the foam, dreaming my dreams, a lost and found-again soul, a transient who will be lost again in an instant, like you, Fanon, like you, drenched by slants of freezing rain one night and then next morning stunned by huge white flakes dropping slow-motion, a pale universe disintegrating around you as you prepared for battle in another region of this country, this France, where I sit tonight in a time of peace you could say, or say I'm lucky to be peaceful this moment in it. Lucky as you, Fanon, or anyone watching snow fall even though war's never-ending.

*

To leave his island Fanon must risk the sea. The sea itself an island, one of many floating islands in a greater sea, itself an island in the sea he must risk to escape his island.

Does one trip lead to another and another, the threads of a life bound together as threads in a fabric, the whole pattern known, decided before the first stitch, a bolt of cloth finished before it's begun. Fanon could have saved himself lots of worrying, lots of wear and tear if he'd believed what he'd read about the old hags or was it mad-women, strange sisters who doled out the threads of human lives, so much for this one, less for her, more, more for him and cut each length to please themselves. He thinks of them cackling, squabbling, ill-tempered, foul-mouthed, gossiping like the women selling man-goes, cloth, vegetables, doughnuts, cod cakes, telling fortunes, telling news, black women in the marketplace measuring out short life there, long life here for each passerby who buys or doesn't buy the stacks of merchandise the women arrange on the tamarind-lined Savanne. If some witch or god knows his fate — and he was sure the market women privy to his, impossible to sneak past without their appraising eyes, their sharp tongues peeling his secrets, pulling down his khaki shorts so he was a naked, tender boy again — if his life a finished thing tied with a cord like the roll of cloth he'd stolen from his father to pay for passage to Dominica, why worry and plague himself, *should I, shouldn't I, go-stay-no-yes-no* . . . his mind tossing like the sea tosses this flimsy boat in its passage to another island, the chop, chop sea, waves splashing, sea sloshing in the boat's belly soaking his feet he can't see in the black night, feet darkness can't hide from the women's cat eyes, Lookee that boy's long feet him long hand. Hello dere, Mr. Boy-boy, Sweet-boy, boy, Mr. Long boy hide-in-grass snake.

His father's skin. Must the son squeeze into his father's skin and wear it forever. Skin father like son had no choice about, except to slip inside and wear. If it had been a sack of coins not a bolt of cloth his father had cached away, would the son have stolen it to pay for passage to Dominica, No, no, he protests to the father. No, no, claims the son who must use this last chance to tell the truth to his father before drowning in the sea because the son Frantz certain he won't survive the rough passage to Dominica, this running-away thread he had believed would connect him to war, to France, a brave warrior risking the sea to rescue the captive motherland, the raped, weeping motherland calling for her son, embracing him, embracing his island, her island she'd neglected till her time of need. Ancient marriage. Dark bastard children. A timeless link severed by the here and now of treacherous waters between two islands, wind that whips and cuts, hungry sharks, shotgun blasts of rain, no mercy, nowhere to hide, a guillotine slices the watery neck between Dominica and Martinique, his picked-clean skull will wash up on a rocky, deserted beach. Stealing money different, Papa, from stealing skin. His father's skin belonged to both of them. To neither. Always. Wasn't he born wearing his father's skin. Money belonged to no one. Money's stolen and you only hold it till it's stolen again. But he'd die wearing his father's skin. His fate. Their fate. No choice. The father had purchased cloth for a suit he intended to wear to the wedding of his first son, Felix, the wedding tomorrow afternoon in Morne-Rouge, the day the drowning son, drowning brother Frantz won't see or will see in a new way, learning how sunrise appears if you watch it from inside the ocean's belly or from inside the belly of a whale. Thread by thread, saving pennies for a year, the father paid for that wedding suit never cut from cloth the son stole. The elegant fabric destined not to cover the father's shoulders but to be unraveled by the son's thieving fingers, picked apart thread by thread, respun into gold, the gold traded for a ticket, the ticket a passage to a different life a different fate for Frantz who must wear it forever as he wears the father's skin no matter how far from the island of Martinique the stolen ticket transports him. Nothing lost. Nothing changed. In the son's skin his father is saved thread by invisible thread, threads accumulating like the precious pennies set aside each week for the cloth.

The father, Casimir, had purchased the cloth from a mule-faced woman in the Savanne who nodded and smiled while he recited his happy story — a son's wedding in Morne-Rouge, family and friends gathering from all over the island, a goat killed, a pig roasted in a pit, the father's story unfolding as she quick studies him with her cold, measuring eye, unrolling a portion from a bolt of cloth, cutting it she promises to meet exactly the specifications he desires, assuring him that her single swift glance — as swift as the glance unveiling in a second all a boy's secrets — was enough in every case to ascertain precisely how much material needed to tailor a fine suit for a fine gentleman's fine frame. She unfurls from her best stock a generous portion, not too generous, just a tiny bit of slack, not too much, sir, not too little, after all, she smiles, you must pay for every square centimeter. She hums to the cloth as her scissors snip, snip, snipping an unmarked, perfectly straight line, hums as she listens to his plans for a son's wedding, absorbed it seems by the man's story, but all the while another tale passes through her practiced hands, a tale like Braille she reads in the nap of the fabric, the man's fate, the fate of Frantz, his son, bound and twisted in the threads of this good cloth, cloth the father thinks is one thing, a thing purchased and owned, when in fact it's another, a story the market woman sees and the man can't. Behind her hooded eyes she watches the father looking back at himself from a mirror, admiring the suit he imagines he wears, the suit he dreams will cover skin he can't shed, skin he can't hold up to the light and assess and say yes, this, or no, a bit more color, less stripe, a tad thinner perhaps or thicker, sampling, pinching it between thumb and finger, a little less blue, let me think about it overnight, I'll decide tomorrow. The father with no more power to change his skin than the son, the son Frantz she sees stealing the cloth a month before the wedding, denying his crime, bearing his secret shame, fearing the theft has doomed him when he's dropped off the solid earth's lap into a cauldron of boiling sea, the son riding a skimpy boat woven from his father's never-to-be suit, dreaming with other clandestine volunteers that he's joining the fight to free France, son like father unable to go back in time and reverse false steps. Son can't unrob his father, unlie, unsteal himself, recross the goat track over the steep, ravine-crisscrossed mountains between Le Prêcheur and Morne-Rouge, arrive forgiven, guiltless, drink rum punch, eat roast pork and conch fritters, dance tomorrow at his brother Felix's wedding.

To perform your duty you must forfeit your duty. To save yourself, to save France, you must be pitched into the sea and drown. Always too late to change what you struggle to learn. What you don't learn no help either. Crazy old crones haggling over your fate, then forgetting you as soon as they dispense your portion. So what if you believe that myth or some other myth. Yes, all threads connect. Yes. No way you can follow how or why. No. You can't choose, even if you could guess where this particular thread or that one might lead. The same step leads everywhere, nowhere. To France. Back home to his island. Glory. Shame. Hitler's fatherland. The motherland. War. Peace. The bottom of the sea.

The woman he crossed the sea to save does not hiss at him or shriek curses but if a look could kill, there on the dock of the bay in his uniform inspecting the wrecked port of Toulon, Fanon would have dropped to the gray boards, one young dead Martinican hero the German army needn't concern itself about. How was Fanon supposed to recall a day twenty-odd years in the past, a day he was not born yet, when this woman had walked this very same dock, newly married, her pregnant belly round as a sail full of wind, her soldier husband off fighting in the trenches of a war from which she fears, correctly, he'll never return, fear of his death a burden she willingly suffered, as if the worst, made real in her heart, her dreams, might somehow stop the worst from actually happening. Fanon has just arrived in battered Toulon, and ignorant of this woman's history, as she is of his, he cannot guess that his smile of greeting is lost upon her or worse, that she sees beneath the smiling mask atop his cadet's trim shoulders the grizzled face of an old black man, so black he must be an African, an old man sweeping the walkway bordering the water, and she sees Toulon miraculously intact as the city was twenty-some years before, the dock's planks gleaming under the patient strokes of the black fellow's push broom, the entire harbor spick-and-span, water calm, sparkling in the morning light. Perhaps this pitch-dark man she's passing by had swept the sea too, sweeping all night, as far as the horizon so he's tired now, leans on the shaft of his broom, exhausted but proud of his handiwork, the sea clear and bright, the walkway at its best, clean and safe for your morning promenade, madame, a huge African smile smiles these words at her, like that big black smiling African soldier's face on cocoa boxes, the only thing missing the red kepi crowning his glossy forehead black as Bamboulinette's, blacker than the shoe polish Bamboulinette's smile entices you to buy. How could a woman, walking on the dock, anxious, alone, pregnant in that time of terror and war, resist the African's wide grin, how could she not smile back at those white eyes those white teeth, and for an instant her dread quiets when she sees, no, feels his eyes caressing her, no, tracing, no, amening the curve of her belly, and she's slightly embarrassed but proud of her handiwork like the old African fellow's proud of his. Good luck, madame, barely a whisper, barely louder than a nod, which perhaps is all it was, an unspoken blessing she believes she hears, no, sees, no, feels directed at her between one slow, easy stroke and the next as he resumes his sweeping. Good luck, she thought she heard him wish her, and sure enough she'd enjoyed luck since that morning over twenty years ago, lots of luck, plenty, plenty luck, endless goddamn luck, all of it bad, a bad, bad, sad portion of misery and misfortune she dated from that exchange twenty-odd years before, blaming her bad luck on the old black devil's evil eye, his fat white African lips and heathen magic. Her young man lost at sea, the lost child drowning in her rotten-apple womb, boatloads of sailors pawing her, stomping her, one famished man after another gnawing on her breasts, wrecking her body like the bombs raining down in this new war wrecking Toulon's harbor. Old widow, old whore, who'd want her now, a ruined city this fresh brown boy mocks with his smile, his nod, because he'd been there that clean, dreamy morning and cursed her, this black demon who changes color and shape at will, returning to taunt her with his perfect white teeth.

Are there semblances of plot, of direction, purpose, and necessity, in Fanon's story. Someone or something in charge — weird sisters, a deity, Progress, History — wouldn't that be preferable to no one, nothing in charge, only random permutations and combinations of desire and fear, slaughter and love, the relentless cannibalizing of ourselves, our offspring. Why not you in charge, Doctor Fanon. A physician who first cures himself, then cures us, the world, of its ills. Why not you. Seize the bit in your teeth, horse and rider, and ride.

A false start the first time Fanon risks the sea. Two weeks languishing on Dominica, a neighboring island very close to his, though it seemed a million miles away the night of his crossing. Boring duty on Dominica. A handful of lucky ones steam off to the fighting in Europe. The rest, including most of the volunteers who'd cowered with you while rough waters battered your frail boat, become toy soldiers, marched, drilled, bullied by veterans in faded uniforms — here a tunic with gold epaulettes, there trousers with a thick red stripe — the buttons remaining on the officers' coats polished bright as mirrors, mourning, doing double duty for buttons missing. Twiddling your thumbs and waiting on Dominica, groaning awake in the middle of the night aroused by the ache of your sex, the ache of impatience, impetuosity, of guilt, your eighteen-year-old body sweating, fiery from mosquito bites, skin raw from scratching, from the sandpaper rub of your father's suit you can't remove even when you collapse exhausted on the plank serving as a bed in the crude barracks. Why do you daydream knights on horseback, fair damsels, besieged castles, fire-belching dragons. Why not a maroon in the hills above a plantation, counting the guards, killing careless whites whenever you get the chance, stealing back your people one by one, patient in your impenetrable hideaway until the odds tilt to your favor and one flaming dawn or moonless night your band sweeps down from the mountains and snatches what's yours. Your fate, your destiny, your portion not something you can wait for or beg or borrow. No one can grant you freedom. If you're in charge, you never wait. You prepare. Gather the threads in your hands, connect them, braid them, take the next step you must take. That next step the only truth, all truth. But isn't truth, Fanon reminds himself, also true if you don't take charge. Your fate's your fate, whatever steps you take or don't take. No way out. And this reversible truth a kind of bittersweet comfort or a good laugh at himself squeezed out of the worst times when he lies awake, beyond the possibility of sleep, empty-handed, famished, waiting for something or someone he couldn't say what the fuck it might be, trying like a prisoner in a cell to remember in the middle of the night what he had believed was worth the risk of winding up in prison. Would he recognize the thing he desired, the thing he'd been willing to steal or kill for, if it rose up and shook its feathers, fur, wings, bared its fangs, its pussy, at the foot of the hard plank where the little generals and sergeants and corporals order him to sleep.

Here is the itinerary or log so to speak of Fanon's Great Escape, his journey from an old New world to a new Old world, after a false start on Dominica. I learned the details of his getaway in a book Fanon never had the opportunity to read so the information's thirdhand at best, an outsourced search for truth, documented by the plausibility of facts, facts unconfirmed by Fanon, untouched by his hand dead forty years before the book published. Welcome information in any case (thank you Mr. David Macey, assiduous historian), welcome as some of the facts might have been to Fanon on those fitful nights conflicted, stalled on Dominica. A healing glimpse of the future. Proof the rumors of the wanderer's return home are true. The flock of vulture suitors will be routed one bright morning and Penelope will never be forced to wear the wedding gown she weaves in public by day and unravels in the secrecy of her bedchamber each night.

First a voyage of four days from Fort-de-France, on the island of Martinique, to the island of Bermuda. A night's layover to take on supplies etc., then an Atlantic crossing of fourteen days in a convoy of one hundred twenty ships to Casablanca, Morocco, arriving in North Africa March 30, 1944, after departing from the West Indies March 12. (Coincidentally, my Seiko said March 30, 2005, when I wrote the words above and today as I reread them, believe me or not, it's March 30, 2006.)

In Fort-de-France (the former slave port Fort Royale) Fanon had boarded a decrepit transport ship, the *Oregon*, with a thousand other myrmidons, all men of color except for a tiny cadre of officers. The *beke*, Fanon's fellow countrymen, descendants of the old original white French settlers of Martinique, chose not to volunteer for war. Why participate in old Europe's bloody orgy of self-destruction. Why not stay home and mind their island business. Perhaps the shameless *beke* were still pouting over the ouster of their champion, Admiral Robert, Martinique's Vichy governor. Why should they take sides. Who could say which side's the good guys, which the bad, and in the final analysis, the *beke* reasoned, whichever side wins, war is good for *beke* business.

This tub should fly a black flag, Fanon quipped, surveying the brown faces mustered on deck for inspection.

A skull and crossbones, his homeboy replied.

And speaking of threads, check out the place names on Fanon's itinerary. A surrealist poet spinning the globe and tapping it blindfolded couldn't have lucked up on a more numinous trio of names. *Oregon. Bermuda. Casablanca.* Perhaps the unscheduled touchdown (1941) of André Breton, fleeing Nazi Europe and encountering fascist Admiral Robert's police and prisons in Martinique, had infected the island with seeds of *hazard objectif.*

Check it out. *Oregon,* the name of the troopship on which Fanon crossed the Atlantic, is also the name of one of the states of the United States of America. Oregon a western state on the North American continent's Pacific rim, as far west as you can go on land before you begin going west on the sea, the edge of the west where we all agree the sun must set after it rises in the east. Oregon not only identifies how and where Fanon's journey commences, Oregon foreshadows where it terminates, here in the good ole US of A, Fanon drowned by a surfeit of white cells, leucocytes, in a hospital in Bethesda, Maryland, a state on America's eastern coast, a fact that predicts the inevitable arc of his story, how his star will rise again from the east and return to light up the west.

Bermuda: an island giving its name to a fabled black hole of lost ships, lost souls. A liminal zone, a magic triangle of darkness and destruction in the Caribbean: Forsake hope all ye who enter here. Bermuda a mysterious New World isle surrounded by waters that devour intruders, inspiring Shakespeare to shipwreck a band of Neapolitans in a place very much like it, or as much like Bermuda as he could imagine, given that the real place and the place in his play exist nowhere but in his mind. A *brave new world,* wrote Mr. Shakespeare, that passeth the understanding of the shipwrecked newcomers, a world where Prospero has been awaiting them, dreaming for years of revenge upon a city and its citizens who transported him, unjustly he's certain, with his infant daughter, Miranda, to exile on a faraway island for the alleged crime of practicing black arts. Prospero equipped with an arsenal of fairies, gremlins, elves, and high-tech clones who serve him as surveillance cameras, listening devices, a posse of visible and invisible presences spreading rumors, telling tales, telling lies, sowing disinformation, mounting simulations. Marooned on the island the new immigrants are ensnared and befuddled by a multimedia spectacle of illusions, a garden of virtual delights Prospero's crew creates. Prospero, whose more powerful magic had defeated (slaughtered) the resident witch Sycorax and appropriated her island, her secrets. Prospero displacing the rightful heir, Caliban, her son, *the first shall be last,* demoting him to hewer of wood, bearer of burden, a dispossessed beast-man, man-beast sentenced to dwell in darkness because Prospero fears Caliban will be tempted by fair Miranda's beauty and dare to desire what Prospero must deny himself. Prospero teaching poor, segregated Caliban the language of shame, language of sheep — baa-baa — blah, blah, blah, you know the rest, Caliban's only profit on it, he learns to curse.

Casablanca: "white house" in Spanish. In American English *White House* means the big house on Pennsylvania Avenue, Washington, D.C. El Presidente's headquarters. Government property, white outside and inside from its first days to this very day, no matter how many dark ghosts you observe shuffling in and out of offices, galleries, conference rooms, bedrooms. *Casablanca.* The big whitewashed houses of *beke.* Chateau. Hacienda. Manor. Mansion. Castle. All the king's white houses. All the king's white men and black men riding roughshod over the poor who huddle in tiny hovels and sprawling shantytowns under the shadow of the Casablanca, the peasants, slaves, serfs, grunts, the many, many, many, many who serve the few.

The many who are enthralled, zombied like Prospero's castaways by artfully administered doses of spectacular sound and light. Fill in the blancs. Fill in the little casas. Catch Humphrey Bogart in the movie of the same name, *Casablanca*. A classic from the epoch when Hollywood the king. Long live the picture show. Cornucopia of images. Hollywood proving life's a dream. As it is for Prospero's Neapolitan prisoners. Just a dream, a game, a video game, you know, like these mini-Hollywood studios you can carry in your pocket, hold in your hand. Turned on. Tuned in. Tuned out. Hey. It ain't nothing but a party, a game show, sponsored by the makers of a gadget soon available in a model installed before birth, no bulky gear you got to lug around, a chip in your brain, so no chip on your shoulder, soldier. A peaceable kingdom, invisible, weightless, wired to our internal wiring, delivering twenty-four-seven virtual voices in the air, bells and whistles tolling the hours, Tinkerbell, Ariel at your service, this sprite or that, musaking you along and here comes old cuddly teddy bear Caliban, your sidekick, ancient boon-coon Tonto buddy loping along beside you, grinning, eager to please, to bear your sorrows, your pain, all your tons of luggage, no problem, just a little-bitty extra lump or two on his broad, sloping, furry, bowed back, hey, it ain't heavy, he's your brother, and a man, my mon, give the old guy a penny, watch Caliban smile that old black magic full of cunning and guile smile he learned in the mirror from Prosperous Prospero, the pair of them, master and slave, watching the shaving ritual (as Fanon used to watch Casimir and I watched my daddy Edgar), two pairs of eyes scanning the same mirror, all four eyes spying on Miranda through the open bedroom door behind them, naked Miranda who rises knuckling sleep dust from her eyes, thumb-nippled breasts rising too as she stretches, yawns, sits up in bed, letting silky covers settle around her hips, part girl, part woman, maybe part fish with her mermaid bottom concealed under the white heap of sheets, Miranda half one thing, half another, like me, Caliban thinks, perhaps my sister, he thinks, a beautiful princess awakening from a five-thousand-year sleep, her skin fresh, sprawling hair to her waist, careful old horny frog Caliban, don't jump to conclusions, just watch like your master watches, Miranda's not real, she's on the tube, a pale maiden behind you dreaming, rising from her dreams. Don't wake her. Enjoy her on the same split-screen channel featuring Prospero's old cleft chin, his square jaw scraped hairless after he wipes away last gasps of lather, of blood left behind by the blade, and with the same towel unsteams the mirror because he doesn't want to miss anything, he paid big bucks for the flat plasma screen, the split screen belongs to him, after all, his mirror after all, and everything it holds — the half-naked daughter, naked beast-man he watches watching him, the dark creature's eyes taking beastly notes all the time, learning to mimic me, whistling the same tunes I whistle working on a new face each morning, grooming myself for the business day, my mirror, my gaze, two identical talking heads, silent on the screen, four eyes alert, hungry, dangerous as the gleaming razor, as the teeth of my doggie slaves, see the fire of my resplendent suit of lights, creature, behold the dazzle and fly dash of my chain mail, Caliban, my boy, you may look, but never touch, never wear the fabulous fabric of my skin, shining like the pitted, running sea, white as the sail of a tall ship suddenly breasting a blue horizon, *bright ships loom, bright ships loom* rising fully formed as my Venus daughter from an oyster shell.

Oregon. Bermuda. Casablanca. Many names, many stories embedded within the barest outline of Fanon's journey. Sampling just a few ought to suggest what could be garnered if we learn to listen, sound the depths of each clue to divine Fanon's fate. His many fates in one. How Fanon's fate connects to ours.

Paris burning in an African campfire. Fanon's journey from Martinique to the metropole to America crackles there too, smoke rising into the darkness, the false start to Dominica burning like all the stories true and false, threads that a curious, determined boy must follow, teaching himself to risk anything, everything, even squeezing out of one skin into another, his life, his fate always unknown, always in his hands. Will he steal from his father again, lie, kill. You never know, do you, what life will require of you, Fanon, what kind of skin you must learn to fit into or when a life begins or ends. Maybe a French patrol will spot a spark from the campfire. Led by a Senegalese scout, commandos in camouflage gear — their brown faces, beige faces, white faces all painted black — are inching closer, slithering silent as a python through tall grass.

On Martinique, part of a crowd lining a broad avenue in Fort-de-France, Fanon had watched a saint's day parade. Why did he cringe, lower his eyes. Why couldn't he just laugh out loud, shout, clap his hands, sway in place to the infectious rhythms thumping from drummers on a flat-bed truck, search out a familiar face in the swirl of old-school *beke* planters' white linen suits, straw hats, the long, spinning dresses with matching madras turbans and aprons, beige men, beige women high-stepping, cakewalking, white grins splitting brown faces ear to ear. Then next, more marchers dressed like ghosts of themselves, this time in traditional Breton costumes, men in dark suits and Saint Paddy's Day hats, shuffling along with the stiff-legged wobbly gait of punch-drunk boxers, women with heads detached from their bodies by wimples, pale faces displayed like pies on platters, this unit cadenced by more drums, bagpipes, flutes playing Breton country music with something somehow very African, very Arab Fanon hears — nasal whine, counterpoint, falsetto keening and wailing. Simple melodies repeated, faster, slower, almost monotonous, then an unexpected note graced, rising, falling. Like memory Fanon thinks. Something new squeezed out of old air trapped in bagpipes, whistles, accordions, breath compressed and released. Inhale. Exhale. Air squeezed into many different noises — grunts, screams, moans, yelps — animals rushing from a cage. He'd read that men from Brittany crewed France's slaving ships, the swift *blackbirds* flying from Nantes to West Africa to the Antilles to Nantes. Bretons manning the sails, cracking the whips, drumming chained Africans up from the suffocating hold to exercise on deck. Is that why he heard Africa, the East. Heard the shameful, evil exchange. The deck on fire. Breton drummerboys and pipers hustling to keep up with burning, jumping African feet. Is that why no eyes in the shuffling cortege of Bretons meet his. Does the music remember. Music mourning dead tribes, dead players, dead lovers, unrecoverable nations. Could any of these ordinary folk spruced up for a saint's day celebration say the names of the dead they pretend to be. Could you, Fanon, say the name of one African ancestor whose dark skin is your costume. Whose history, whose dead mimicked by these mummers, these fake Celts, Goths, Vikings, Arabs, Indians, Mandingos, Igbo parading through the streets of Fort-de-France. Mummy history. Bandages wrapped round and round the living. The public buildings of Fort-de-France, of Paris, Algiers, draped by flags, tombs for gloriously dead Greeks and Romans.

Though he's near enough that afternoon to touch the musicians, the music plays at a great distance, reaching him only as an echo, as a memory. The music refuses to honor his claim to it, though it opens a space, a melancholy absence he hears and feels and yearns to fill, yearns to close. A place that neither lets him in nor lets him go.

The old Breton music stubbornly, single-mindedly itself, yet it couldn't help echoing other music, each repetition of itself affirming the silent ground of all music. To become itself, it recalls more than itself, recalls the silence it shares with other music. Each music plays that silence differently — as his life will play out differently from any other life against death's silence, his life a small truth like a particular music's small truth. No revelation small, Fanon guesses, if you can learn to listen.

Many years later, camped in the bush, listening to the noises of the African forest, he hears Breton pipes and drums, an unexpected layer pushing up through the silence, pushing down to raise the silence, a kind of creature breathing in the immense black night. Something's out there, a story about him, if not exactly him, out there breathing in the night. An empty pocket waiting for him to fill it. Would the pocket disappear if he stepped out to fill it. Would he disappear. Of course, he'll never know. Only knows he's risking his life, the lives of the men he commands, searching for a road which might very well be a fiction. A fiasco. A quixotic obsession. Mumbo-jumbo. Hoodoo. Power from the barrel of an imaginary gun. Dreamy Frantz. More poet than warrior. Rhymes instead of reasons. Rapper before his time.

He'd watched the saint's day pageant pass the Palace of Justice, then continue along the Schoelcher Library toward the grassy park of the Savanne where the statue of Napoleon's *beke* wife Josephine stands headless, a monument to her treachery. The stone empress decapitated by terrorists, her guillotined head rolling down the street, vanishing, never seen since. The missing head proclaims her guilt, the absent lips confess crimes against humanity. Her bee-stung *beke* lips which had begged a favor from her emperor husband: Just a few more years of slavery. What harm could it do, my sweet. A little more bondage for blacks who've never been free, who know only slavery. Just a few more years, a decade and change perhaps, my darling. You wouldn't want to bankrupt my family, would you, beloved. Why would you deprive them of their hard-earned property. And you mustn't forget that your wars cost money. Empty coffers can't be taxed. If you let us keep our slaves a few more years, we'll make it worth your while. *Beke* gold as good as gold, sire. France is not an island, my master, and that distant island of Martinique a purse, not France. Black is not white and never will be. There nor here. Despite the Convention's mad proclamations. Her words poisoned honey she pours in the emperor's ear before she finishes off the blacks with a squeeze of her thighs.

Empress Josephine, Napoleon's kidnapped island prize. Her blackened Creole whiteness a fashion statement in Paris. Court ladies imitate the lilting island lisp of her French, her jungle cat's tread and stealthy grace. Gold chains drape her neck, many silver rings spool like threads around a single finger, cascades of tiny, multicolored trade beads are miniature curtains dangling from her ears. How elegantly she stands, her long, lean back arched like the trunk of a palm tree, her rump protruding like a slave's, her corkscrew curly hair sprawling like the palm tree's fronds. She wears silk sarongs cunningly wrapped, their transparency more revealing than nakedness. India-cloth turbans twist around her hair in the style of mulatto concubines whose sultry glances decorate a lavishly illustrated book, executed at the emperor's command, his window on the exotic islands he rules but would never risk the sea to visit.

On page 1794 of the *Shorter Oxford English Dictionary* the word *savannah* appears below the words *savage, savagedom, savagery* and above the word *savant.* The English savannah, *savanne* in French, derived perhaps from an African or Carib word *zavanne.* Martinicans borrowed *savanne* to name the green market square of Fort-de-France. The word *savannah* employed in French and English to name a type of landscape common on continents and islands Europeans believed bore no names, no history, lands whose inhabitants babbled in multitudes of baa-baa tongues, none worthy of the name of language, lands whose natives wouldn't think of attaching words to ideas because thought didn't dwell there, no one, nothing there humanized by the touch of words, only a wilderness of anonymous mountains, flora and fauna, murderous weather, deadly insects, disease, endless grassy, treeless plains, an emptiness awaiting baptism, awaiting conversion to the real. The word *savannah* a sign of inclusion in god's plan, his kingdom — one day nothing, nothing as far as the eye can see, only a vacancy of nodding grass and then, miraculously, the *savannah* stretches forth, a green sea, green plain, a bountiful green park, God's will, his plenty and power made manifest, a green ark, a green playing field stinking of sewage some Sunday mornings from the backed-up Levasseur canal when Fanon and his brothers Joby and Felix gather on *la savanne* with other Fort-de-France brown boys to play soccer beneath the stone ramparts of old Fort Royale that loom above one edge of the island, protecting it from the sea.

A towering fence of ragged tamarind trees marks another border of *la savanne* and one morning Frantz Fanon, galloping after a scuffed white ball, stuns the other boys by bounding higher than the tamarinds, hanging in the sky a moment, tongue in cheek like Michael Jordan, grinning at the others. Every player's mouth wide open, eyes popping before Fanon soars beyond the treetops, never to be seen on the island again.

Felix to his right, Joby to his left, Frantz attacks. A magic triangle. Crisp passes back and forth, a flying wedge cutting through the other team's defenses. The field rough and uneven, a tilted, scuffed, pebbled surface but on mornings like this with his brothers on the wings and him in the center charging the goal, they skim across the Savanne like skaters on a frozen pond. Their opponents, helpless as tarbabies, are signposts nailed to the ground, unread by Fanon as he zips past, an arrow speeding to its target.

When the game's pumped up to its swiftest pace, it slows down for the best players. Calm in the eye of the storm, Fanon watches the game unfold frame by frame, watches himself watching, directing. Plenty of time, all the time in the world between one moment and the next. Running full speed down the middle of the pitch you head-feint right, cock your knee as if surely you intend to blast the ball to Felix on the right, Felix who is your brother so he's seen that feint, that hitched leg before and doesn't hesitate, doesn't wait for a ball he understands isn't coming, but accelerates, sprints ahead into the gap between two defenders his brother's false pass creates, and in that space open only an instant Felix receives a pass from Joby, a shot on goal a split second after Frantz has punched the ball ahead to Joby on the left.

Fanon scans the field quicker than thought. Thought's trumped by action. Pumping hard down the middle of the pitch or bounding high above the tops of worm-eaten tamarind trees, he is as stunned as the others by what's happening. He drives the ball with his instep, then he's alive inside it. Not exactly surprised, not exactly in control, driving, accelerating to weightlessness. You've prepared for this moment, been here before, you've done this running this passing this micromeasuring and parsing and orienting, this assessing of other players' skills and habits, this breaking down of lanes, angles, distance many times on the field and in your mind and there's no time to be wrong now, wrong would be slowing down, falling out of the flow. Wrong would be not playing on. In the rush of the action, speeding faster, speeding past, you exercise options you don't recognize as options until after you've executed them. No choice, no right or wrong decision, only a goal or no goal, a pass completed or not, a deeper, more dangerous penetration, or nothing — stalemate, the dissolve of the action, the clock slowing down, your feet back on mangled turf till the next chance if one ever comes.

Fun while it lasts, Why doesn't it last. Why so many cells squeezing the life out of time. Stealing time. Killing time. Unlike most of his fellow dreamers and revolutionaries of the sixties, Fanon neither was gunned down nor served time in prison (in spite of numerous alleged plots to capture or kill him). Thus his life evades those myths of martyrdom so handy for settling accounts. For closing the book. Fanon's accounts of his life prevent him from being written off in other people's accounts. We have his words; we can count on them. Fanon uninventible, or you might say resists invention. He's no more or less a fiction than any person writing about him. Fanon's been here and gone. Free. Played the game till it was too dark to see the ball. You can't touch that.

When I think about it, bro, I don't know why you keep beating yourself up trying to write intelligent shit. Even if you write something deep, you think anybody wants to hear it. Everybody out there just like the guys in here. Everybody just wants out. Out the goddamn slam. Quick. Why they gon waste time reading a book. Book ain't gon get them out. Deep down they know they ain't never getting out. Don't need no book telling them how fucked up things is.

Anyway, real smart motherfuckers don't listen to nobody nohow. They know better. Busy wit their own scheming. And dumb motherfuckers don't understand shit even if they standing ass-deep in it. So when I think about it, big bro, I give you credit for being an intelligent guy, but, you know, I got to wonder if writing an intelligent book's an intelligent idea.

In 1942 Frantz and Joby were sent from Fort-de-France to board with their schoolteacher uncle Edward in Le François, a small town about an hour from the capital. The Fanons' idea was to remove their sons from the dangers of a rumored Allied invasion of Martinique, which would undoubtedly target the French warships stranded in Fort-de-France's harbor and the Vichy government that had installed itself in the city. Removing Joby and Frantz to Le François would also rescue them from a city unsettled by war, plagued by poverty, crime, school closings, its population near starvation and harassed daily by the increasingly ugly racism of mainland French sailors marooned with their vessels by the Allied blockade.

Ensconced within the relative safety, quiet, and isolation of Le François — more country village than town — Fanon, under the tutelage of his uncle Edward, would have begun reading more and thinking more about what he read, habits encouraged, as biographers and critics have noted, when Fanon returned to Fort-de-France, by his new teacher, poet Aimé Césaire, who stimulated not only Fanon but a whole generation of students, including Edouard Glissant, for instance, young men who become pillars of Martinique's intellectual and political life. But wouldn't enforced rustification in Le François also have been experienced by young Frantz as punishment. Fanon a city kid exiled to the country. I think of Emmett Till, teenager from Chicago's black South Side, bored, restless, inventing mischief to pass the time during his summer in Money, Mississippi. Fanon an urban outsider in rural Le François, learning to turn inward for company. Cultivating studiousness, self-reflection. Infected by more than the standard measure of adolescent alienation, resentment, anger, and anxiety at being abandoned by his parents, separated from his comfort zone in the city streets. Or is another story intruding here. Thomas's story. Thomas a stranger in a strange land. The *only one of his race* in classes and extracurricular activities at his 97 percent white high school.

During a tour of a local chateau with classmates from his uncle's school, Fanon heard a guide's tale about the *beke* who'd purchased the chateau from the *beke* who'd constructed it in 1750. Whether the guide addressed the story to the entire group or one-on-one to Fanon, whether the story was part of the official tour menu or a spontaneous aside, whether it was narrated in standard French or Creole, what the teller intended by the telling and whether the teller was male or female, whether black, white, brown, beige, red, yellow, or an inextricable mix of all the above, I can't say, and in a sense none of the above matters. What matters is Fanon listened and must have remembered the tale years later when he decided to write about how some groups of people control the lives of other groups of people.

The story the guide recited a simple one. Familiar to all the *beke*'s neighbors and their slaves because when he was drunk, the master of the chateau loved to brag about his success and wealth, his army of slaves, the chests full of gold he'd stashed away in the woods. Brag how with a single bullet he'd protected one chest's secret location and sealed Old Tom's gossipy lips, dooming the lazy good-for-nothing slave to guard the chest forever. A good trick played on cranky, balky Tom whose meddling tongue had forgotten too often over the years who was master and who the servant. Fanon didn't learn from the guide's story whether the *beke* said or didn't say goodbye to his ancient companion, only that the *beke* drew a pistol, pulled the trigger once, and left Old Tom silent, bloody, crumpled across the chest in the pit Tom had spent half a morning excavating, the pit over whose edge Fanon stares, tracking a sweating, grizzled brown head after the rest of the body disappeared from sight when Tom wrestled the heavy chest down with him into the hole he'd never leave.

At school next day, instead of an essay extolling the architectural splendors of the chateau and listing the inimitable artifacts imported from Europe gracing its rooms and galleries, Fanon produced a short story. Unfortunately it has not survived. However from Joby's testimony (and Mr. David Macey's summary of that testimony) we know the story involved pirates, stolen gold, murder, a ghost's revenge. Autobiography in other words. Young Fanon's version of the guide's tale. Only with a different twist, I bet. An eye for an eye, most likely. The last becoming first, etc.

Years later, composing *Black Skin, White Masks,* Fanon must have recalled the legend of the *beke* who sentenced Old Tom to eternal servitude. Wouldn't Fanon have admired begrudgingly the *beke*'s cold logic. Slaves belonged to their owners from cradle to grave, the law declared, but the *beke* had demonstrated that a slave's usefulness could be extended beyond the arbitrary limits of birth and death. After all, didn't unborn slaves serve the master, visions of sugar plums dancing in a master's head, the added incentive of profit if lust not enough motivation for humping his slave women. If work could be squeezed from virtual slaves before they reach the cradle, why not work after the grave. Fanon was familiar with the scary tales about Haitian planters who poisoned their slaves and transformed them into living-dead zombies. The problem with zombies is they possess bodies — powerful, tireless, mindless bodies able to wreak havoc on a plantation. The Le François *beke* had a better idea. A scheme more efficient, elegant than his Haitian peers'. Though he left the head on his slave's bloody shoulders, he separated Tom's mind and body. Freed Tom for eternal servitude. So what if Old Tom invisible. So what he's a ghost. The clever *beke* invented ghost work for Thomas's ghost body to perform. The circle unbroken. An endless cycle of production and consumption. Slaves sown to produce slaves, slaves producing babies that grow into trees that become lumber that becomes wealth that seeds more wealth that purchases more slaves, etc. No escape alive or dead as long as Old Master rules, Fanon concluded many years later, writing about how some groups of people rule other groups of people by transforming those others into phantoms. The colonizer dooming invisible natives to ghost work. Scaring them with ghost stories of irresistible, godlike *beke* in charge during daylight hours, fearsome monsters and evil spirits reigning after night falls on the island. The circle unbroken.

Each person an island in a sea of time. Isolated by the sea, each person's fate determined by the sea's traffic, by voyages that risk the sea's treacherous currents and vast distances, voyages that may seem to master seas they navigate, but any sea mastered is also, always, an island in a greater sea.

Until he tells the woman in the wheelchair, Fanon had never admitted to anyone except his brother Joby how much the snow blanketing the French countryside had frightened him. More frightening than death, he had confided to Joby. Winter's whiteness a season experienced only in picture books, and then, fighting a war in frozen forests and mountains east of Lyon, he'd become more certain each day the people who lived there had forgotten how to turn the page. Did Fanon turn the page, peek ahead to the end of his story, and see snowy cells of leukemia drowning him.

No preparation for snow. Only island stories about *petite neige*, strange white flakes falling from the sky, white dust each morning after Mount Pelée grumbled at night, pale ash powdering roofs of villages and sleeping cows in the weeks before Pelée erupted and unleashed a pyroclastic blast leveling St. Pierre, incinerating in a minute the capital city's thirty thousand inhabitants in a firestorm rolling down the mountainside (a black prisoner in an underground dungeon cell the only survivor, the story goes). *Petite neige.* Little snow. Now he'd crossed oceans and found big snow. Or snow had found him. Not the snow of postcard France. The postcards lied like the smiling brown faces on postcards of Martinique. Winter besieged France as relentlessly as war. Trapped you in a kind of living death, a skin-cracking and -splitting zombie in-betweenness. No escape because snow squeezes inside you. Back home on his island, death turns things soft and runny. Things rot, stink, change colors. Here his flesh and blood would harden, become a transparent chunk of ice, exploding finally, the swirling particles of him swept up by the wind, then drifting slowly back to earth, indistinguishable from the snow, buried forever in a cold white sheet.

His first snowfall arrived obscured by darkness, mixed with freezing rain, cold blots on his cheeks, his eyelashes, pellets of icy rain pinging the column's vehicles as the men bivouacked for the night. Not until the next morning did he see big flakes hovering everywhere around and about him, countless particles descending in slow motion. The dust of his shattered, frozen bones floating in front of his eyes. How could he have slept through Pelée's fiery hands tearing him apart.

Was snow drifting down or was the entire earth rising, slowly, slowly, climbing into the sky like the fir trees crowning a ridge in the middle distance, feathery trees lifting themselves and drawing up behind them the hills in which they're rooted.

Snow falling slowly, thickly, unbelievably quiet as war before war starts up each day. He's the first to burrow from a jumble of tents pitched under a truck's giant, dragon-toothed tires, a truck whose canvas-covered bed is packed with frozen sticks of men, and for a moment he believes he's the only one awake in the world. But why him. Why here in a place so far from the green *mornes* and golden beaches of his island. Why is he imprisoned in this fortress Europe that has beckoned then betrayed him, this hell of killing and being killed. Peering up through the screen of snow, he sees a sky bright blue already at dawn, an unexpected, unnerving blue like the eyes many years ago burning cold in the face of an ancient, tarry-fleshed *martiniçaise*. Blue not a sign of the sky's presence but its absence, he decides. Nothing above the falling snow except a vast hole, a hole punctured by countless other holes to let through the white flakes surrounding him, this snow tasteless on his tongue, a net dissolving into nothing when his mittens bat it.

It is a year since I left Fort-de-France. Why. To defend an obsolete ideal . . . If I don't come back, and if one day you learn that I died facing the enemy . . . never say he died for the good cause . . . the idiot politicians must not delude us any longer. I was wrong . . . nothing justifies my sudden decision to defend the interests of farmers who don't give a damn . . .

Crossing the chilly Atlantic he'd wondered if snow falls on the ocean. It must fall on the seas at the top and bottom of the globe. White bears, white seals, floating white islands. Snow must fall there. No snow on the Atlantic passage. Unlike his first run to Dominica, the sea calm. No weather to speak of, except the restless weather in-side him, the turbulence of a soldier's excitement laced with dread. From birth he had lived surrounded by water so his uneasiness the first days at sea surprised him, the water, water in every direction as far as his eyes could see, water close up too, constantly lapping the troop transport's side with the gross weight of its tongue. Water sloshing on deck, stinking of gasoline and salt, vomit, piss and shit. He was sure the shadow the ship dragged beneath its hull was also a black hole thousands of feet deep and any second the ship's ponder-ous bulk would be lifted then dropped by a wave, breaking the hole's seal, sending the ship plunging down, down, the sea instantly closing without a single pucker or bubble to mark its plunge. Almost sick the first few days, then the unease subsided. Surely the huge armada pro-tected by size, its sluggish pace, its tedious routines, the obliging, neutral weather. The convoy just might steam on forever. Why would a foe attack ships sailing nowhere so slowly. Fanon imagines a giant naval operations table with a map of the seven seas painted on its surface, miniature ships nudged by inches east, west, north, south by officers with sticks like pool cues (maybe they are pool cues) who speak in low, secretive tones of grand strategies and tactics whose success depends upon the ballet of little ship-shaped, colored chips. No danger to his transport unless a steward (brown perhaps) carry-ing a tray of coffee and croissants bumps the board, knocks their convoy's marker to the floor, kicks it under the table. Forgotten, the convoy a Flying Dutchman. No destination, no home, no port, shut-tling back and forth over the sea, ghost ships worn thinner and thinner by the elements till they're invisible, mired in the green Sargasso Sea or locked in the crushing ice of Antarctica. But one con-solation of being stuck on the bottom of the globe, Fanon thinks, is yes, he'll be able to answer for himself the question about snow fall-ing on the ocean.

*

White snow. Why doesn't it fall in other colors like leaves, Fanon asks the kind woman sitting next to his bed. White the color of ghosts. Of fear. White-hooded lynchers in America. White-wimpled nuns and nurses in France. Snowstorms scramble the hospital room's TV. White chaos sometimes silent, sometimes buzzing and screaming, limbo scenes neither alive nor dead. The lily-white chill of bloody France. White sheets shrouding blackened faces of the dead. White *beke* linens drying in the sun after washerwomen have beaten them against black rocks lining the riverbank. He narrates for her the story of a flash flood in Le Pilot that drowned two *blancheuses*. Howling wind drove water in a foaming rush through a river's narrow channel, toppling the women, ripping sheets, towels, pillowcases from their hands, sending the *beke*'s whiter-than-snow laundry high into the sky. The bare-legged washerwomen, skirts hitched up brown thighs, never had a chance. Knee-deep in the water, gossiping, singing when the storm hit and then years later in a country where war rages Fanon hears their mourning voices. What else could snow be. The fiery breath of Mount Pelée frozen, drifting in the air, white ash on blackened corpses and charred stones of St. Pierre, a white curtain dropping to hide the carnage in France. Show's over, folks. Time's up. Shame, shame. Nature fed up with rumbling artillery, the screams of mangled animals, the bloody mud, the suck of marching jackboots, jeeps whining, tank treads crushing seeds stillborn inside the earth. Fanon's cold brown skin ashy, his feet dead lumps of ice in snow-encrusted boots.

Who promised you death by drowning in a warm, clean sea. Many maroons died sealed inside the chill fastness of mountain caves, icy caves turned to cooking pots by flame-throwers, Afghan caves mashed by percussive, bunker-busting bombs, an Algiers cave behind a casbah basement wall the paratroopers could not penetrate with their eyes but electronic listening devices inform them terrorists crouch like mice behind the bricks listening to the paras' ultimatum, the countdown before plastic explosives blow them to smithereens . . . seven . . . six . . . five . . . four . . . three . . . two . . .

What do you do, Fanon asks Death, and Death answers, I connect the dots.

Perhaps Fanon's first snow also the first for many of his comrades who, like him, hail from tropical zones — Algerians, Malians, Moroccans, Tunisians, the island men of Guadeloupe, Martinique in this motley brigade of colonial infantry. Some of whom will be dead by nightfall. Is that why the day had dawned so miraculously serene and bright. A reward. A tease. This first snow your last, my orphaned children, so here's a sample of how beautiful snow can be. A taste of what you're going to miss you can take to your graves, my sons. See. Open your wide, hungry eyes. Look. See. Here's what you're not going to get, this spilling white rainbow of wonders never ceasing. Enjoy it before the brutal wind kicks up, before gusting snow blinds you and bullets of ice penetrate your layers of protection and you're sopping wet inside your uniform, as if bathed by sweat, good sweet tropical island sweat, until you begin shivering and freeze. Button up, gear up, move out, and hit the road, Jack, Jacques, Amin, Mohammed, Caesar, Abdul, Michel, Kwami . . . Time to stop thinking dumb thoughts, trying to make sense of your first snow by comparing it to things familiar or frightening, Fanon, things desired, things lost and neglected during war. Forget love. Your sex exploding would shame you, a cold puddle in your drawers as you hurry off to more war.

Baptized doubly by the fire of battle, the winter of France, how could he explain to Joby, let alone any stranger, the fear, the beguiling ache of loneliness each rare snowfall since. Why is he trying to tell this woman who sits beside him, touching his cold flesh with her warming hand. Is she the one humming the *blancheuses'* song.

You could insert something like the spooky *Twilight Zone* riff now and flash forward, Mr. Jean Luc, Mr. Lucky John, ringmaster and emcee, flash ahead to the end of the movie. Snowflakes we've been watching become a blizzard of leucocytes, a lynch mob of white cells attacking Fanon's body, stripping, choking, stomping him, hacking off souvenirs of his flesh, beating him black and blue, obliterating any trace that a man might once have dreamed and suffered in the hospital bed, vacant now, covered by a rubber sheet, a stack of snowy, folded linen at its foot. Depending on the meaning you wish to attach to Fanon's death in a Bethesda, Maryland, clinic, if you've taken my suggestion and segued from a screenful of gently raining snow to a frenzied storm of white cells, you might as well go ahead and bring on the angels at this point — pale, translucent, computer-generated special effects, like gigantic anthropomorphic snowflakes or diseased white cells that have metastasized and stylized themselves into vaporous, part-human, part-bird snow things, alien and scary almost but also graceful, even elegant as they descend, wrap Fanon's dark, limp body in appendages not quite arms, and then rise, returning through the hospital room ceiling that their unlimited powers render porous. Spectral, winged messengers. Snow angels. An intelligent viewer will make the connection and understand the meaning of the transition. In any case, if you think the scene's too supernatural, too Hollywood, later in interviews with the press, blame Fanon. Blame the patient dying in the bed, his feverish condition at the end, his delirium, his liminal not-quite-dead/not-quite-alive zombie consciousness, his convulsions, his body furiously evacuating itself from every orifice like a hanged man. Blame Fanon who can't manage his own swollen tongue, surrounded by hostile strangers who can't speak his language even if he could articulate his thoughts, Fanon desperately seeking a way out and not surprisingly when a way out appears that might free him, free him at last, the imagery of escape figures itself in terms of the Catholicism remembered from his youth, his mother's religion, the holy relics and lithographs on her bedroom walls, the rites of confession, absolution, and salvation, those weirdly persistent, overheated, cross-cultural, multidisciplinary ceremonies so often evoked by his patients, the tortured and the torturers, Christian and Muslim, Fanon treated in Algeria at the Blida psychiatric clinic. You'll be off the hook if you blame Fanon. Sympathetic viewers won't exactly fault him, either. A real temptation at the end, *in extremis,* to revert to comforting childhood memories, to wishful thinking, to baroque fantasies and magic realism with their once-upon-a-time happy-ever-after promises. Why wouldn't Fanon go there during the few semilucid intervals when drugs liberate him for a minute or two from a constant drubbing of pain.

Or if you choose, Mr. Director, none of the above, score the end in a different fashion. Downplay it. Perhaps skip it altogether. Click. In the middle of the action the screen goes black. Click. After a decent interval, the house lights come up. No gory details. The end's the end — no intervention, divine, directorial, or otherwise. The end arriving at a different point each time the movie plays. Arbitrary. Random. Untranscendental. Unheroic. No end. Just letting go. Why not just let it go. Let it end. Click. *The end.* Fini. Always the same story. Leukemia, like life, no respecter of persons. An agonizing, relentless assault, the disease dispatching whomever it lays low, no matter how many surreal, special-effects angels dancing on the head of a pin or snow drifting down, covering a black iron fence, then all of Dublin, the whole wide world. No. There's nothing pretty, nothing worth saving in Fanon's last hours. Not anything that would fit on the screen, anyway, emptying it or filling it with meaning. Certainly nothing to drop in an audience's lap as the film's final shot and expect people to rise in their seats and applaud. Let it go.

Instead of dwelling on the end, jump cut to the African wilderness. Stygian night. A fire burning bright — yes, yes — as a tiger's eye. It crackles, dances, throws up sparks, reassures Fanon, who pees and breathes deeply for the first time in days, sure no marauding mercenaries will visit the camp tonight. In the morning we'll be on our way. In four days the mission complete and we'll be back safely at headquarters in Tunisia. The senior staff, spotless in knife-creased khaki, will gather and listen to my plan in a different way now, with different ears and eyes because we will have demonstrated the feasibility of a supply line from south to north, through Mali to Algeria. Like Lawrence of Arabia in the film of the same name, when he returns from his mission of stirring up the Bedouins, I'll wear the map of the journey imprinted on my weary body, on the filthy uniform I won't change until after I brief the high command. The certainty of victory will blaze in my tiger's eye as I form each word of the story.

Whatever happened to Fanon's plan. Did any of it really happen. Is an ancient Malian trading route still patching itself together through the jungle, fossilized on stones, written on water. At night, if you peer up between black towers of twisting, snaky foliage, will you find the road's bright shadow mirrored in the sky, a road of light carved through dark treetops, a path mirroring the long scar on the ground, the old wound scuffed into the earth by camels, men, horses, and mules a thousand years ago, the wound Fanon would rip open to heal Algeria, heal Africa, heal himself.

In a way the world situation ain't all that complicated, my brother declares to me. Then he says words to this effect: What it is is the right hand don't know what the left hand's doing. Simple as that. You know. Cause it's all about one person, really. Hey, I don't know shit about biology and shit but it's like we all in one body, we all the same person who lives spread out over the whole world, everywhere, you know, one giant body with people the cells of it, different cells but all part of the same big old body. Ain't about no two lonely people like Adam and Eve in a garden fucking and making babies and babies making babies till you got all these different people ain't never seen one another, spoke to one another. Huh-uh. We's all one person, all the same body. Fuck color and countries and religion and male and female and she-male, that's all bullshit. You got this one human person trying to make a life for itself on the planet. Seems like a lotta us, but we's all the same one, doing the same thing — hunting for something to eat every day, a safe place to lie down at night. Wanting good loving and good talk. Some singing and dancing and maybe getting a little high now and then. We stay alive by having babies, growing new cells cause the old cells get tired and wore out. You and me and everybody else all rolled up together into one big One. But the trouble is the hands of the body done forgot each other. Everybody into they own mind, they own thing, they own little world and that's cool, maybe that's how it's always spozed to be. Plenty room for that as long as the big old body's hands keep track of one another. As long as they don't forget they working for the same person. I mean, the way it is today the hands don't speak no more. Squabbling. Fighting. Grabbing. Hands hate each other in a way, you could say. Trying to strangle the one neck they own. People so stuck up in they own little worlds they forget they live in the same body and got to depend on the same two hands.

Like when he was in Peabody High, my brother reminds me, and they killed King, my brother says, and me and the fellas tore up Homewood Avenue and started a strike in school. Mr. Glick the principal, same principal as when you were there, right, bro, anyway, ole Slick Glick all shook up and called us strike leaders down to his office on the first floor. What do you want, he asked. Straight up. No hello, how you doing bullshit. *What do you want.* Just like that and I thought to myself, you little, bald, four-eyed motherfucker, what the fuck you think we want. We want what you want. We want what you got. Want your money, your watch, your nice house up on Hiland Avenue, your car, some pussy from your cute little four-eyed daughter. Want a good job like your son gonna get. I wanted everything I thought Mr. Glick had, and maybe even before all that stuff, I wanted him the fuck out of my fucking face asking questions. That's the shit I think I really wanted. I wanted to be asking the questions. I wanted my goddamn cops outside the door so I could call them in to haul Glick's ass to the slam if he didn't give me the right answers. Thinking all that kind of bullshit or something like it it seems to me now sitting here thinking back on it. Course I didn't say nothing. Just glared at Slick Glick cause I didn't know what to say or how to say it. But what I should have said, even if it didn't do no damn good, which it probably wouldn't have, is this — We the same person, fool. Get your foot off your own neck. Stop choking me with my own hands. Don't you know you're dissing yourself when you disrespect me. Ain't you figured out that you hurting your ownself when you hurt me. Go ahead. Toss my ass out of school and pretty soon ain't gon be no Peabody High. You out a job, sucker. If I ain't got nothing, one of your hands is empty. The empty hand won't be there when you need it. And when that hand goes to stealing and shooting to get what it needs, who you think it be sticking up. Whose kids gonna be out there in the street running crazy wit me or from me. Who's gonna be sorry when raggedy Pittsburgh ain't fit for nobody.

That's what the world situation's about. What the terrorism shit's about. One hand trying to outhurt the other. Stone confusion. People scared of they own damned selves. Cutting off heads, cutting off hands like we got heads and hands to spare. We done forgot we the same person. Killing off our own body, part by part and soon ain't nothing gon be left. We scared cause we doing the bad shit to our ownselves. Scared and can't stop.

A cruel world, bro. Every mother's child knows it's true. Mom's right but she's wrong too. Trouble does last always. Sure it does. A person can't hardly get along even with all the body parts in good shape. Every day on TV you see these pitiful crazies. Serial killers, folks who snap and kill up everybody they can shoot before the cops kill them. It's like people locked up in dark little rooms with a pen-knife and so fucked up scared and lonely they start whittling little pieces off they own body. Tiny bits so it don't hurt too much at first. You know. They keep slicing away at theyselves and afterwhile don't feel nothing. Maybe even start liking it. Damn. One hand cutting off the other and they think they solving they problems.

The younger Fanon was tardy. Very late indeed. Only a quarter-hour remaining of the afternoon session when he sidled into the rear of the classroom through the back door and slumped onto his seat. He'd been missing since recess. Earlier I'd asked my nephew Joby the whereabouts of his brother and received no satisfactory reply. I assumed a sudden illness had indisposed the younger Fanon. Or rather, that had been my most charitable supposition. Neither Joby nor Frantz a bad boy, and among my sister's children, Frantz plainly had something especially salvageable about him, though I'd detected good minds and abundant natural talent in all my Fort-de-France nephews and nieces. However, Fort-de-France bad habits and perni-cious influences cannot be eradicated by a few weeks here in Le François attending my school and boarding in my home. Absolutely no backsliding can be tolerated, so the fellow would be punished for his offense. Illness no excuse, if illness it was that caused him to absent himself from school without seeking either my permission or instructions as to where and how he should spend the vacated afternoon.

Ordinarily the disciplining of my young charge would have begun the moment he attempted to slink into the classroom, assuming his place as if it's his prerogative to come and go as he pleases, as if his presence or absence were purely his affair and would not be noticed by every single pupil sitting at his desk, nor the professor at the lectern intent on the business of instruction. I would have pounced upon this disrespectful disruption of the usual routine and stung the young man immediately, employing the occasion to impart a general lesson to my struggling scholars, yet something about the manner in which my nephew slid, no, crumpled onto the bench of his desk warned me against greeting his very late arrival with too harsh, too peremptory a reprimand. A beaten look about him. The look of one who had been severely disciplined already. I was reminded of some of our country people, poor cane cutters, domestic workers, landless peasants, their shoulders bowed eternally, resigned to whatever punishment their betters impose. That guilty-before-charged submissiveness of slavery days retained in the bodies and minds of far too many of my island brethren. Pained, ashamed by what I saw, I decided, for the moment, to let an exasperated nod, a withering glance suffice as response to my nephew's trespass. In vain I waited for him to raise his eyes and dare meet my gaze. I was denied a full view of his features until I'd resumed my lecture and then I observed him snapping — *snapping* the only appropriate word — snapping to attention, stiffening his back, squaring his shoulders, drawing himself up as tall as he could be while seated at his desk, the posture I taught my students their first day in my classroom and insisted upon every day thereafter. Clearly this organizing of himself came at a considerable cost. Directed finally, as they should be, toward the front of the room and the lectern behind which I stood, his eyes were utterly devoid of expression. I was unnerved by the blankness of his stare and could not repress a shudder. The boy's eyes looked through me, through the wall behind me, his empty gaze shaking the school building, toppling it, demolishing the town, sending the entire island to hell, beginning with this small corner of it I believed I'd consecrated to learning and progress.

Empty eyes. Shattering eyes. No disrespect, no challenge in them. Nothing. Nothingness I cannot expand upon because finally that's all the eyes held. Nothing. An island superstition says that mirrors must be veiled during periods of fresh mourning to spare the living a glimpse of the newly dead's fear. One lifts the veil at one's peril, and perhaps unwittingly I'd committed just that trespass, blundered into the abyss of my nephew's uncovered eyes.

I learned later that he had sneaked away at recess to spy upon the autopsy of a drowned man being performed in the basement of Le François's municipal building. Secreting himself in a narrow passageway at the rear of the town hall, he'd crouched at a tiny ground-level vent and, hidden from the view of passersby, witnessed as many stages of the gruesome operation as he could bear, the horror accumulating until he became ill watching the slicing and draining, watching the scalpel digging deeper and deeper, the prying and sawing, dead flesh peeled, split, butchered till it was nothing but gore, nothing more, nothing, not man or woman, not horse or cat, nothing. The nothing I saw in his empty eyes when, like one of the shades Ulysses observed haunting the shore of the River Styx, he materialized in my classroom.

In November of 1961, the year he composed *The Wretched of the Earth*, which could have been titled *Notes from Underground* or *Invisible Man* or *Black Boy* or *Things Fall Apart*, flogging himself to write fast because he's aware death is closing in and might overtake him before he finishes his book, the same year whose last months he spends in a hospital bed in Bethesda, Maryland, guest of the government of the United States, Fanon learns his book has been published.

The urgency, compression, conviction, and force preserved in certain sections of *The Wretched of the Earth* remind me of Martin Luther King's "Been to the mountaintop" speech, which was delivered as Fanon delivered his book, just before dying. My point here is that when death is imminent, whether a person stands at a podium in the Mason Temple in Memphis or lies terminally ill in bed or waits at the bottom of a trench to be shot, any place will do as actual location or metaphor to snap truth into focus with resounding clarity. Being there, bearing witness as the end approaches grants unimpeachable authority, a final truth, truth lost as it's found and perhaps that's why such witnessing convinces when it is eloquently reported — convinces and also overwhelms. Another's life shaped into words — Fanon's book, King's speech — how much of it can anyone else really use. Its truths belong to the witness. Darkness abides. The witness's words are evidence of a known world closing down, its light, however bright or small, piercing or shallow, swallowed by the unknown. Fanon's words, King's words reveal a glimmer of truth earned by them, experienced by them, their lives large, their witness compelling because they struggled to know, though the unknown shrinks not one iota.

The first thing a baby be thinking, my brother says, when its little self lands here and it's laying all cozy and warm, snuggled up on its mama's titty, what it thinks is, Hmmm, hmmm, this ain't such a bad place here, I love this place, the baby's thinking and the next thing the lil rascal thinks, my brother says is, Lemme see if I can eat it.

One day Thomas thinks if he hadn't been born black maybe a good second choice would be French, then realizes what a stupid thought he's entertaining. Plenty of French people are blacker than he is, or so it seems anyway, so his choice of French not a choice of an alternate color, and since toying with the idea of changing who he is by erasing his color and trying on another color was the intent of his thought experiment in the first place, he's getting everything assbackwards, because French not a color and he's not a color. His thought no thought at all, just daydreaming, just remembering he loved Curtis Mayfield singing "If you had a choice of color, which one would you choose my brothers" but could never decide what the words meant.

We some mean animals, man, my brother said. Mean. Just plain mean. Don't know about women — my woman tells me women just as mean in their different way — but guys, I know guys is just plain mean. A guy needs somebody he can fuck wit. Look around here. Inmates punking inmates. And the guards got us to fuck wit. A few good guards but plenty go out their way to be evil and mean. Hard to believe sometimes. Like the way they teased Goines the day he was screaming and begging to go to clinic. Everybody knew Goines got AIDS. Everybody knew measles going around and Goines shoulda been taken out the population. Huh-uh. Measles got in his sores and they just let him rot in his cell. Laughed at him flopping around. Shit. All us got good days and bad days but how come guards make it their business to aggravate inmates. Answer is they mean. Answer is they miserable unless they hurting somebody. Ain't that the reason generals let soldiers tear up a town after they capture it. The reason some nothing dude with a nothing job and a nowhere life brings home the shit people dump on him all day and beats on his wife and kids. Little king. Lil motherfuckering tyrant at home so he can go on back to his job next day feeling like he's somebody. Way the whole world works, my brother. Here in the joint. Everywhere. Cause men deep down in they hearts and souls is mean. Mean. Like that evil, grinning president we got, man. Got the whole world under his thumb but his cowboy ass ain't satisfied unless he's fucking with somebody.

Mom,

I am entrusting this information to you, these stories some people might call an unauthorized version of your life because once upon a time you were entrusted with me and here I am today still alive and paddling around in the greater sea I passed into by passing through you, through a storm of beans and farts, passing through the sea within you that was also my island, as I am yours, Mom. You didn't choose me, no more than I chose you, but when I consider the possibility of you being other than you are, I understand I could not have chosen anyone not you, so in that sense of being fated, married to one another in a sense, I guess we're stuck with each other always for better or worse since that's the way it's been for as long as I can remember and is now, no other options possible, yet it's also true that the alternatives — what we could have been, the different people, maybe — are part of us too, the unborn children of ourselves, my lost brothers and sisters, your lost daughters and sons, my son in prison like yours, my son, your grandson I haven't mentioned till now, though every word present and the words unspeakable are addressed to him, to those others not chosen, not here because instead we chose what we did. Those different stories exist too, buried in the stories we remember and tell, unspoken parts, unseen parts like the shape of a room we're not aware we hold in our memory unless the lights go out suddenly and we have to negotiate the room in total darkness.

Last night in a Q and A following my reading from work-in-progress called *Fanon*, a young woman with cropped, very black hair, maybe twenty-five or thirty, definitely intense I could tell from her eyes, her posture, how she thrust up out of her seat, out of herself when she began to speak, reminding me, reminding herself that the person I saw, the place where I saw her sitting and she found herself, the body, the seat that seemed to contain her, would never be more

183

than a thrust of her shoulders, a rearrangement of the weight of her ass from losing their hold on her. She could snap her chains with a question. *Why do you write.* Though I'd answered that question in public many times, in various settings, last night I said something I'd never said aloud. *I write because I'm lonely.* Exactly those words. No hesitation, not skipping a beat, almost as if I'd conspired with the young woman earlier and knew what was coming.

THOMAS DISPOSES OF THE HEAD

Whatever happened to the head — the next question asked the evening of my reading. A question Thomas had posed to himself countless times. A question I'd asked myself at least as often. And even if no one asks that question the night the black-haired, intense girl asks hers, I owe an answer. Owe it to myself. To any good soul who stays the course this far. My reader. My fan. Fellow traveler. I owe it. Because yes. This is a story intended to save a life, and people (including me) want to know what happens at the end.

One morning, on one of his walk/runs along the East River, Thomas recalled the ending of a story he'd written many years before whose title, "Damballah," he had bestowed on the collection of short stories in which it had been published. At the end of that story a slave boy on a plantation in the American South rescues the severed head of a murdered fellow slave, carries the head to a river, and tosses it in. A kind of burial. A kind of grim wish for more life. The ending had worked once. Reviewers had praised "Damballah" and the collection it named. Why not recycle a good thing. Thomas had invented the ending, the boy, the head. They belonged to him. Couldn't he do with them as he pleased. Off with the head.

No one paid any attention to the droopy black garbage bag, its twisted neck wrapped in his fist, along for the walk, along for the ride one morning beside the East River. Black plastic garbage bags a common sight on the riverwalk Thomas plied. Fishermen employed them. The homeless who slept beside the river stuffed their belongings in black plastic sacks they piled on shopping carts. Senegalese vendors on their way to fleece tourists in Battery Park rolled their bulging cardboard boxes on dollies and like black Santa Clauses toted black plastic sacks slung over their shoulders. Black garbage bags, some tied, some spilling their guts, are parked beside the metal trash cans they'd once lined, cans chained to a steel fence bordering a long straight stretch of the walkway at the foot of Chinatown where ancient, bony men and women exercise slow-motion at dawn, and later, on steel benches riveted into a concrete deck at the river's edge, just beyond the shadow cast by the noisy FDR parkway, people browse newspapers printed in Asian alphabets, copping sun when the sun's out. Too early for sun, for witnesses the morning he said *Sayonara* and watched his handful, head full of black bag splash into the water and sink without a trace. No halo of ripples spreading as far as Africa, no shivering crown like he'd imagined around the old African's head after the boy had heaved it as far as he could, farther than he'd guessed he'd be able, out into a lazy southern river, a river broad, as cloaked in mist at daybreak as the reach of Joseph Conrad's fabled Thames.

No problem. Splish-splash. The water always there, always running to the sea, to the ends of the earth. Always patient and available. For a head. A body of any size shape color gender. The river absolute. Indiscriminate. He smiles, wondering a second if such is really the case. What he'd just thought. That simple thought about a river. Didn't this river ebb and flow and change with the tide. Run two directions at once sometimes — upstream, downstream — between its twisting banks. Never the same river twice. Falling. Rising. No. Keep it simple. Heave-ho. Splash. That's what happened to the head.

Writing "Damballah" he'd found it easy to identify with the slave boy. Liked him. Likes him again now that he proves to be a useful fiction for disposing of the head. A kind of avuncular fondness for the young man/boy and for the story in which he'd discovered him. The last time Thomas read "Damballah" aloud it had sounded okay, maybe a bit better than okay, given the audience's respectful, attentive silence. A simple story. Old story. Father/son/ghost story. Playing to simple emotions and expectations of his readers. A boy performing a simple act of devotion. A slave boy believing he could help an old, dead African's spirit find its way back home.

He envies the boy's belief in home. His youth. His credibility in general. Believing scary, funny stories told by other slaves on the plantation. Believing he'd caught a glimpse of freedom in the old man's strange ways and strange talk despite the fact that those ways and talk had gotten the man killed by white folks. Believing he could spy on the old fellow and learn how to escape from the chains of color, the drab, smothered lives the others around him endured. Believing an ancient African could catch fish by coaxing them from the river with song. He admires the boy's courage, how he steeled himself to toe the head gently away from a bloody mess murderers had made of the troublesome old slave's scrawny, naked body. The boy scooping the drippy head up in his shirt, fleeing from a barn thick with droning flies. Those were the good ole days. He'd been young and daring. Almost as naive, as innocent as the boy. Intoxicated by possibility, drunk on his talent like those fat, buzzing, blue-black flies drunk and surly on blood when the boy shooed them from the mutilated corpse.

Much easier back then to be sure of himself, easier to imagine it would never end. Easier in those days to fabricate endings and tack them wherever an ending seemed necessary or natural or expected or shapely or portentous. He handled that part of storytelling as he had believed he'd be able to handle whatever else came along in life. Deftly. No looking back. No second guessing. Charmed.

Ah, youth, Thomas sighs. Yours till you desire it and then it's gone. You know. Like you are who you are, Thomas, until you think you're not. So what. Let it go. Heave-ho. Splash. That's what happens to the head. An ending, if an ending's needed. As good as any other.

In Lyon pacing up and down the cage of his mind, like a lion in Lyon pacing up and back, he listens to her pounding nails into his book, pounding nails into his cross, his coffin. Fanon's voice rises and falls, louder, softer as he tells his wife his book, his thoughts flying almost, but since he doesn't possess the skill of typing, this dictation as close to flying as he can manage, his wings nailed to a noisy machine. He writes by speaking and trying to listen to himself think aloud, his voice — is it truly his voice he hears — propelled by various tides of confidence, presumption, sadness, anger, imitating other voices, or recalling them, conversing with them, challenging them, this voice he wants to save, that voice he needs to forget, or his voice solo, trying to hear itself weaving something from nothing in the air, his words now floating, now bouncing off the walls of the small apartment with almost a view of the Rhone River from one of its tiny windows, then his voice still, swallowed by the silence that comes before and after and during every word, or stopping because he reaches the peak of a promontory he's been struggling up for an hour and now on the summit, swaying, dizzy almost in the thin air, he surveys a white sea of snow-packed ridges and valleys spread out below him tame as a postcard, not daring to raise his eyes to the heights still to scale, catching a deep breath, gathering his strength, waiting for his legs to stop trembling, his eyes to unmist, content to absorb the wonder of a moment so high and precarious, the reward for an arduous journey, a multitude of doubts surmounted, his professors shamelessly airing their doubts in public, and worse, the unspoken private knot inside him, his color, his origins, a dark pinpoint of doubt, a single pebble which if kicked loose has the power to precipitate a rockslide, a pebble picking up speed and mass, tumbling into the abyss, his body tumbling after it, huge boulders splitting, splintering, explosions that hammer the stillness, blow after blow, her fingers on the typewriter shattering his complacencies, his spidery web of convictions and hunches, the typewriter clattering to keep pace, tumbling down after him as he flees the thunderbolt of each stroke, the nails, nails, nail after nail puncturing his skin, pinning him down, nailing down his words in black and white, white and black, sentences pounding one after another, her fingers chasing him, gaining on him while he sucks in a deep breath, his legs quivering from exhaustion, from the suppressed sprint in them as he resists the urge to escape, gallop, jump, fly, and instead pauses, paces the room in measured strides, cool in a crisp white shirt, dark tie, his style, his rhythm professorial, reserved, precise, counterpoint to the machine's sprawling, lunging, jackhammer yammering.

What rough message is she fashioning over there behind his back, sawing, chiseling, drilling, driving nails, that racket, that chaos, that cage erected bar by bar for his words. Whatever his mood, the speed of his thoughts, he must remember to pause regularly so she can catch up, let her join him in the silence. Silence. If he stops dictating once and for all, the book not completed just *finished* because he refuses to utter another word, will the machine die too. Or will he always hear it, awake or asleep, working on the book or not, hear the clacks and clicks, the bells and banging of it, the shattering, smacking shift of the carriage, a crash then slide that's also a knife honed on a whetstone, a blade sharp as a razor slices through your neck before you feel the cut, only hear the bump of the bloody head that's yours, hear it rolling unhinged across the floorboards, faster and faster, hurrying out of the apartment, out of Lyon on little chicken feet it's grown, high-stepping, splashing in blood from itself gushing everywhere.

Just talk your book to me Josie had offered. Trust me. Say your book aloud the way you talk it to yourself inside your head. I'm a good listener and you know I'm a very good typist. It might be fun to work together. Even though what you're writing can't be fun for you. Or me. I'm more than pleased to type your book, fun or not. Your book means so much. You mustn't say no. I'll stay quiet as a mouse. Pretend I'm your pen. Forget another person's in the room. Read from drafts or dictate your thoughts. Either way, any way you wish. I only want to help. I promise I won't miss a single word.

Do you know your mouth twists up sometimes when you're writing. As if you taste the bitterness of what you're thinking. I can almost hear your eyes moan. You're so close, yet so far away. I really believe I feel what you're thinking. Sometimes you look like a person struggling with a foreign language, as if you're watching a word being spoken, then you carefully work your lips, saying the word silently to yourself, getting it right before you're ready to try it aloud. I don't hear them, but I see words taking shape. If you speak your book to me, I'll learn to listen without listening. I'll be too busy typing to spy on you. I promise I won't disturb you or distract you. Probably couldn't if I tried. If I step one inch closer than I should, I'm sure your eyes will freeze me in my tracks, won't they, my love.

He stops. Arches his spine. Lets the weight slide from his shoulders, ripple down through his flexed buttocks. Relaxes the tension that had pumped him up on his toes, *moulet de coq* trotting back and forth across the apartment's ancient floorboards. He envisions himself as he must have appeared to her just moments before, hears again the words he was speaking and they close over his head like the sea undeceiving a drowning swimmer. He must have sounded ridiculous. Full of assurance and pleased with himself. His muscles remember how they'd performed the classic puffed-up rooster strut of island men, men who practice swelling and preening, pleasing themselves when no one else is around to please, admiring themselves if no one available to admire them.

Remembers and continues anyway: This new section will be titled "Colonial War and Mental Disorder." *We have brought together certain cases or groups of cases in which the event giving rise to the illness is in the first place the atmosphere of total war which reigns . . . the bloodthirsty and pitiless atmosphere, the generalization of inhuman practices, and the firm impression that people have of being caught up in a veritable Apocalypse.*

Case Number Five: European police inspector and torturer — thirty years old — married — three children — came to clinic on his own accord — stated that for several weeks "things weren't working out" — loss of appetite — insomnia — nightmares — smokes three packs a day — what bothers him most are fits of madness. [I quote the patient] As soon as someone goes against me I want to hit him. Even outside my job. I feel I want to settle the fellows who get in my way, even for nothing at all. Look here, for example, suppose I go to the kiosk to buy the papers. There's a lot of people. Of course you have to wait. The chap who keeps the kiosk is a pal of mine. I hold out my hand to take my papers. Someone in the line gives me a challenging look and says "Wait your turn." Well, I want to beat him up and say to myself, "If I had you for a few hours my fine friend you wouldn't look so clever afterwards" [end quote].

The particular incident that precipitated the patient's visit to the clinic happened in his home. He dislikes noise. His children were squabbling and he started hitting them. His wife screamed at him and tried to separate him from the children. He recalls saying to himself, "I'll teach her once and for all that I'm master in this house." He tied her to a chair and began to beat her. Fortunately, the children's wailing and tugging brought him to his senses. He realized the madness of what he'd done and the next day decided to consult a nerve specialist.

Stop a moment, Fanon says. "Nerve specialist" is the patient's way of saying *psychiatrist.* Be certain the text distinguishes the patient's voice from mine. When I quote him I'm reading from notes transcribed during interviews. I'm quite scrupulous about the accuracy of my transcriptions so that consulting physicians have access to a reliable record. In this book I want readers to hear precisely the language with which a patient describes his or her situation. Perhaps you could insert an extra space to separate blocks of text when one voice gives way to another. Perhaps the patient's voice typed single-spaced to contrast with the normally double-spaced format of the narrative. Underscoring or brackets or quotation marks perhaps around short phrases of the patient's I include in my summaries of their cases. The business about "master of this house . . ." etc., for instance, or "nerve specialist." I don't want to fall into the trap of treating my patients as the *beke* treat me. Never letting me speak for myself. Or turning my words into evidence against me. The proper representation of these cases is immensely complicated. Perhaps hopelessly compromised by any form of writing. I suppose in some sense I'm always speaking for my patients. Though, in fairness to myself, I often feel the patients speak for me. Not only do I quote them at considerable length. I also find myself splicing into my accounts their exact words or words not exactly theirs not mine either, words I try to imagine the patient might employ in a particular situation. An odd, secondhand, alienated structure's being formed as we proceed in these book sessions. A process that controls me as much as I control it. A sort of bricolage of free-floating fragments whose authorship is unsettlingly ambiguous. Two men or perhaps several attempting to go about their business, each with a leg in the same pair of baggy trousers.

Shall we carry on with Case Five. I'm ready if you are. I quote the patient: "Those gentlemen in the government say there's no war in Algeria . . . [ellipsis his]. But there is a war going on in Algeria, and when they wake up to it, it'll be too late. The thing that kills me most is the torture. You don't know what that is, do you? Sometimes I torture people for ten hours at a stretch . . . [ellipsis mine]."

I ask the patient, "What happens to you when you are torturing?"

He answers: *"You may not realize, but it's very tiring. It's true we take it in turns, but the question is to know when to let the next chap have a go. Each one thinks he's going to get the information at any minute and takes good care not to let the bird go to the next chap after he's softened him up nicely, when of course the other chap would get the honor and glory of it. Sometimes we even offer the bird money. Money out of our own pockets to try to get him to talk. It's a question of personal success. You see, you're competing with the others. In the end your fists are ruined. So you call in the Senegalese. But either they hit too hard and destroy the creature or else they don't hit hard enough and it's no good . . .*

"Above all what you mustn't do is give the bird the impression he won't get away alive from you. Because then he wonders what's the use of talking if it won't save his life. He must go on hoping; hope's the thing that'll make him talk."

Fanon.

Fanon shuts the famous book of empire. What lessons could he draw from Rudyard Kipling's novel. Where in his book might the Englishman's fake tale ring true.

This is the great world and I am only Kim. Who is Kim. He considers his own identity, a thing he had never done before, till his head swam. Whose head swam. In what body of water did it swim. The River Ganges? How far. Did the head ever return. Who is the *He* in Kipling's sentence that begins *He considers* . . . Who the reported. Who the reporter. Whom addressed. Kim or Kipling. In any case both names begin with the letter *K*. Perhaps that conscious or unconscious slippage and conflation and punning as good as it gets, as close as author gets to character, subject to object, fiction to truth, black to white, representation to reality, as close as many truths get to one truth indivisible with liberty equality fraternity for all. Who knows what Fanon thinks as he closes Kipling's *Kim*. Who says he ever opened *Kim*.

(Aren't you cheating, he asks Kipling, asks Fanon, asks himself, asks Thomas. All these shifts, substitutions, translations, and denials. Or Fanon asks him. Doesn't biography or, worse, autobiography serve readers primarily as a source for gossip, rumor-mongering, titillation. Thinly disguised voyeurism. An absent life substituting for a reader's absent life. Did you sleep with your lieutenant in a field tent. Did the pair of you rise at dawn and stroll along the riverbank, bathe each other out of sight of the other men. You, Fanon, in carpet slippers, foulard dressing gown, and Hugh Hefner PJs, rather shamefully excess baggage on a bare-bones, tightly packed expedition into the heart of darkness, wouldn't you say, old chap. We prefer your suits, your manners impeccable. Dark, tasteful ties, stiff white shirts adorning your taut athlete's torso. Creased gabardine trousers swaddling your beguine-dancing limbs. Biography a costume drama. Dresses up and undresses. Performed for whose benefit. To whom addressed. Why would anybody bother to open the cumbersome package. It's too late to enjoy your touch, Fanon, your commanding voice, too late to sample your spoor on the breeze, see the aura spun by your quicksilver thoughts bright like a halo in the air above your head.)

Now that we know what happened to the head, here's a better Fanon quote, a better message to deliver in the box with the head: "*A permanent dialogue with oneself and an increasingly obscene narcissism*

never ceased to prepare the way for a half delirious state . . . where intel-
lectual work became suffering and the reality was not at all that of a
living man, working and creating himself, but rather words, different
combinations of words and the tensions springing from the mean-
ings contained in words . . . Shatter this narcissism, break with this un-
reality."

Fanon.

Lyon. A tourism brochure advertises two of the city's main attrac-
tions: Rabelais' villa and the studio of the brothers Lumière, Auguste
and Louis, the light brothers, no, no, not the Wright brothers, stupid,
the light brothers, but you're also correct, my brother, the Lumières
invented flying, up, up and away, lighter than air, faster than light
craft, witchcraft some would say, devil's work, our Mr. James Baldwin called it, the trick the Lumières conceived that animates the
dead, revives dead images of things, the images people and all other
things discard, sloughing off images like skin sheds dead cells, you
know what I mean, constant traffic too swift for human eyes to follow as people and things are dispatched molecule by molecule from
one world to another world or to many worlds, how would we who
are left behind clinging to this one know, but we do understand that
we live in at least two kingdoms, a known and an unknown, a visible
kingdom and a kingdom we cannot see, the invisible one a mysterious otherness, a counterreality we guess might exist in darkness or
inside mirrors or underneath the surface of water, and between
or among those kingdoms always traffic, shadowy, dreamlike exchanges, comings and goings, some things gone for good, for sure it
seems, then the unpredictable returns of people and things so stun-
ningly reconstituted, as the Igbo insist, we're sometimes halted in
our tracks and wonder how we'd believed the things or people had
departed forever, anyway what the French Lumières accomplished
was a practical means of harvesting and preserving dead images con-

tinuously shed from our live bodies, the images that reside swimming, hurtling, frozen in the invisible Great Sea of Time, fast or slow not relevant since everything travels at the same rate there, here, where we are, if not now then in the blink of an eye we're there, here, then gone again, back again too fast for eyes to track, anyway, the Lumières taught themselves — those pioneers and wizards and necrophiles — to fish in the dead zone, the other unseeable kingdom where we leave the consequences of ourselves behind, as falling leaves leave summer behind, marking one season's end, another season's beginning, fall leaves falling into some place that is no season not summer or winter or fall or spring when they let go and drop or the wind shakes them loose and they blow away airborne awhile yes but definitely treeless and on their way out, exiting to make room for the next, next leaf next and next and next, time's up, drifting seldom in a straight line given the randomness of wind tide temperature and fate but falling just as unerringly, inevitably as the arrow fired at your heart that will enter exactly when it's time for you to fall in love or die, exactly that straight and true, bingo, it's over and done and these cunning French brothers developed a technique for recording the time people lose living, the deceased time, used up, depleted, shorn time people in the dark ages had assumed was useless, an empty set, time emptied of time, time given up for dead. Then transformed by the Lumières' magic, the dead images dropping from me and you and the people and things around us, that invisible snowstorm of expired particles, became moving pictures. Think of light as my old pal Charley's assbackwards brush unpainting a sticky dark sky or think of a tongue coated like our tongues with masses of sticky multi-propertied chemicals and chemical reactions, a stew or broth we exchange and consume when we eat something or lick something or stick our tongues in each other's mouths, French kissing, hungry, alive but always also the site and medium of decay and death and change exchanged, no matter how good or bad it tastes, anyway the brothers Lumière discovered how to catch, cook, fast-freeze the dead images which are always dropping and dissolving like dead cells from the skin of the world, from our bodies our breath from every move we make or don't and after preserving this stuff on strips of celluloid, they shined light through them and the rest is history. Astute businessmen, the Lumières realized they'd stumbled upon a goldmine and toured the world to exploit their moving pictures, their movable feast of dead things frozen, packaged, recycled, served up fresh and edible on the screen, real as the real thing, better, many insist.

Lyon all high-tech clean, dot.com, pharmaceutical now, but once an untidy city of fractious workers, of spice sellers and puppeteers, merchant princes whose castles commanded the bluffs along the Rhone River, makers of musical instruments, river pirates, weavers, cosmopolitan immigrants, a funky international hub of France's commerce with the Orient. Lyon a European depot of the fabled Silk Road that once wound through Asia, Lyon's workers spinning gold from thread from mulberry leaves Chinese worms chewed and excreted. How many soldiers from Lyon died at Dien Bien Phu, how many killed and killing, tortured and torturing in Algeria's mountains, Frantz. Do you know the statistics, could you see it all coming over a half-century ago, written on the walls of your flat above the Rhone, through the tiny, frosted bathroom window just missing a view of the river that was as much luxury as you and your new wife could afford or perhaps you could afford more, a nicer flat with ravishing views of Lyon, but, you know, the pair of you forced to rent where you are welcome, white woman, brown man, Lyon not paradise after all, then or now, is it, especially the quarter housing Arab immigrants in kennels and hives where you labored each day in your clinic and occasionally drank tea with Muslim men, you a foreigner too, in a Lyon back-of-the-wall ghetto that previewed the casbah, souks, and medina of Algiers, the same poverty and wretchedness, crime and despair you and your future comrades of the FLN will struggle to reverse into a kind of health, as healthy as it's prudent for the oppressed or your patients to become in a sick world, the sickness you saw first festering in Fort-de-France, then Lyon, Paris, and North Africa, different each place and the same, old and new, familiar and alien as your island birthplace, a disease dooming all those cities, all the seas and countries you risk to dispense your freshly coined skills, a native doctor administering hope to the natives, to Africans, Europeans, to brown and white and black, tortured and torturers. Unpeeling Lyon an endless tumbling through history. Like unpeeling your skin. Down which path should your biographer pursue you to catch a glimpse of your true face. The same question dogging you, Fanon, as you pursued your many faces, through many cities, many pairs of eyes. Will I get lucky and unearth a definitive portrait of you. A view of you freeze-framed on the screen, like I chanced upon Emmett Till's battered face once upon a time, a closeup, millions upon millions of fugitive dots momentarily aligned just so to represent a conundrum recognizable as a human face and also undoubtedly your particular face, your likeness, a still photo fixed so I can study it, you know, like an image from the Lumière archives, an original print stuttering, impaled on the end of a quivering spear of light, a ghost face, dead leaf, its stare crossing mine, staring back as I stare, staring till the ancient stock overheats, begins to smoke and curl.

All that to say or unsay what, he said, Frantz Fanon said to himself so no one heard he barely hears himself in the noisy hospital ward, and if he couldn't hear himself think, obviously it was necessary to bend down, place his doctor's lips at the level of the patient's ear, the level of the prone patient's heart and glazed eyes, eyes immobile as dark stones lining the rocky bank of a river he remembers from his green island, water from high on the volcano's steep slope gushing cool over his bare toes, sun hot on his shoulders, sunlight blackening the unmoving stones as if they were sunken in a shadow of themselves the light deepened, the shimmering light solid as skin stretched over the moving water's surface, a speckled skin — could he, if he tried, reach out and pick off a glittering mica chip of it. The patient's eyes still and dark as those black island stones, all the life in them sucked down to the sockets. Open pits and you know better, don't you doctor, than to step too close to the edge. Though emptiness beckons, you resist. After all, what's to see, what's to find down in there. The lesson learned as a boy in Le François, then part of your training as a physician. You learned to brush aside cobwebs of illusion, of hope when you enter the sick bay, but as you're leaning down to speak into the patient's ear you can't help casting another glance at those dead eyes, a glance slowing as if it's entered a medium sluggish as porridge, slow motion the only possible motion across a strange, bumpy, untidy terrain, the patient's flesh magnified and distorted as your gaze crawls over the wasteland once a man's face, blurred now by nearness and intimacy into something alien, unruly hairs, gaping pores, pimples, creases, rubberish lumps, craters, your eyes trying to sneak mercifully past the disaster of his features and keep the patient at the periphery of your vision where you see but don't really see, you don't need to look, you're not a captive dragged naked across burning coals, but in order to speak to him, to this patient, to say whatever it is you don't know yet you're going to say to whomever this patient might be, this person you've caught a glimpse of by not minding your business when you allowed your gaze to stray too close, linger too long, Fanon, if you're going to speak it's necessary either to holler loud enough to be heard above the chaos of the ward or bend down so your lips are next to the patient's ear and then perhaps he'll hear the words that you're still forming, the words you couldn't share while you towered, doctor, over his bedside. Your pity, your fear aroused, as always, when you consider a millisecond after you read his chart how you might feel if you were him. Then you sneak a look at him and don't look away quickly enough. You see the eyes you'd imagined just a few seconds before as stones, as black holes, are cartwheeling, rolling, swiveling, bursting with wild energy, eyes that would emit bloodcurdling yells if they had tongues. Don't listen, doctor. You must do your duty, you must forget those eyes and regain composure and deliver the message you compose as you lean closer to the stink and dying of him, this patient now wrapped totally head to toe in bandages like a mummy, holes in the swaddling for eyes, nose hole, shit hole, piss hole, one ear hole waiting now for your words, words good for nothing, of course, except to make yourself feel better, doctor, remind him, remind yourself, you're doing your best though you know and he knows your best always far from enough, this throwing yourself on his mercy, on your knees, no, not praying, you would despise yourself for even thinking of prayer, for trying to recall words of prayers you used to perform, kneeling beside your bed, praying out loud so your mother could share the false comfort of that humiliating, fearful ritual, and now you can't go down on your knees without feeling silly, raunchy, no, your mother is not somewhere hovering in the darkness of the room listening, you are a man, standing erect on your own two feet, doctor, so you must not kneel, you must lean down and say whatever words you should say to the patient, not a prayer dammit though it's okay to borrow prayer's rhythm and Bible words, the whispered singsong *now I lay me down to sleep,* or *Yea, though I walk,* my, my, how those island habits, island voices, island sad songs and prayers persist, you can't help weeping, moaning a little bit now, *in extremis,* Frantz, wishing your gimpy old man's legs could dance. Legs stiff under the twisted sheets. His frozen legs burning. He remembers his mother soaking her tired feet at night in a bucket of water, remembers water covering the washerwomen's feet, *les blancheuses* who squat on black stones lining the green riverbank or sit dresses pushed above their knees, shiny brown legs dangling, toes chopped off, anklebones broken and bent, you'd think, seen from the angle where he crouched one spring afternoon spying on the women, the swift water purling around their shins, around their thighs when they step out deeper, deeper, swaying, singing, their dresses balled around their hips, stepping till the river rears up and drowns them, drowns everything, every part of the washerwomen gone but their voices and what his eyes had stolen creeping up on them, hiding on his knees in the bushes, peeping like the river up their wet dresses, at their wet brown skin, the women laughing because they knew a boy spied on them, they'd get their revenge soon enough, boy, looky, looky, long boy, the roar, rumble, and thunder of the surging river like chaos in the ward he bends to be heard above, bends down to hear, down to an ear, his own ear, little Frantz's grown-up little failing, decaying, stinking black ear, Doctor, save me, kill me, save me, kill me, the message blinking on and off in the patient's darting eyes.

(No. You tell *me* how my mother and Fanon wound up in the same place. You figure it out. Me, I haven't reached that point in the story. Maybe I never will, so don't hold your breath. An explanation might unravel itself along the way in spite of me. If an explanation's necessary. As if an explanation ever changes facts, the fact for instance that in this movie an old woman, my mother in a wheelchair, encounters Doctor Frantz Fanon as he lays dying in a hospital bed.)

The first time she rolls herself by Fanon's room it's an accident, a coincidence because his room happens to be on a route she follows for no particular reason the day she invents her route for that day, wheeling here and there through the hospital corridors, riding elevators to various floors, tooling through various wards, anywhere within the sprawling, built-yesterday-already-old-today health-care complex neither signs nor nurses shoo her away from. The next time she goes by the room that turns out to be Fanon's, it's less innocent because her curiosity has been more than aroused by the very unusual circumstance of a policeman on a chair guarding a door she'd chanced upon during her previous run, so on her next run, last of the three per day she's authorized and encouraged to undertake, she hurried back, a beeline this time, to ascertain whether or not a cop still sat outside the door of the third-floor room and sure enough there he was, or there *one* was on a chair (one a woman one day), nodding off my mom thought till he raised an eyelid like lazy old Teddy, who was a girl dog not a boy dog in spite of her name, used to one-eyeball anybody who cracked the frame of the kitchen doorway when Teddy snoozed on her ratty blanket next to the stove. Of course my mother wondered fiercely who could be behind a closed door with a cop guarding it, a burly brown cop who smiles at her the next time she passes, Smokey the Bear with his big leather belts and boots, cowboy hat and a gun in the holster on his wide hip to keep people out or keep somebody in, she wonders which and thinks to herself it's always some of both, no doubt, rolling past again, then many times again, one time the door cracked and a crowd inside, doctors, nurses, suits, uniforms, spilling through the door, hiding the room's occupant, whoever's in the room and a couple people who can't fit inside squeezed outside with the cop in the hall who's standing not sitting on this occasion to keep track, it seems, of what's going on inside as well as outside the room. Cracked that once, the door closed since. Always a cop and always closed. Closed. Closed. She didn't count the closed times because she wouldn't want to lie when the detectives questioned her with a lie detector: How many times have you wheeled past that room which is none of your nosy-old-lady business, old colored lady, why do you sneak past peeking so many times a day, at least once every morning noon and night, don't think we don't see you on your so-called exercise runs you claim the doctor ordered to keep your blood flowing and maybe raise your depressed spirits but we know beyond a shadow of a doubt the doctor sure didn't advise you to scoot straight to the back elevator and up to Three, your old heart beating faster and wheels turning slower the closer you get to the closed door with nothing to do with you behind it, ten, twenty, how many times a day, you tell us, lady, and tell us who pays you to spy and she wouldn't confess anything to them or yes, forgive me lord, if they torture her, she'll tell them, hand on the Bible, every barefaced lie she can dream up, because her business none of their business if the closed door's none of hers. Tell the truth, she'd lost track of how many times she passed the door. Same thing every time. Same ole. A shut door. A big blue bear with a big gun scaring people away.

On his side of the closed door Fanon misses nothing. He hears the spinning wheels, the old, thumping heart. The door not exactly transparent, so her likeness took a while to seep through it, and now a clear image of her face available each time she rolls by. He's developed a preternatural awareness, a kind of Humbert Humbert spidery acuity in the lonely vortex of a web which trembles when a butterfly's wings agitate a breeze in Peru. How Fanon feels from time to time anyway, chained to a bed, lying there helpless, naked except for a diaper, hour after hour, or days or years, neither awake nor asleep, throat parched, a swamp of sweat, shivering, choking, assaulted by the frantic traffic of cells constructed, cells demolished and trucked away, cells remodeled, scraped, scrapped, workers and machines coming and going, a great excavation at the center of him, a constant thudding of wrecking balls and hooting bulldozers knocking down older quarters of the city, slums cleared, fresh construction tumbling down as it's completed, new and old consuming each other, collapsing into the same pit at the center of him into which everything, hands, eyes, memories, bowels, disappears, the cells clamoring, screaming because loud brutal tools are pulling them down faster than other tools can shape and secure them, love them, their walls giving way, giving up. There is nothing, no solid ground inside him to stand upon, cling to, just the lost city of him, demolished, sliding away, dust, rubble, and noxious waste. Each cell on a suicide mission, self-destructing, the raw walls buckling when the first dab of paint applied, bright panes of glass maneuvered into place on a top story, then crashing down into the emptiness where his island once floated, the city of him unfit for habitation, its foundations quicksand, his flesh sinking into mud, becoming mud, he breathes mud, tastes mud, swims in a slick wet ooze, he's drowning, the thick, smothering intimacy of the mud bearing dead messages from everywhere, nowhere, news of pain at the tips of useless fingers, pain messages delivered by follicles of hair with burning roots like a torturer's cigarettes stubbed on his chest.

But on his side of the hospital room door, as on her side, you can't even depend on pain or death to get you through the night. It lifts. Not death. Not night. They don't lift, my brother. Pain lifts. A torturer's trick Fanon knows well. The torturers schooled him — all pain no gain, my brother. Keep hope alive. You must keep hope alive or the stubborn ones overdose on pain and die on you. A black mark mars your record, not theirs. You suffer the consequences, not them.

Pain lifts. Temperature rises. Not fluorescent lighting searing your eyes, Doctor Fanon, it's the tropical sun. Shield your gaze. Scan the postcard view. Forget your skewered, blistered, bloated, blackened body roasting over a pit. Run toward the laughing ocean. Your legs are strong and sturdy again. Soccer trim. Run fast but not too fast. Your muscles have grown sluggish. Allow them to warm up. This is not a dream, not paradise. No wings. You'll need your legs. Remember, you're no better at imagining paradise when you're awake than when you're asleep. Don't sprint, a gentle lope because a small person with legs shorter than yours clasps your hand. Can't you feel the warm, wet squeeze. Can't you hear her squeals above the thudding surf. Waves loom ahead tall as skyscrapers. A city's famous face painted across the horizon rushing toward them. He'll sizzle when waves break over him. Salt will heal the charred threads of his skin. It will only hurt a moment, my dear, he shouts, smiling down at her crown of dready locks. Her small hand grips his tighter than skin. I won't let go this time, my daughter, my flesh. Soon we'll be free, home soon, as soon as we step into the cool sea we'll step out on the other side. See the rows of braids, the white ropes, blue ropes, green ropes of rolling and pitching water, see the rainbow fish, their bubble eyes and needle teeth, look down their tongueless mouths into the pink wells of their bellies, my sweet girl. Gentle strides but he must hurry too. Her short legs scissor to keep up, old sores popping and bleeding, his, hers, your flesh after all, your bad seed sprouting in this daughter, blacking up her skin, scarring her hair. It's not far, baby, hurry, hurry, don't pull her small hand off her small arm, Daddy.

She survives you, whatever that means, and in an interview I imagine or read she talks briefly about her name, your name, Fanon, the difficulties claiming a famous name so neither she nor it's forgotten. A balancing act, the difficulty of shedding the famous name when she wishes to be known by another, the difficulty of wanting others to remember her different name yet not to forget her father's name her mother did not take but asked him to give to her daughter, your daughter, Fanon, your flesh surviving after you're gone, and though you were in love in Lyon, about to marry another woman, you said yes and signed the appropriate documents bestowing your name *Fanon* on your daughter, thus giving her the legal right to claim the name, but you did not include her right to claim more than you decided you were willing or able to give, and you never met her, this girl child Murielle, bearing your dead sister's name, the daughter whom I imagine further on a rainy day, your birthday perhaps, July 20, perhaps walking alone under a purplish umbrella down an aisle of the cemetery in Fort-de-France, a two-tiered cemetery, one tier a crowded, sprawling ghetto on the hillside's steep upper slope, the poor as you predicted at last on top, and at the foot of the hill the rich folks' cemetery, a walled village of miniature stone dwellings. Your daughter Murielle finding you where she knew you'd be waiting, at the base of the hill, her father handsome, dignified, in a photo encased on a marble page of an open book atop the stone crypt inside the iron fence enclosing the family mausoleum that sits at an intersection near the cemetery wall farthest from the little stone shed at the entrance where I asked directions of a goateed attendant and he pointed down a lane between two rows of elaborate, aboveground tombs *tout droit, tout droit* and I followed his finger along this street lined with monuments and mansions of the dead to arrive at the spot where I'm imagining her under her large mauve umbrella staring at photos, plaques, wreaths, dead flowers, imitation flowers arranged on a chest-high stone vault containing various remains, I assume, though not her father's, he lies many islands, more than one sea away, back where he came from and therefore she came from and where he has returned and she will too, but not yet on this rainy afternoon I imagine her paying her respects in the Cimitière de la Levée, the so-called cemetery of the rich, in Fort-de-France. Although her father's buried, they say, in Africa, he's also memorialized here by his family in the final resting place as they say of his mother, father, brothers, sister, etc., the Fanons, her people too, her name inscribed on mementos, carved in the tomb looking back at her as she waits dry-eyed in Fort-de-France under her umbrella. An easy day for mourning, no need to cry or tap deep private reserves of sadness. All nature's grieving. Dismal sky, dark puddles on the asphalt pavement, a small damp chill in the air that counts as cold in the summer tropics. The gray stones of this town of the dead blacker, heavier when they're wet. Tears from the sky gently tap, tap, tapping on the purple umbrella shielding her plastic-scarfed hair, and she's glad no wind today, no howling, no whipping, no snatching. She stands aside quietly, lets the universe mourn, the sliver of it anyway revealing itself here, on this gray day, lets nature cry for her father's absence so she's free to listen for him, to greet him if he arrives unexpectedly, lets the quiet in her deepen until she can hear the *plink-plink-plink* drip from yellow beaded tips of the umbrella's struts, slower, more lugubrious on the pavement than the tap, tapping above her head. It's a soundtrack appropriate for doing this dreary thing, being in this difficult place. Without looking at them she recites the words inscribed on the marble book holding her father's image, a lament honoring a beloved son and brother. The words dissolve, scatter as she repeats them to herself, fading like in a movie she thinks to take her from one scene to the next. Effortlessly she's thousands of miles away in a green place she's never been. Africa one name for where her father rests, where he or whatever's left of him rests in peace, she hopes, impressed as she always is and isn't that numerous nations now lay claim to her father's bones, his dust, while none claimed him when he lived and breathed and wrote and spoke his changing mind. She worries his spirit may be drifting, unsettled and restless like the elders say fresh souls wander, just beginning their voyage back across the water. She wishes she could help him. Launch him where he needs to go or be his anchor, the tether her mother couldn't be for him . . . but that's old, gossipy business, after all, they need each other now, all of them, us, these dead, the Fanons, in new ways none of us can dream properly yet. On gray days like this one she fears her father's lost forever, his name forged on empty graves, his body scattered to the winds by politics of naming and claiming. Her father kidnapped, then refused and abandoned like her. How could you give your name to a person and not claim that person, not allow that person's claim on you. How long does it take to make a daughter. How long to name her. Is naming a mere technicality, a cold, formal signing on or signing off, as simple as sleeping in one woman's bed one night, another woman's bed another night. The somber skies, the rain pouring now are mourning for her so she's free I think to imagine forgiveness or other less imposing possibilities beside a replica of the Fanon home, a representation in stone of the family parlor except one wall is iron bars so the living can spy on the dead as we peer at lions in a zoo, as lions in a zoo peer at us. Don't fret, don't mourn. Don't blame the years lost waiting for your father to claim you. He was busy in his way, intent on doing just that — claiming you, my mother would say. Fighting a war for you. A claim's not in a name. He'll know you by your footsteps, your knock, my dear, not by your name, your country, your color, your fate. Just step toward him. He'll meet you halfway when the iron gate swings open. And open it will, my mother would insist. Don't weep, my children, she would say to the Fanons, father and daughter, say to us, to Fanons gone and to come, huddled on either side of the door, if she could.

And because she's old and can't work miracles, often my mother thinks of herself as a roach. Nasty and useless, scared and doomed as one of those panicked roaches scrambling everywhichway after her mother, my grandmother, Freeda, crept tippy-toe before anybody else out of bed winter mornings and lit the kitchen oven to warm the frigid ass-end of the rowhouse on Cassina Way, and the big dumb bugs — still busy picnicking on scraps and crumbs, forgetting like they do every time that fire's coming and the all-night party the last one for a whole bunch of them — would come flying and scooting away from the heat to discover Grandma Freeda waiting for them with both feet alert and a carpet slipper in one hand whap, whap, whap, deadly as god. My mother, scurrying along one of the hospital's long, gleaming, piss-stinky corridors, is sure god has his reasons she wouldn't understand any better than roaches understood my grandmother's murderous slipper, good reasons for being angry with creatures he fashioned in his likeness who behave no better than dirty, pesky, good-for-nothing insects even though she wonders why god on his high throne would waste much anger or time on them, wouldn't he just roll his eyes, suck his teeth, and go on and do whatever else he needed to do, no surprise, was it, human beings still hurting and killing one another by ones and twos and hundreds and thousands these Last Days, just like they been killing for thousands of years, people killing people almost as fast as birthing people it seems, even though it seems the people population growing fast as roaches every day. She could see why god would despise such sorry creatures, but he wouldn't *despise*, would he, after loving us into being, *despise, hate* the wrong words for what he'd feel toward humans he'd given a human nature, just as he gave roaches roach nature, why would he be surprised roaches act like roaches if roach is what he put in them, why crinkle his brow or fuss or punish the things people do to one another and to themselves, it's not news, not the score of a Super Bowl he didn't already know before it started which team would win, so not a matter of hating or despising, maybe, more like just being bored, like he's tired of the foolishness and ugliness on TV, and strikes a match, and quick, opens the oven door, and quick, sticks it in the fire to catch the swoosh of gas filling up the oven. Jerks his arm out the way and quick slams the door. Waits with a slipper in his hand for them to come tearing out the holes they had sneaked into. Whap.

He's coming down the hall, slipper in his golden hand. Whap. She smiles to herself thinking what a foolish thing for an old crippled-up woman in a wheelchair to think the master of the universe didn't have nothing better to do than chase her down a hospital hallway. Mashed-up, bloody old slipper in the same fist had squeezed light from stars and set planets spinning like tops and shaped her out of mirey clay and lifted her up close enough to his sweet lips to blow in a breath of life. All those wonders performed and here she comes this morning busybody minding some other body's business, as if she didn't know better, as if she didn't know she should leave well enough alone, as if she could play hide-and-seek with him, as if her old stick arms, these wheels for legs could scoot her along too fast to be noticed from where he sits on high. As if he's finished with her. Nothing to lose, nothing of her left worth breaking or stealing or humbling she's down so low down to a bitter nub and all alone at last with nothing but her pitiful roach self in this pitiful chair he got to be done with me she thinks out loud and wonders why he isn't, why she feels his breath on the back of her neck, why her skin's hot with shame and guilty knowledge because here she goes again poking her nose into somebody else's business, whoever the person was behind a door she guesses is locked and the key in a bear's pocket.

A few nurses in this hospital she wouldn't blow her nose on or wipe her ass with and then again a few of them tending her couldn't be nicer. If being a nurse her job, would she be one of the nice ones, the angel kind who never said no, never said too much or too little, who poked and stuck and drew blood the same gentle way they tucked her in or said good morning how you doing today, Mrs. Wyman, so the words sounded new, not like a scrap of food swept up off the floor nobody decent would think of putting in their mouth.

Nice like nice Nurse Mimi who reminds her of Cora Brunson at church in her all-white missionary uniform leading old folks to the particular pews where they been sitting each Sunday since way before Cora Brunson — who ain't no spring chicken — born, since before there was a Homewood AME Zion church on the corner of Bruston and Homewood, old people occupying the same exact seat every Sunday, a seat some of them couldn't locate if it wasn't for Cora Brunson remembering and leading them to it, poor old brains fuddled and fogged, further gone than hers, my mother thinks, worried about her little bit of roach brain left, enough left in those old ghost people to get dressed and out the house on Sunday morning and know the wrong place if somebody don't lead them to the right place they'd refuse to sit down in the wrong place, wag their old heads *Huh-uh. No indeed,* and vanish, carrying off Homewood AMEZ with them if it wasn't for angels like Cora Brunson her hand guiding an elbow or taking the papery fingers slipped into hers. Cora a large woman, heavyset, you know, looks twice as large in all that missionary white with her bowlegs and overstuffed white gym shoes and little weensy white veil pinned like a bride on top her head. Even if your head bowed and eyes shut praying you knew when Cora Brunson passed up or down the red-carpeted aisle by the squeak of her bound up in fully packed nylon undergarments rubbing against the white uniform with not an inch to spare, squeaky like a man breaking in a new pair of Stacy Adams. Just like Cora Brunson, Nurse Mimi too big and black to be any kind of angel my mother would have thought before she knew better, way back when in Sunday school, a pale, empty-headed little color-struck girl, but today no doubt about it, an angel's what Nurse Mimi is. Thank you, dear. You're a real angel. You know you're an angel, don't you, Nurse Mimi. If nobody's told you lately, somebody sure needs to, so I will.

Oh, Ms. Wyman. Thank you so much. Do my best around here. Surely I do. But I sure ain't growing no wings.

You're kind, patient, respectful. As good as wings in this mean place.

Thank you. Like I said I do my best. When I change my mind about that, I'm outta here.

Stay as long as you're able, please, Nurse Mimi. Can't be easy, is it.

Know something, Ms. Wyman. This ward the easiest I've worked in a good while. Hands stay plenty busy, but this ward far, far from the worst.

Where's it hardest, if you wouldn't mind me asking.

Course I don't mind. It's preemies. The neonatal ward, Ms. Wyman. Doctors keeping newborns alive younger and younger. Means smaller and smaller. Some them poor little things look like they ain't got no business out here in this cold world. So tiny and shivering and shriveled-up, you know. First time I worked the preemie ward I could hardly believe some them was real babies. More like shrunk-up old people dolls. Or little pink mice or puppies. Too tiny and funny-looking for human being babies. But that's what they surely are. Little-bitty people got personalities no different from you or me. Afterwhile you start thinking the big, fat, healthy babies lined up in the nursery window down the hall is the strange ones. But them preemies do take some getting used to. So small and weak. You be halfway scared to touch them. Ain't easy for the parents neither, Ms. Wyman. Can't blame them in a way. Who wants to claim a child look like it from Mars. Some scared the baby ain't gon make it, so they just can't touch. Some the mothers too young and dumb to be mothers. Babies theyselves. Pass on they crack habit and that's about all the preemies gon get from them. Anyway, we gown and glove up the mothers and some would hold the babies all day if we let em. Doctors better and better at keeping the wee-little ones alive but some come here ain't spozed to stay here. No way. So we still lose babies and it's hard. Little things ain't done nothing wrong to nobody but they ain't never had no chance. Me, I always be picking one the worse-off ones and giving it special attention. The little fighters ain't got nothing going for them but fight and your heart's rooting they make it even if your head figures ain't no way. But you hold them and talk to them, keep them fighting breath by breath. You ain't slighting the others. A particular one just plays on your mind all day while you working. When you home you hoping she still be there when you go in for your shift. Stay on an extra shift sometimes trying to keep one breathing. Don't pay to be softhearted if you working with the preemies. Lots the nurses up there don't sleep well. You on double double shift but what good's double days off if you can't sleep. Some the girls get into drugs, you know, to keep theyselves going. I wasn't no better, Ms. Wyman.

Anyway, it's hardest on the preemie ward. I been on post-op and critical care and cancer but preemies the hardest. Takes the most out a person. Don't know how the girls work there regular stick with it. Did my rotation many a time, then I had to let it go. Never forget the day I walked in there and thought I was in jail. Seem like all the preemies in little cells, tied down with those tubes and wires hooked up to the monitors and alarms. See, you got to have alarms cause they cry so quiet. Can't holler to get your attention. Lungs one the last things grow in right. Lung problems finish most them preemies don't make it. I walked in one morning and seems like all them making that pitiful *peep-peep-peep* like baby chicks' noise you can barely hear instead of crying and hollering out loud like full-term babies. That quiet little sound got to me, Ms. Wyman. I thought to myself these babies asking me why they locked up in here, in this goddamn slam, excuse my English, Ms. Wyman, and nothing I could do but march my big self on by like some goddamn prison guard.

The preemie ward on Five, isn't it. Tried to visit the newborns once but the nurses turned me around.

Uh-huh. Only parents. Sounds like you getting familiar with this place. And getting around better too, ain't you, Ms. Wyman. Good for you.

Did you know there's a policeman guarding one of the rooms on Three.

We get police and paramedics in here when they bring in hurt people off the street. Sometimes they bring an inmate from over the prison for an operation. Usually the poor man's half dead before they bring him in here. And after they cut on him he ain't hardly ready to jump up and run away. Guard on the door kinda silly if you ask me. The man up on Three a different story. Whole hospital talking about him. Buzz. Buzz. Buzz. Did you know this. Did you hear that. Poor man can't walk, can't talk, barely breathing but they scared to death of him. Guard him night and day. You'd think they got Bin Laden himself with those sad, pretty eyes up on Three. Say he's from another country. Say he's black as me and can't speak no English if he could talk. Say he hates white people and wants to kill them all. Now if he don't speak English what I want somebody to tell me is how any these fools round here know who the man hates and don't hate. A troublemaker big-time, they say — you know, like they say about our Dr. King and Malcolm. Say he was a bad fellow back wherever he came from and he's very sick now, but they must still be scared cause he's locked up in here so they can keep an eye on him till he dies. Heard people say his name but I can't call it to mind. A funny kind of name I ain't never heard of. If he's like our troublemakers, bet somebody somewhere sure knows his name. And ain't gon forget it. Know what I mean, Ms. Wyman.

So that's how they got together, my mom and Fanon. One likely story anyway. If you need a story to stay on board my story. And now that I've showed you mine, it's your turn to show me yours. Isn't that how it goes. Isn't that only fair.

One day, though the weather outdoors rainy and dismal, inside the hospital it's dry and bright as artificial illumination can fake, and inside Fanon's head a sudden and from his point of view suspicious clearing. As a psychiatrist he'd been trained not to trust his patients' sudden turnabouts or conversions. Such dramatic swings more likely symptoms of disease, signs of deterioration rather than progress toward a cure. A light bulb flaring up just before it quits. Is he being manipulated by the constant flow of drugs pumped into his body. Truth serum, poisons, placebos, consciousness-altering substances. Is this instant, wonderful clarity a reward the doctors can give and take away. Are these Americans, these lynchers, softening him up, beginning a calculated process of conditioning. Training him like a Pavlov dog. Will they addict him to pleasure, then manipulate him by withholding or administering sweet doses of what he can't bear to live without. Pleasure some argue more persuasive than pain — catch more flies with honey than vinegar the old folks say. Couldn't the simple absence of pain bring pleasure. Especially after an intense, prolonged session of torture. Doesn't this momentary truce, this bright, unbelievable interval of simply being himself, depend upon the threat of pain, *pain* always there just below the threshold of consciousness crouching in the shadows around the next corner ready to spring. Please, doctor. Don't talk this reprieve to death. Don't waste it. Enjoy yourself, my brother. Fly as high and happy as you can fly.

Fanon can't remember any stories about torturers extracting information from captives by making them happy. Inflicting pain more efficient than throwing a party. He makes a note to himself to raise these issues with his patients. Do torturers or the ones tortured understand pain better. Whose pain. Are pleasure and pain inseparable. Please, doctor. Stop. Why ask questions. You know damn well there's a difference between pleasure and pain. Don't spoil this gift of clarity. Believe it for as long as it lasts.

The explosion of gushing water is not a river overflowing its banks, not Mount Pelée erupting, not a black hole swirling open in the sea and sucking down the troop transport *Oregon,* it's one of the policemen flushing the toilet they share with him. Why are they afraid. Why don't their eyes meet his when they enter and leave. Not *they.* Though different policemen guarding him, and once a policewoman, it's one, always one at a time ignoring him, fearing him. One at a time in the tiny cubicle just inches from his bed, so he tries to resist *they.* But *they* lock the stall behind them. *They* flush to be certain the toilet clean for their dirt. Then *they* unroll paper, reams of paper, to wipe the toilet, the sink, line the seat, cover the floor, wallpaper the walls. *They* grumble, maneuvering their large bodies in a small space. He thinks of cowboys in American movies, awkward as armored knights in their leather chaps and vests, giant hats and holsters, belts, bandoliers, spurs, and boots, cowboys dismounting, jingle, jangle from snorting broncs. Even for a stand-up piss, the *flics* can't get at their pissers without unbuckling, lowering the beltful of rattling paraphernalia. A big sigh when finally they plop down. Their giant pillows of ass smothering the hole his shrunken hams would sink into if not for a nurse bracing his arms. Routinely, their shits move the earth. Then they flush again. Or flush twice. Leaving no shit for the prisoner's shit to contaminate. More water running, more paper, more rattling and squeaking, zipping, buckling up. Enough water consumed flushing, washing, and rinsing to quench the thirst of a drought-stricken Algerian village. If famine deprived them, he had no doubt these husky carnivores would devour one another. Imagines himself flat on his back, legs poking up like a roast chicken on a platter, while *they* big-bellied their way to the dinner table, polite hippos waddling on their back legs, napkins under rolls of chin, knives and forks in their fat hands.

Doctor Fanon, you have a visitor. A lady, doctor.

He touches his necktie's assumed perfection, the dark knot of it exactly centered bulging from white wings of his collar. He's prepared. This ushering and announcing of visitors a formality. He knows perfectly well the shape of his day, the sequence of appointments and phone calls scheduled between them, the bedside consultations in the wards, evenings observing and interacting with his patients in the therapeutic social activities he arranges for them. As resident psychiatrist at Blida, with endless demands on every thimbleful of his time, he must organize and prepare meticulously. Much of his energy exhausted planning how to execute a thorough yet efficient passage through the maze of his patients' illnesses. Their symptoms create the shape of each working day, working days neverending it seems, all his waking hours and most of his fitful sleep consumed by his patients' demands, a situation bearable, perhaps, only because the alternative is worse. Anything better than empty time alone when the ever-present sous-conversation, sometimes a barely perceptible murmur, sometimes a roaring in his ears, takes over, that conversation with other voices and himself about the inevitable failure of all undertakings, the cruel setbacks, total crash of cures patient and doctor devise, unspeakable exchanges he cannot ignore whose only theme is futility, a running negative commentary from the world outside the Blida clinic critiquing his efforts inside the Blida clinic. *What about the massacres, doctor. Have you heard there's a rebellion in the hills. doctor, doctor, I'm mad, I'm ill, I'm a native, a god, a dog. You could help us defeat them, doctor. You're one of us. Not one of them. Whose color. Whose skin. Whose flag do you serve, doctor. You're a doctor, not a soldier, doctor. If you touch me with those black hands, doctor, I'll scream.* In the muddle of voices, his often the loudest, mocking the logic of his routines, his plans, the hopeful words passing between patient and physician. Endless hours in clinic and ward dull the sous-conversation, sustain the illusion that all's well, or partly well at least. He's a doctor, after all, performing his duties, ready for the rigors of the day. He knows his name, his trade, he'll be prepared with practiced face to meet the first patient's trepidation or relief or hypocrisy or naive faith or loathing.

To amuse himself he pretends he's forgotten who he is. Forgotten who waits on the other side of the office door. Plays dumb. Feigns total ignorance of what he's supposed to be doing in the next eighteen or twenty hours. Forgets the consequences of forgetting, forsakes the safety zone where he can pretend to be one kind of man, a doctor in charge, running the show, at least until fatigue and the weight of self-deception, the weight of lying to his patients brings him to his knees again and he hears the rattling of his chains, the moans and screams of the others locked in the hold with him. He plays innocent. Slips the yoke and turns the joke. As if he doesn't know what's come before and coming next. As if he can't look through the wall and see who's being announced when the nurse descends from the sky and pokes her head in the door. You have a visitor, doctor. A lady . . .

Good day, madame . . . sir . . . let's see . . . hmmmm . . . are you a torturer or one of the tortured. The question he never asks though the mischief-making part of him entertains asking it, goads his professional persona by pointing out the usefulness of such an inquiry. Why not commence each interview with simple questions. Insane or sane. French or Algerian. Black or white. Living or dead. Allow the patients to declare themselves and thereby begin to cure themselves. The physician's job no more nor less than grasping whatever thread the patient offers, holding on, following it through the labyrinth. Saving each other.

From the podium he sees a brown sea of faces, brown broken here and there by a few islands of whiteness, particularly in the rows closest to the stage and then as his gaze lifts toward the auditorium's rear the faces become one color, no color where the house lights dim and an overhanging balcony sinks all faces in uniform darkness, and out there, just beyond and below the balcony, a busy traffic of delegates through a pair of double doors admitting and expelling light each time they swing open, doors at the ends of the aisles that divide the interior into three sections, a massive wedge of seats in the middle, a narrow band of seats along each wall, the hall's design configuring the audience just like politics divides he thinks or like the divisions of human nature that politics mirror, he thinks, the center squeezed by the margins, the margins squeezed out by the center, and he wonders who will come forward first, someone from the right flank or left flank or center to seize one of the microphones set up for a Q-and-A session scheduled to follow his keynote speech, one mike at the foot of each aisle, just before the pit or apron or moat dividing stage from the first row of seats. Will the conference delegates descend to the mikes with the same urgency and determination they exhibit hustling out of the doors at the back of the auditorium. A steady stream so the doors are blinking eyes or like flashbulbs popping to steal snapshots of each delegate who enters or leaves. Perhaps urgent state business summons the fleeing delegates. Or too much wine at lunch for overworked middle-aged kidneys perhaps. Doubtless these diplomats and bureaucrats and reporters and exiles and spies and intellectuals without portfolios are all extremely busy people, busy men he should say since almost all are men, men who, before they enter rooms where conference business is conducted, shed the young women you see them chatting up in the lobbies, the halls, the streets, the women they escort to bars and restaurants surrounding the conference center. Where do these women disappear when the men are here, Fanon wonders. Wherever the women are, is that where the delegates are running. Running to take care of business. State business. Man business. Woman business. Monkey business. Who knows who's paying whom to do what. Who finances the errands, meetings, exchanges in the city's best downtown hotels where even in this so-called black man's country at least half the guests look white.

At the swinging doors delegates get in each other's way, no labored courtesies, no bows or handshakes, no you-first-Alphonse-no-you-Gaston comedy, the delegates busy men too much in a hurry to acknowledge one another, unhappy to be caught a naked second in the lobby's glare, rushing away from the glare of this important conference hosting important people. Fanon follows them after they escape through the doors, patting ties, neatening the drape of briefcases, smoothing a rich fabric's invisible wrinkles, brushing dust from immaculate lapels. Delegates wearing the tight-lipped smile of a well-dressed person emerging from a public restroom who avoids the gaze of the next in line, declaring himself or herself innocent of shitting or pissing like an animal on the other side of the door.

Scanning through the auditorium's walls into its bright lobby, Fanon observes delegates displaying conspicuous lack of interest in whatever might be transpiring inside the hall, there a delegate hovering near the entrance for the next chance to enter unobtrusively as a delegate departs, here a cluster of delegates smoking, chattering a discreet distance from the doors, there delegates forming a second front in the lobby around a bearded, well-known attendee's impromptu lecture, here a pair of delegates, each sneaking peeks over the other's shoulder while nodding vigorous assent to the other's words, words, words — words you might guess, from the concerned, earnest gazes the delegates pass back and forth, at least as significant to humanity's struggle as any speech delivered from the podium. Some delegates pass in or out of the doors and glide through the lobby elegantly, expertly as they shuttle through VIP lounges of international airports.

Seated on the podium, Fanon despairs. How will anyone hear him, how will he hear himself above the buzz in the lobby, limo doors slammed, helicopters taking off, planes landing, terrorist bombs exploding, the whisper of expensive trousers rubbing well-fed thighs. He watches a hand sliding down a row of plush seatbacks as a delegate extricates himself from a front center seat, excuse me, excuse me, please, thank you, thank you, the delegate guiding himself by the feel of the seats, politely trampling others' feet, battering their knees, then hurrying, almost a sprint on tiptoe up the aisle to the door where his picture is snapped, and he blinks and bumps slightly a delegate entering as he leaves, the newcomer's eyes accustoming themselves to darkness, searching out an empty space to occupy until pressing affairs summon him away.

Who passes out masks and forces the delegates to wear them. Who decides the masks must be black or white. What colors lie beneath the masks. Will I live to see their faces unveiled, Fanon wonders. When delegates return home, would they be visible without black masks or white masks. Will they ever be free to remove their masks or only exchange white for black, black for white.

It's too late. Masks do not disguise truth. Masks are true. The pure, absolute, reassuring truth of black or white. Pure illusion. Pure white or pure black. Masks truer than the gray shadow staring back from a mirror, your unconvincing reflection that does not disguise the blazing emptiness behind it you pretend not to see.

Stop, Fanon tells himself. Delegates are not wearing masks. They are blind. The conference a school for the blind, teaching delegates to manage a world they cannot see. A world where sightlessness an asset not a handicap if you learn the rules, follow instructions. Everybody's blind, equally blind, equally secure and terrorized by blindness.

And who am I if not a delegate, Fanon asks. A delegate representing myself first and then others, perhaps. Yes and no, because who am I without those others. But I am not those others. Who pays my way. Whom do I owe. What am I demanding from other delegates attending the conference. Why should they risk anything on behalf of Algerians fighting for independence from France, Algerians I claim to represent. Do delegates gathered here represent anyone besides themselves. Do they love anyone.

My brother, my likeness. He often recites those words of Baudelaire to remind himself that what he despises most in another is also always his own face mirrored in their features, his actions doubled by theirs. No matter how clinically accurate and irrefutable his observations of others, in the end he is the balky mule he lashes, the impatient rider straddling his own sweaty back.

Who am I. Why am I here, pretending to be someone solid, substantial I cannot be, someone pure and true I think I might wish to be. The circle unbroken. Delegates are hostages. Hoods over our heads an act of mercy. Blinding us to the truth of our blindness.

Speak. Rise to the podium and speak. It's your turn now, Fanon.

A sea of faces waiting for him to strip off his clothes, dash into the water, and drown. His brothers armed with volleys of applause to fire at speakers who parade to the lectern, rooting them on, shooting them down one by one to cleanse the stage for the next pretender to the throne none of the little monarchs at home or sitting out there on their regal butts is prepared to relinquish until brute force deposes him, *vive le roi, vive le roi, le roi est mort.* Why such dire estimates of your brothers, Fanon. Why the small, suppressed tingle of excitement, of complicity upon sighting white faces scattered here and there in the front rows. In the hall colored faces could swallow uncolored faces as easily as tall waves gulp down churning limbs. Only a spattering of white faces. Some of those colored, no doubt. No doubt some of the uncolored more friendly, more simpatico, as is often the case, than many of the colored. Why is he quibbling over the meaning of these different shades of color or no color his gaze supplies. As if color makes a difference. Why ponder this incompleteness, these uncolored spaces that with a little effort could or should be painted differently. Would the absence of uncolored faces render a unanimous verdict on who belongs here, who owns the conference, who it serves. Why. Is he secretly pleased by a sprinkling of so-called whites, by the irony that the issue of their removal is on the conference agenda. Will they have a vote, yes or no, to erase themselves. Which is it — the presence or the absence of their faces that signifies the conference's success. Though few, are the few precious because without them the sea he's facing from the podium doesn't exist on the map of the larger world, the map that ancestors of these precious few drew centuries ago, the ancient map of wishful thinking, a cartoon map, really, outmoded then and now, *Beware, dragons be here,* a map with distortions of scale, flat-out lies and conscious misrepresentations, embedded superstitions and ignorance, a map of dreams, a prettied-up picture of Europe's unspeakable nightmares and aspirations, a map adorned on its margins with occult symbols, coats of arms, saints, imps, mermaids, monsters, portraits of pale faces and pale bodies beautiful as angels, a fairy-tale map abiding till today, this very instant Fanon unseats himself and slowly walks toward the lectern for his turn to speak. Won't these very steps take their measure from the old map, his six or seven strides meaningless, not counting as steps, unless they are plotted on that old map of continents, countries, islands, and seas, the map drawn by a few dreaming hands, by the same ones, their numbers still small, who retain the power in their hands, their heads to draw the old map again and again and squeeze a whole world onto a parchment grid, making it, then and now, everybody's map, white brown black red yellow green, establishing scale and relationship among peoples, among things, determining the place of things, their absolute largeness, smallness, significance — Near East, Far East, West, First World, Third World, on top or down under — the map missing the sea of faces Fanon looks out upon, and no matter how deep and dense this sea appears to him, that immensity does not exist, cannot be located, a blank site, a *terre inconnue*, emptied of meaning once and forever by the mapmakers because they chose to render no shape for it, appended no names but theirs, left it as an invisible island floating, drowning, a hole, a fearful void in a greater sea that surrounds it, washes over it, conceals it from sight and time. Unless the map, as Fanon understands it, the map that erases him by erasing itself by erasing him, can be flipped over to its unwritten side and then perhaps you could begin a fresh drawing of the world.

Speak

POSTSCRIPTS

A university professor, Peter Worsely, describes Fanon's speech as electrifying, "an experience to set the pulse racing . . . remarkable not only for its analytic power but delivered with a passion and brilliance that is all too rare." Worsely also writes that he noticed Fanon come close to tears during the speech and afterward asked him why. Worsely reports Fanon's response in the words below, words included in the Macey biography, page 432.

Suddenly he felt overcome at the thought that he had to stand there, before the assembled representatives of African nationist movements, to try and persuade them that the Algerian cause was important, at a time when men were dying and being tortured in his country for a cause whose justice ought to command automatic support from rational and progressive human beings.

◇   ◇   ◇   ◇   ◇   ◇   ◇

In 1961, Jean-Paul Sartre wrote a preface to *The Wretched of the Earth* that upset his fellow countrymen more than Fanon's book upset them. Many influential French intellectuals were at least as mad at Sartre for championing Fanon as they'd been when Sartre championed Stalin, a Russian tyrant with the blood of tens of millions on his hands. "Oh fuck. There he goes again, our Voltaire, stirring up the natives, Sartre as wrong about the blacks as he was about the reds."

❖   ❖   ❖   ❖   ❖   ❖   ❖

These field notes, compiled while I operated undercover disguised as a journalist, trace some of Mr. Frantz Fanon's recent travels, his speeches at various international gatherings, the reception his speeches received, the fellow travelers who attended. I've included my analysis of the significance of his activities and a number of recommendations based upon my observations and concerns. I hope we will meet and discuss my recommendations ASAP when I return to Washington this Thursday. I'm certain we're heading for a full-scale crisis in this matter and should act swiftly, decisively to avert it.

❖   ❖   ❖   ❖   ❖   ❖   ❖

Mom,

Greetings. Hope you're fine. Hope the weather's nice so you can sit outside on your terrace. Romeo is growing locks. Not goldilocks. Nappy brown dreadlocks. Even though his mom's fair-haired and blue-eyed. You never know what to expect, I guess. Given the crazy, mixed-up quilt of folks of all colors rubbing shoulders in Pittsburgh, nobody should be surprised sea-green eyes like brother Dave's pop up in our brown, burr-head clan. Why do those eyes make some people want to kill him. Anyway, Romeo's dready cap is flourishing and looking good and tomorrow the three of us fly to Paris. Believe it or not, I'll have a draft of the *Fanon* script (couldn't have done it without you) in my briefcase.

Heard from Romeo's grandmother in France it's unseasonably hot there. I say bring it on. After this long, nasty winter, I'm ready for sunshine and ocean. Other news from over there not so good. Immigrants burning up in government hotels. Algerian kids and kids from Mali, Senegal, Ivory Coast, Martinique burning cars.

Economic woes. People trouble — Muslims vs. Jews, Jews vs. Christians, Christians vs. Muslims, blacks vs. whites, immigrants vs. natives. Some folks shocked France not as cozy for everybody as they believed. Other folks shocked anyone in their right mind could have believed things cozy for everybody. You know how that one goes. I'm afraid the trouble's going to get worse because the loudest, dumbest voices are grabbing this chance to be onstage, stirring up shitstorms the knuckleheads and opportunists and optimists of blind goodwill always kick up. At least the French are starting to take to the streets and to fuss at one another instead of the blah-blah-blah like here that's worse than no talk. Next time you see Fanon, tell him we need him. Need the best of him. Like we need the best of you. The part that says we're all in this mess together, and says *question* and says *keep pushing*. The ice is cracking, Mom, but we're on our way across the pond, whatever. Wish us luck. Will try to write soon again.

Love.

ACKNOWLEDGMENTS

Since the 1960s I have followed Frantz Fanon in the Grove Press translations of the original French publications of his work. I wish to express my gratitude to Grove Press for keeping Fanon's writing available in English. The English translations of Fanon quotations that appear in the text of my novel are from the following Grove Press editions:

The Wretched of the Earth (1963), translated by Constance Farrington
Black Skin, White Masks (1967), translated by Charles Lam Markmann
Toward the African Revolution (1967), translated by Haakon Chevalier
A Dying Colonialism (1965), translated by Haakon Chevalier
The Wretched of the Earth (2004), translated by Richard Philcox

Special thanks to David Macey, author of *Frantz Fanon: A Biography* (New York: Picador, 2000), an indispensable source book for Fanon's life, thought, and times.

Thanks to Myron Schwartzman, author of *Romare Bearden: His Life and Art* (New York: Abrams, 1990).

A general thanks to scholars, critics, colleagues, and biographers of Fanon, who will not allow Fanon to be forgotten.